LOVE AND THE
LAND BEYOND

JAMES LEASOR

LOVE AND THE LAND BEYOND

HEINEMANN : LONDON

William Heinemann Ltd
15 Queen Street, Mayfair, London W1X 8BE

LONDON MELBOURNE TORONTO

JOHANNESBURG AUCKLAND

First published 1979
© James Leasor 1979

SBN 434 41027 6

Printed and bound in Great Britain by
Morrison & Gibb Ltd, London and Edinburgh

Chapter One

It was the evening of Marshall's fiftieth birthday, and so, in his opinion at least, something to be celebrated.

At breakfast that morning, he had announced to his wife that he was now half a hundred years old, and she had smiled with that purely muscular contraction of the face which wives adopt when they have been married too long to the wrong man and nothing he says can be amusing.

Marshall stood, thinking about this birthday, elbows on the ceramic-tiled wall of the rented house in Praia da Luz in southern Portugal, looking out over the beach and the sea. Across a small field of sweet-corn near the house, the six o'clock wind rattled dry stalks like dead men's bones. This wind, so unexpectedly chill, seemed a trailer for autumn and for evening.

It had been a hot day, and now, too quickly, the heat was dying. Marshall felt vaguely uneasy, as though there were a warning in this. But of what – and why? What could go wrong now with his plans? So long as he stayed unrecognized here for the next few days, he would be safe, and more than safe, rich to the extent he need never take such risks again. For ever and ever, amen. The words had a melancholy echo to them, like a response murmured by a new-made grave. He shook such thoughts from his mind.

Marshall was proud of his firm muscles, his thick black hair, still without a trace of grey. He wore dark blue slacks, a blue tee-shirt, white-soled canvas yachting shoes because he felt that such clothes emphasized his fitness and virility. Around his right wrist was a thin gold chain attached to a gold plate engraved with his name and blood group. The representative of an insurance company had given it to him years ago, when he had taken out a large life policy in his wife's name, explaining that it was a good idea to wear one, 'in case of accidents'. They had both laughed, for Marshall never had accidents. He looked like any advertisement's idea of a successful man: leaving an executive jet, enjoying a six-inch cigar, buying a £40,000 car. He was, in fact, a crook and on the eve of the killing – again that unfortunate association with death – which he felt certain would enable him to enjoy the life to which a man of his looks and charm should surely be entitled.

He watched a barefoot Portuguese beach attendant in white jeans and rakish peaked cap, like a sailor who never went to sea, fold up canvas sun-screens, and wondered what the man did in the winter. Perhaps he took to the hills and lived rough, or maybe he moved in with one of the middle-aged Middle West widows who lived here all year long? Several local fishermen, blue jeans rolled above oddly pale knees, carried flagons of wine and small containers of food to a heavy wooden fishing boat. Soon they would join others out beyond Sagres where, hundreds of years earlier, men like them had set off in ships little larger to chart a way to the East. The fishermen would wait all night, engines off, floodlights flickering like fireflies to dazzle the fish, and then return early on the following morning to sell what they had caught – sole, octopus, swordfish, sometimes even a baby dolphin, looking too human for Marshall's palate. Theirs was a simple, uncomplicated rhythm of life, relatively unchanged for generations; the eyes painted on the bows of their boats in blue and reds were a direct link with the ancient Egyptian goddess of good fortune. In a world where men reached out to the moon, these fishermen looked back to a past beyond recollection.

But why, Marshall wondered, would a man go to sea every night in all weathers if he could sell for a huge sum a field his father had left him, and live off this money for the rest of his life? Fishermen's cottages were fetching fortunes from foreigners; new white villas covered land where no-one had ever lived before. Marshall was not one of those who regretted this disruption. There had to be change. Only the dead stayed still. Life was like riding a bicycle; you either moved forward or you fell off. Marshall was a mover.

Through the Moorish archways of the rented house, he could hear his wife, Marilyn, chattering to their daughter against a clatter of dishes, as they washed up after a late tea. The Portuguese maid had gone home early for some reason not clear to him.

He glanced to the left, past blood-red blooms of hibiscus and purple bougainvillaea. A gardener stood watering a flower-bed through a green plastic hose. The tide was coming in. The fishing fleet from Portimao, bigger boats with cabins and thumping diesels, streamed in formation across the bay, past the anchored speedboats, out west towards Cape St Vincent, where the ancients believed the earth ended.

Marshall saw all this, but was not really concerned with it. He was wondering uneasily what two men, part-time colleagues of his, would say if they discovered he was in the Algarve. He had promised them he would not leave England until they had given their permission. Of course, they would never discover he had broken his word, so his concern was academic; notional, as his accountant would say. Marilyn had heard glowing reports of Praia da Luz from a friend with whom she played a lot of bridge, and when this friend and her husband told her they were coming down for two weeks, and knew of a villa the Marshalls could rent, he had been unable to produce any convincing reason why they should not accompany them. So here he was, but prudently keeping to the house as much as possible.

He was also wondering about the girl he had seen on one of his evening walks. She had a boldness that attracted him: firm rounded breasts, a slightly quizzical eye, and fullness of the lips that he found exciting. He had enjoyed girls like her all his adult life; the wonder was that he hadn't married one of them. Or was it really that he had married at all?

Memories teased him of amusing and sometimes energetic afternoons spent with other girls in rented hotel rooms with a bottle of Krug by the bed. There had been flights to Nice (by different planes, of course, for Marshall was a cautious man), even to New York, stopping off at Bermuda on the way. This particular girl was never on the nearest beach, where canvas sun-screens flapped like the flags of an army, and a few Portuguese children, watched by sallow nannies, still played on the darkening sand. He had only seen her some distance away, under Black Rock. The beach, indeed the whole village, took its name – the Beach of Light – from the strange configuration of these dark cliffs overlooking the sea. By some angle of refraction or reflection, Marshall was not sure which, the setting sun poured light on the cliff face so that each evening the whole curved cliff and bay was bathed briefly in an ethereal glow, green as the depths of the sea.

She had been picking up shells when he had noticed her first of all. He had said 'Hullo', but not introduced himself, because he did not wish to advertise his presence in the Algarve. She had replied in English, and he had looked for odd shells for her – some long razor-bills, others flecked with pink, and they had walked on together for a few yards. They both saw the same shell at the same time and reached for it together yet individually, and their hands had touched, and they had looked at each other. There was something in the girl's eyes that convinced Marshall he was on to a good thing.

He glanced at his watch. This was the hour he had seen her. He would seek her out again and they would walk along the shore together once more, and this time he would find her address in England, and from then on all would be simple. Manners might make man, but in Marshall's view, when it came to making a woman, money also helped.

He stood up, smoothed back his hair, called to his wife with elaborate and practised casualness: 'Just taking a stroll along the beach, darling. Back about seven. We're going to the Rosses' party, aren't we?'

She replied, almost accusingly, not even coming to the door: 'You know we are.'

'I'll be back in time, don't worry.'

He would enjoy the party because by then he'd have made

4

some arrangement with this girl. And why wait until they returned to London? The cliffs were honeycombed with discreet and convenient caves, and huge round boulders gave cover from prying eyes.

Marshall walked briskly down the steps into the paved courtyard, nodded curtly to the gardener, as a superior to an inferior, taking it for granted that both knew and accepted their social position, and set off towards the beach, past a promenade where a few cars were still parked under the dusty trees. At first the sand was soft underfoot; then, nearer the sea, it grew firm and hard. The tide was coming in quickly. Within a few minutes it would wash away all traces of the summer day. The wooden spatulate sticks that had once speared ice creams, the wrapping papers and empty Sumol bottles that some visitors were always too lazy to put in the litter bins, would float out into the Atlantic, to be deposited eventually on another beach.

He passed a canoe, drawn up beyond high-water mark, then some fishing boats propped upright with stakes; then he was among the rocks, brown and slippery, pocked with holes. Tiny crabs and transparent shrimps swam frantically in shallow pools, eager for the safety the incoming sea would provide after a day avoiding the nets and spades of children.

He had not noticed the evening to be so cold before. Maybe the weather was changing. The sirocco – or was it the mistral or the Levant? – was due to blow in from North Africa. He glanced at his watch. Six fifteen. She should be there. She could not have collected all the shells she wanted, or maybe that was just an excuse to meet someone like him? He had never seen her with a man, or indeed with anyone else, for that matter. Perhaps, like him, she was basically a loner. He travels fastest who travels alone. But to what eventual destination?

Marshall's shoes slipped and slithered on slimy rocks. Once, salt spray iced his legs. The tide here ran in very quickly. He had heard about couples who had gone to kiss or copulate under the rocks in the afternoon, become understandably oblivious of the tides and have to swim back to avoid being

5

cut off, and arrive embarrassed and soaking on a crowded beach. That would never happen to him, of course: he was too careful. Or was it because he was too clever? Others were caught in all kinds of compromising situations; not Frank Marshall.

He rounded a brown spine of rock, edged with sand that led into the sea, like the tail of some huge landlocked animal, half in water, half on land. He was now out of sight of all the houses, and the striped cliffs brooded above him. There were no birds, no sound but the roar and bellow of the surf on the rocks and the suck and hiss of the sea. The beach lay empty as a dead man's eyes. He'd give her ten minutes, and if she still didn't turn up, he'd have to go back. There was something about the scene, its impersonal emptiness, the heavy pounding of the waves, that depressed him.

Marshall walked on more slowly, half wanting to turn back, to be one of the crowd at the Rosses' party. Not that he really knew the man well – he was a friend of the friends who had persuaded Marilyn to visit Portugal – but he liked people around him. People were witnesses; with people, he felt safe.

The beach was still empty. Perhaps the girl was walking farther along? He'd go as far as the next spine of rocks and see.

To his left, under the cliff, caves opened like tunnel mouths, black, arched, rimmed with rock formations, refuges for lovers or others caught short in urgent needs of nature. Marshall picked his way over some larger boulders, slipping on the wet, mossy rocks, and jumped down, dusting damp sand from his palms. Immediately, he felt a spasm of annoyance. Someone else was on the beach.

A man was sitting, back to him, on a round rock, knees drawn up. He sat locked in thought, looking out across the sea. He wore a skin-diver's black rubber wet suit, the mask over his eyes. He must be about to go into the water.

This man heard loose shingle rattle beneath Marshall's shoes, and turned towards him. Marshall thought he seemed vaguely familiar, like a face from a photograph he had seen long ago but could not quite place, because it was out of focus; and of course the mask concealed his features. Finding someone else

6

here made Marshall decide to turn. His desire to meet the girl had died completely.

The skin-diver stood up. He held a gold cigarette case, thin as a wafer, in his hand, and lit a cigarette.

He hasn't offered me one, thought Marshall, although there was no reason why he should. But somehow he saw this as unfriendly, almost hostile. The prudent antennae of his mind sent their signal: Go back. Keep away. Retreat.

He turned and began to climb back over the slippery boulders.

The man called to him in English.

'Wait a minute!'

Marshall looked back at him enquiringly. He thought he knew the voice now, but he could not be quite sure. Maybe his memory was playing tricks on him?

'Weren't you collecting shells out here with a girl last night?' the man continued.

'Yes,' Marshall agreed. But who was this bastard? Her lover, someone who thought he could put the button on him? Maybe, heaven forbid, her husband? But she hadn't worn a wedding ring; he would have noticed if she had; he always did.

'There are some most unusual shells over in those rocks, nearer the sea.'

The voice sounded different now; more foreign than he had thought. He had made a mistake. Or was this a false accent adopted to conceal the man's identity? He'd humour him, anyway. Marshall jumped down and moved towards the waves. A breaker rolled in, all power spent, pulling a heavy floor of water, streaked with salt. Then it was sucked back. Air bubbles burst in the damp and shining sand.

'Where are they?' he asked. 'I don't see any.'

'Right in front of your feet. Turn round.'

Marshall turned and glanced up enquiringly at the man. He was standing on the rock, feet apart, cigarette in his left hand. But it wasn't his left hand that surprised Marshall; it was his right. For in this had grown, like an extension of his arm, the long menacing five-pronged fork of an underwater spear gun.

7

Five sharpened arrow-heads pointed at Marshall's stomach. His flesh crawled on his bones like worms.

'What's the matter?' he called hoarsely. For something must be the matter, otherwise why should this stranger aim such a weapon at him?

'You know what the matter is, Marshall,' said the man, without the accent. He pulled off his mask.

'My God!' Marshall cried in horror. For this was, after all, the man he had at first thought it just might be. The man drew on his cigarette, so that the end glowed in the dying evening light like a tiny firefly.

'Wait a minute,' Marshall called, bewildered. 'I'm simply here because my wife arranged the trip. I'm not going back on my word, I swear it. For God's sake, don't shoot. You know me.'

'Too well,' the man replied. 'I was warned not to trust you. I should have listened.'

In that second – beyond all measuring of normal time, beyond the time-stream itself – Marshall knew he was about to die. His shirt stank with the sharp sweat of fear; the smell of death was in his nostrils like the salt of the hammering, restless sea.

'Stop!' he shouted. 'Wait! I can explain!'

The man smiled as he fired. The five prongs of the spear caught Marshall in the groin. For a second he watched its anodized shaft sticking out from his body, the long cord attached to its tail flickering like a serpent's tail. Then he saw the blood – his blood – and agony overwhelmed him. He sank down on his back like a huge crab, digging his fingers into the damp sand as waves of water and pain exploded over his head. His anal sphincter muscle relaxed and he voided, and lay in his own dung in the shallow water, streaked with blood, shivering with shock and reaction. His sight was fading; he could only see a vague immensity of sky, cold and darkening, out of focus, without meaning. He heard a voice calling piteously and did not recognize it as his own. Only the pain was real and fierce and unbearable. Frantic tigers within him were clawing a way out through his flesh.

'Help me! Help me!' he cried weakly. 'For God's sake!'

A wave larger than the rest broke over Marshall's head. He felt his body drawn over the vast roughness of the sand, and he tried to scream again. This time his mouth was filled with sea and sand and blood, and he gurgled and choked with weakness.

Slowly, his hands relaxed and his clenched fingers unwound like the claws of a dying bird. Peace slowly and mercifully overcame the pain. The sea beat over his head, and beat and beat again, as he slid, beyond all feeling, all fighting, into a deep green oblivion.

The man crossed the beach towards him, bent down and deliberately cut the cord from the spear. Then he took off his wet suit, put it in a duffle bag, pulled on a shirt and canvas trousers. As though he had all the time in the world, cigarette still in his hand, he slowly walked away, bag over one shoulder. As he reached the rocks, he stopped, turned and waved to Marshall, as though the man was still alive. Then he walked on over the boulders, towards Luz. Fifty yards from the nearest house, a girl was walking towards him. She smiled at him and turned. Close together, so close their shoulders brushed with each step, hands entwined, they walked on.

*   *   *

Dr Jason Love floated on his back, kicking out his long legs lazily as he drifted slowly across the shining blue water of the swimming pool.

Above him, the evening sky stretched in a cloudless blue infinity, and by turning his head slightly he could see a third blue of the sea beyond the Algarve shore. Three shades of the same colour, and all in perfect harmony, just as the crimson blossoms of the bougainvillaea did not clash with the huge scarlet geraniums or the pink of the pelargoniums that grew in the same flower-bed.

He thought lazily, soporifically, how wonderfully planned the world had been, for no colour of nature ever clashed with another, and as Bishop Heber had rightly pointed out in his

9

famous hymn, every prospect pleases and only man is (regrettably) all too vile. He wondered about Heber, what he would think of the world today. He mightn't approve, but then he would enjoy the prospect from this pool. Yes, that would please him. It might even inspire another hymn.

Love turned his head slowly in the other direction towards the three arches that sheltered the patio of the house that a patient had lent to him, complete with maid, and gardener, for all of August and half of September. It was not at all disagreeable, he thought, to be a doctor in Somerset, especially when a patient was generous enough to show his appreciation of services rendered in such a pleasing way.

This was Love's first day in the Algarve. He had arrived on the previous evening, driving from Calais, through France and Spain, in his white supercharged Cord Sportsman, stopping where the Guide Michelin declared the speciality of this region or that deserved a detour. He made several such detours and all had been eminently worth while. But agreeable as passage in an open car through these two countries had been, the last lap of his journey was one of the most pleasant. An early dinner in Lisbon and then the four-hour drive through a warm summer night, with the green-lit instruments on the Cord's engine-turned dashboard accentuating the deeper greens of the forests and darkening hills on either side.

Night moths and other insects danced in the amber beams of his headlamps and his spirits danced with them. The road south was almost deserted. He passed a few country mule carts with a donkey hitched alongside, to be harnessed for the steeper hills, a second gear with hooves, and the occasional lorry trundling down from Lisbon.

Part of his pleasure in the drive was due to the curious car he drove. The Cord had been built in Indiana in the 1930s, in a State and time when roads were empty, and the only limits to speed lay in the car's performance and the driver's nerve. This car was designed for the open, empty road, and Love felt himself in entire agreement with a remark that its designer, Gordon Buehrig, treasured most.

10

'Somehow,' a friend told Buehrig, 'the Cord didn't look like an automobile. It looked like a beautiful thing that had been born and just grew up on the highway . . .'

Love always remembered this as 2,400 revolutions showed on the tachometer and the supercharger engaged with its whistling whine of gears. Then the huge car appeared to take wing. Love felt that this must be the nearest thing to human flight, and having regard to the thirst of the eight-cylinder Lycoming engine, almost as expensive. But as a bachelor, with no dependants or family, he could afford this indulgence. He had diligently attended the funerals of too many former patients who had always intended to enjoy themselves but somehow had never found the time, not to realize that such a theory was folly indeed. The poor used time to make money, while the rich used their wealth to make time in which to enjoy themselves. For as Sir Thomas Browne, the seventeenth-century Norwich physician whose books Love collected, had shrewdly noted: 'There is no antidote against the opium of Time.'

Yesterday was gone, tomorrow could never be guaranteed. And what merit was it for anyone to be the richest man in the graveyard? There might be a better life somewhere, but he did not want to join all those others in the cemetery trying to find it.

Some of his contemporaries at Oxford and St Bartholomew's Hospital would occasionally express surprise that Jason Love had moved to Somerset, when he might equally well have enjoyed a fashionable practice in Ascot or Harley Street. Sometimes, too, he wondered what would have happened had he taken different decisions; but always he felt sure he had taken the right one.

In the country, the seasons of each year were more important than social seasons elsewhere. Most of his patients were also his friends, and so long as he could engage a suitable locum, he could take time off when he wanted, where he wanted. And how many fashionable doctors could honestly say they were as fortunate?

In Somerset he conducted a practice from a seventeenth-century manor house, set in several acres. Over many years he

11

had gathered together a collection of car badges that ranked, so insurance valuers assured him, as third or fourth in the country. And he also enjoyed the ultimate privilege of freedom which, as a Sagittarian, he put quite simply beyond price as being – after health – the most valuable possession in all the world. He was his own man, to make or direct decisions without reference to anyone else. He could accept any consequences because they only concerned him.

He kicked out to keep himself on course, thinking of these things, and then suddenly his body stiffened. He listened at first with surprise, then with resignation. The telephone was pealing.

Its bell echoed with an imperious intensity from the white stuccoed wall around the garden. The maid had gone home and the house was empty; he would have to answer it himself. With four powerful strokes Love reached the steps, climbed out, wrapped a towel from one of the deckchairs around him, and walked into the house.

After the burning afternoon heat, the living room with its polished red tiles and cork-lined ceiling supported on dark wooden beams, seemed cool as a bodega. His bare feet left wet footprints on the carpet as he reached the hall and picked up the telephone. A fruity voice, enriched by years of Five Star Martell and expensively fumed by the smoke of countless Havana cigars, erupted in his ear.

'Am I speaking to Dr Love, the owner of the white Cord I saw in Luz today?'

'You are indeed,' agreed Love.

'Good morrow to you, sir. Or rather, good evening. I am Douglas Ross, late colonel, First Fifth Mahrattas, the fighting fifth. My sister, Mrs Carver, is a patient of yours in Somerset. She gave me the best means of identifying you – your car.'

'There are other ways,' said Love. 'But that, I agree, is the easiest. She mentioned her brother had retired out here. I was going to look you up.'

'Good. The reason I am ringing now, doctor, is to ask you to a little party my lady wife and I are giving at eight o'clock this evening. Sorry it is such short notice, but we did not know you had arrived until I saw the car. The post is not what it was. But then, of course, nothing is nowadays.

'Apart from wishing to meet you, I have another reason for inviting you. I run a stable mate of the Cord, an Auburn 851 cabriolet.'

Ross paused to let Love realize the full effect of this statement.

'Now nothing will keep me away,' Love assured him and listened to the directions for finding Ross's house.

Love had not seen an Auburn for several years, apart from the Speedster in the National Motor Museum at Beaulieu. The car was a sister to the Cord, a member of the Auburn-Cord-Duesenberg triumvirate, which throughout the middle and late thirties had produced three of America's most individualistic cars. His own attraction to the Cord he sometimes found hard to explain. Beautiful as it appeared, and advanced in engineering for its time – front-wheel-drive, disappearing headlights and an electrical gear change which could be used as an ordinary box or as a preselector – the sum of the car's complications sometimes exceeded its good points. Like the little girl in the rhyme, when the Cord was good it was very, very good, but when it was bad, it was horrid, or frequently worse. As one indication of its individualistic mechanical complication, it could claim the extraordinary distinction of being able to engage two gears at the same time, with disastrous and expensive results.

The Duesenberg was a different breed of car, the result of a liaison between Errett Lobban Cord and Fred Duesenberg. One was a salesman of genius, the other a genius of automobile designing who set out to build what he intended would be 'the world's finest motor car'.

Did he succeed or not? Did his majestic creation, that in 1928 developed more than 250 h.p. with 32 valves opened by double overhead camshafts, surpass the designs of Sir Henry Royce or Marc Birkigt at Hispano-Suiza? In terms of sheer brute power, the answer was in the affirmative. Royce was reluctant to reveal the horsepower his engines developed; he simply said it was 'sufficient'. The Hispano T68 put out 190 b.h.p. from

13

9·4 litres, and even the huge 770K Mercedes lagged behind at 200 b.h.p.

Certainly, the Duesenberg was America's mightiest motor car, and a list of owners included William Randolph Hearst, Howard Hughes, Clark Gable and Paul Whiteman. Starting price for one nowadays would be around £150,000 – if it ever came on the market.

The Auburn, by contrast, had been a relatively simple design: a Lycoming straight-eight 4·5 litre engine in a chassis that would not disgrace a lorry, and fitted with an accessory generally now only found on trucks: a dual-ratio back axle. The driver could change the ratio from high to low and back again, as he drove, simply by moving a lever on the steering wheel. There was barely any need to use the gears at all. The Auburn just tooled along, ironing out hills as though they did not exist. It was fast and restful to drive, a champion that never needed to prove its power to any competitor. Like an old heavyweight boxer, the car commanded respect; nearly two tons of metal could never be lightweight. It would be good to see one on the road again, so far from home. As Love walked out through the house he poured himself a Glenlivet, added soda and ice, and then sat on the patio, letting the warmth of the sun dry him. He felt completely at peace.

*　　　*　　　*

In the south of Portugal, as in other sub-tropical climates, every day dies a sudden death. One moment, the sun burns like a torch in the afternoon sky. The next, it has capitulated and slides down into the sea, to surrender to the dark.

At seven o'clock, a wind which had slept throughout the day, was active, rustling the leaves of fig and almond trees by Love's house, lifting powdery dust off the track that led down to the main Luz road. He switched on the two outside lights near the front door and kept a third burning in the living room. As with so many people who live on their own, Love disliked returning to a strange house in darkness. His experiences as a part-time agent for the British Secret Intelligence Service, sometimes known as MI6, had done nothing to diminish this feeling.

Of course, the days were all behind him when Colonel Douglas MacGillivray, the deputy head of that shadowy force, had appealed first to Love's patriotism and then to his personal sense of loyalty to a former army colleague, to help him in an investigation where, as a doctor, no-one would suspect his real intentions.

The two men still exchanged Christmas cards, and sometimes lunched together when Love was in London, but that was about the extent of their association. The last time they met, Love had thought that MacGillivray looked much older than he remembered him, but, of course, had not mentioned this to his host. MacGillivray had thought the same about Love, and put it down to the fact that the doctor complained of an unexpected number of night-calls in his practice during the previous week. These country characters, he felt sure, lacked the fortitude and resilience of city-dwellers . . .

Now Love climbed into his Cord, pressed the accelerator to prime the pump on the double-choked Carter carburettor, and turned the key against the Startix. The engine fired, and he drove down towards Luz.

This was a fishing village, and although now much built around by new houses, its charm remained. He passed the whitewashed church where the bell tolled for evening mass, then a supermarket, the post office, the local bakery. The Cord's two three-inch exhausts boomed back from the walls of old houses built right up to the edge of the street. Wives and widows in perpetual black stood in open doorways, and old men sat on wooden benches outside the wine shop. The road led past the Luz Bay Club, on beyond a vast camp site where the flags of many nations drooped on poles, and joined the main coast road, Estrada 125 from Lagos to Sagres. Half a mile along this, Love saw the long white bonnet of Ross's Auburn parked at the top of a steep drive, and swung off the road. He recognized it as an 851 cabriolet of 1935. Gordon Buehrig had been allocated a budget of $50,000 to facelift its unsuccessful

15

predecessor of the previous year – a sum that nowadays, Love knew, would barely finance the design of a new radiator badge. And for the succeeding year, even this meagre money was lacking; the total Auburn design modification from 1935 to 1936 had been to change the model number – from 851 to 852!

Love stopped the Cord, nose to nose with the Auburn. As he climbed out, he could hear waves of party conversation and laughter against a tinkle of glasses and the beat of Burt Bacharach.

A middle-aged man with grey hair, wearing a copper bracelet against rheumatism on his right wrist and a gold Rolex on his left, and holding a half-pint glass of gin and tonic as though it was a trophy, came to meet him.

'You can only be Dr Love?' he asked. 'I am Douglas Ross. Pleased to welcome you.'

Love admired the neat house with its bright blue shutters, the red and white sun umbrellas around the pool, bougainvillaea bright on white walls, and enough huge earthenware pots to hold Ali Baba and his forty thieves.

Ross led Love on to the patio. About thirty people, some young, others retired and older, stood about. All showed pleasure at the chance of meeting a stranger. Life all year round in a small seaside town in a foreign country meant that of necessity the guests at any party rarely changed; only the places where they met.

A dark-haired woman with horn-rimmed glasses and rabbit teeth held out a limp damp hand.

'I am Evelyn Ross. Do come and meet everyone.'

Someone pressed a goblet of gin, no larger than a goldfish bowl, into Love's hand. A kaleidoscope of faces passed before him: bored, unhappy, cheerful, tipsy.

'Meet Colonel Buckmaster. Here is Jerry Hirst. Mrs Mac-Tavish. And Maureen Grant, who has just got engaged out here to Billie Grout.'

Love always found it difficult to remember the names of strangers or match a name to a face. He accepted that this was a sign of mental laziness; because he might not be greatly

16

interested in meeting someone, his memory would conveniently forget to file that person's name. But now he struggled gamely with names he would never speak again, faces he would never see, let alone recognize, until they all crossed the River Jordan to that last reunion in the sky. He shook hands with people and exchanged small talk so minuscule it was practically not talk at all. His host materialized alongside him, his glass freshly charged for the rigours of speech.

'This will go on for another hour,' he said. 'Then we can have a look at each other's cars. After that, my lady wife and I hope you will join us for dinner. We are going to a new place just opened on the cliffs on the way to Sagres. They serve the best lobster in the whole of the Algarve. No frozen fish fingers there, what?'

As he spoke, Ross kept looking over the heads of the guests as though searching for someone he could not see, a face beyond the crowd.

'Ah,' he said triumphantly at last. 'Two people you *must* meet. Mrs Marshall and her daughter. They are staying down near the sea. Having a celebration too tonight, aren't you, Marilyn?'

Mrs Marshall smiled. Her eyes did not.

'My husband's fiftieth birthday,' she explained. 'If that's something to celebrate. He keeps telling me how old he is. But then he's a pessimist – and a pessimist always talks about his glass being half empty. I like to think of mine being half full.'

'Which reminds me,' said Ross, pouring her another gin of gigantic proportions. 'Where *is* your husband?'

Mrs Marshall shrugged.

'He went off on his own along the beach. We waited for him, until we couldn't wait any longer. But he'll be along soon, I'm sure.'

'Where do you live in England?' Love asked her as Ross moved on to refill the glasses of a couple across the room.

'Mummy says she will live anywhere, absolutely anywhere,' said her daughter.

Mrs Marshall nodded.

'Yes,' she agreed. 'Anywhere between Eaton Square and Belgrave Place.'

They drifted apart. A man smiled at Love.

'A fine car you arrived in,' he said appreciatively. 'Haven't seen one of those for years.'

'Only a few left now,' Love admitted.

'Must be a mark of age,' said the man philosophically. 'But I can remember the days when "vintage" didn't refer to old motor cars, only to drinkable wines.'

'That dates both of us,' agreed Love.

'A little more gin to freshen you up?' suggested Ross, cruising past with another full decanter. 'This stuff's very cheap out here – masses of junipers.'

The other man shook his head. 'Thank you, no,' he said.

'Thank you, yes,' said Love. He held out his glass. The man moved away.

'Who's that?' Love asked his host, nodding towards him. Ross shrugged casually.

'Probably a friend of a friend. No-one I know.'

*   *   *

Dr Love was swimming in water, blue as a police-lamp. Gradually the colour changed; azure to lapis lazuli, and then he was out of the sea, head in the air, gasping for breath.

He was in bed, head beneath a sheet, and the confounded telephone was ringing by his ear. He struggled up and reached for it. Would the wretched bell never be still? His dream faded as he glanced at his travelling clock: a quarter to nine. Sun streamed into the room through horizontal gaps between the green shutters. He had returned in the early hours from a most excellent dinner. The Rosses had both called in for a nightcap with him, and it had been four when he finally went to bed. He scooped up the receiver, shaking sleep from his fuzzy head.

18

'Ross here. Did I wake you?'

'No matter,' said Love philosophically. 'The huntsmen are up in America, and they are already past their first sleep in Persia.'

'Eh?'

'Nothing. Only quoting Thomas Browne.'

'I don't know what you are talking about, but I want you to come down to the Rua Vasco da Gama at once. Number ten. Mrs Marshall's house.'

'Why? What's the trouble?'

'There has been a terrible accident.'

'To whom?'

'Her husband.'

'How? Car accident?'

'No. Worse. I'll tell you when I see you. But hurry, please. The police are already here.'

'I'm on my way.'

Love swung himself out of bed, dressed, washed and shaved. How wrong he had been to imagine he could escape from medical responsibility even when on holiday! A doctor was always on duty. He was expected to leave his seat in a theatre without demur to attend to some drunk who had fallen down in the gents' lavatory. Driving in a car rally, he must pull out and lose all hope of winning, to administer to a complete stranger who claimed to be ill or injured. Now, the absent Mr Marshall. Well, that was part of his job. He had known that before he ever became a medical student. It was too late to jib now.

The Portuguese maid, a middle-aged widow in black bombasine, raised hands gnarled as oak twigs in horror when he waved away the breakfast of fresh figs and two lightly poached eggs she had prepared. He hastily drank a cup of strong black coffee, climbed into the Cord and drove to the Rua Vasco da Gama. This was a short stretch of road running parallel with the sea and paved with small square stones, known as calcada. The residents had planted trees and shrubs which, because they were watered regularly, had now assumed jungle

19

proportions. In the Algarve, with water, anything grows. A police Land Rover, its radio chattering, was parked outside No. 10 behind a white Simca with a medical badge.

Ross stood under a tree out of the sun's heat. He held a round tin of fifty cigarettes in his right hand and was smoking nervously. His face was sallow. He looked older than on the previous evening.

'What happened?' Love asked him. How often had he asked these two words on arrival at the scene of a road accident, or a domestic tragedy?

'You know Marshall didn't turn up at all to our party last night? Well, he didn't come home, either. At high tide, about midnight, a couple of German tourists who were out catching condalipas came across his body on the beach beyond the headland.'

'What are condalipas?'

'A species of sea-food. Tastes like a mussel or a scallop. They live just under the surface of the sand. When the tide is out you'll see people wriggling their feet about in the sand until they feel these things. Then they pick them up.'

'I learn something new every day,' said Love. 'Have you seen these tourists yourself?'

'No. But I have a friend in the Fiscal Guard who has. He told me.'

'Had Marshall drowned?'

'Presumably. But first he had been shot with an underwater spear gun. In the guts.'

'By whom?'

'How the devil do I know? He was found in the sea, of course. Been for a walk along the beach.'

'Doesn't sound like an accident.'

'You mean – murder?'

Love did not answer.

'Have you seen the body?' he asked.

'No. That's in the police mortuary.'

'They'll do an autopsy, I suppose?'

'A doctor examined him. He thought he had been shot first.

20

Then he fell down and the tide came in, finished him off.'

'Someone was making assurance double sure, as Shakespeare said. How is Mrs Marshall taking all this?'

'I would say, remarkably well. You never can tell with wives. Or widows. Many husbands should have as their epitaph: "A happy release." '

'For whom, in this case?'

'Shall I say, Mrs Marshall does not appear inconsolable?'

'So what can I do to help?'

'Well, you *are* a doctor. You might care to see her. Difficult, this happening in a foreign country. I am trying to get the British Consul on the 'phone, but the line's engaged. Lot of trouble with 'phones in the tourist season. Too many people using 'em. If she wants to take the body back to England, there are all kinds of formalities. You'd never imagine.'

'I can, very well.'

'Personally, I'd plant him here. Very good cemetery, you know. And in this heat, the sooner the better. I remember, once, in India, a fellow . . .'

Love interrupted him; he had no wish to hear of burial customs long ago and far away.

'Did she ask to see me?'

'She didn't actually *ask,* but it's always appreciated in a time of trouble. You know, rallying round, all friends together, that sort of thing.'

As Love opened the wrought-iron gate at the bottom of the entrance steps that led up to the patio, two little cow-bells attached to it tinkled their demure advance warning. This was the local way of advising anyone who might be sunbathing nude that visitors had arrived. But no-one was sunbathing. A Portuguese maid stood shaking out a sheepskin rug. In life or death, housework must continue. Love heard a faint busy buzz of voices behind smoked glass doors. Mrs Marshall saw him, and slid open one door.

'How kind of you to call,' she said, hand outstretched.

'Just in case I could help in any way,' Love replied. 'But I see a doctor is here already.'

21

'Yes. Dr da Silva. A neighbour, who has a telephone, very kindly rang for him.'

'I don't suppose I can do anything, but if you need sleeping pills or something to help you over the next few hours or days, and you don't like to ask Dr da Silva, I travel with pretty well the whole pharmacopaeia.'

'Thank you, but I don't think I'll need anything like that, doctor.'

'You are taking this very well, very bravely,' Love told her. He had visited too many bereaved homes where loneliness and misery stared out of bewildered eyes, dim with disbelief at the sudden, unheralded presence of death. But there was no moistness, no grief, in Mrs Marshall's bright hard eyes.

She lit a cigarette with untrembling hand.

'A drink, doctor?'

'It is a little early for me, Mrs Marshall.'

'My husband used to say that if it was too early here, then it must be too late on the other side of the world, so he'd even things up. He could always equate drinking with very good reasons.'

'He must have been quite a character.'

'Yes. But I do not wish to be hypocritical. Frank and I were not on the closest terms. We shared a house, and in a factual sense, a bed. But don't imagine I am a weeping widow, inconsolable in my grief. We both lived our own lives.'

And now Marshall had gone to his own death, for death was the ultimate individual happening in everyone's life, thought Love. We all entered this world unannounced, often unwanted and alone. Many lived out their existence in the same way and left as they had arrived, quietly, without fuss to anyone, and without friends. As Sir Thomas Browne had remarked long ago, 'Death is the cure of all diseases'. Even so, most preferred the ailment to the remedy.

'What about your daughter?'

'She was closer to her father, of course. But then she only saw one side of him. She is lying down in her bedroom. I have given her some aspirins and black coffee.'

22

'No news of how this – ah – accident occurred?'

'It was no accident, Dr Love. It was deliberate.'

'By whom? Was he robbed?'

'No. Nothing was touched. His watch and his wallet, his credit cards. Nothing.'

'But you've no idea who would do such a thing – deliberately?'

'Of course not.'

She paused.

'And yet he *was* a bit on edge from the moment we got here. Even a bit before, looking back on it. As though he didn't want to come to the Algarve at all. Funny, really. For he liked travel.'

She paused again. There was no mileage for Marshall now; he would only travel as far as the cemetery on the hill behind Luz, if she did not have his body flown home.

'Well, if I *can* help at all, please let me know. You know where I'm staying.' He gave her his telephone number.

'Thank you, doctor. You are very kind.'

Love turned and went down the steps, past pelargoniums that tumbled out of blue and white porcelain pots. The bells tinkled again as he shut the iron gate.

The sun on the sea was blinding in its light. He felt somehow withdrawn in the heat. He had never met Marshall, and no doubt he had been a rough, tough, hard fellow. On the other hand, he had met Mrs Marshall. Perhaps they had deserved each other? And yet, and yet . . . ?

He climbed into his car and drove slowly back through narrow streets already heavy with heat, up the hill to his house.

Chapter Two

The stranger sat in the black leather driving seat of the Ford Mustang GT he had stolen in Seattle that afternoon.

He was in his late twenties, with bright red hair, almost orange, a colour that attracted instant attention, and a large moustache. He wore horn-rimmed spectacles with slightly tinted lenses. He was not a man to miss in a crowd. An American Automobile Association road map lay open on the passenger seat beside him. The ashtray was filled with the bent-over stumps of half-smoked Camels and Lucky Strikes. The stereo played Henry Mancini.

He was parked off Highway 101 in Oregon on the west coast of the United States, outside the little town of Waldport. He drove in over the bridge, across a muddy river. Its banks were littered with huge logs, bleached grey by wind and weather. A notice outside the town caught his eye. 'Waldport – Population 777. Drive carefully.' The last figure was on a small plate screwed into the sign. This could be removed when a new member of the population was born – or when another citizen died. He wondered idly when or even whether his business that evening would cause the local authorities to make a change in the number. Perhaps they were never hasty over individuals; a birth could instantly cancel a death.

He passed a yellow revolving ball advertising Ball Realty; then the red, white and blue chevron of a Chevron gas station; then the invitation, 'Big Wheel Drive-in. Burgers to go.' And not only burgers, he thought. We've all got to go one day. The only certain thing about life was that one day we would all be required to leave it. Yet not everyone expected to be ushered into eternity by a stranger. He smiled at the thought.

He rather liked the turn of that sentence. If he were not kept so busy in his own job, he often thought he should have been a writer. You could work then when you wanted, as you wanted and where, not as he had to work, when he was ordered to do so.

The sea between a row of single-storeyed shacks rolled and glittered in the fading afternoon. It was poor weather for August. A mist hung low over the water. More signs. Charboiled Burgers. See Vue Homes. Homes in a Tree. A Drive to the Dunes. Drive a Train through a Tree.

He turned off at a motel entrance, parked the car outside the long, low building, walked through the swing door. The hidden switch beneath the Welcome mat rang a clattering bell, and a girl appeared from a rear office.

'A room,' he said.

'On your own?' she asked.

'On my own.'

She pushed the card he had to sign towards him. He filled it in, pushed it back across the reception desk. The air was heavy with a stale smell of cotton seed oil, of bacon long grilled, coffee newly ground. She gave him a key, number seventeen. His room was like any other motel room, impersonal as a grave.

Outside his window a green neon arrow jumped nervously to and fro: 'Vacancies. Free T.V. Bathrooms in every room. Free coffee.'

The stranger dumped his case on the bed, went into the bathroom. A ventilator began to whir as he opened the door. He ran some cold water, patted his face with his hands, dried himself on the towel and looked at his eyes in the mirror. He had read somewhere that eyes were not windows looking out of the mind, but windows through which strangers could look in. Clever, these writers, to think of something like that. But he would challenge any of them to discover his thoughts. He kicked off his shoes, set his alarm watch for five thirty, and lay on the bed. When he awoke an hour later, he felt relaxed, at ease.

He took a washleather pouch from his jacket pocket, opened

25

it, and checked the 9 mm. Walther that lay inside. The action was carried out almost unconsciously, as a plain woman always looks at her image when she passes a mirror.

The stranger sat down on the bed and began to thumb through the local telephone directory until he found the name and address of the man he had come from New Jersey to see: Dr E. S. B. Cartwright, Dentologist and Surgeon. He picked up the telephone, dialled International, and gave the operator details of his telephone credit card. Then he asked her for a number in Southern Portugal.

'I would like the call to come through one hour from now. Six thirty exactly. At this number.'

He gave the girl Dr Cartwright's number.

'Person to person?'

'No,' he said. 'My friend in Portugal is expecting the call.'

He replaced the receiver.

We are all expecting a call, he thought. But some callers were most deadly when they were unexpected. He rather liked the sound of that sentence, too; he must make a note of it. Humming to himself, he rang Cartwright's number. Then he went down to the front office.

The girl was putting up new postcards in a wire rack for tourists. Oregon views. Felled logs lay on eight-wheeled trucks. Large men in bright tartan shirts stood with axes inside giant hollow redwoods. A long empty coast bared its curiously distinctive grey beach and the grey-barked husks of trees, like a moonscape.

'Have a nice day,' she said with bright insincerity. He nodded and walked out to his car, drove to Cartwright's house. Small floodlights were staked out among plastic verbena on either side of the front door. He wondered when Cartwright lit them. The evening was already approaching the edge of darkness. A white, woolly mist blew in from the sea. The car windows were frosted with condensation.

He reversed up the drive, cut his engine, walked to the front door, pressed the bell. A nurse in a white coat answered it.

'I rang earlier to see if Dr Cartwright could help me. A

filling is giving trouble.' He gave her the name he had used then.

'Oh, yes. Well, Dr Cartwright *has* had a cancellation.'

The waiting room was like any other room of its kind. Leather-covered chairs, a low table, covered with thumbed magazines. French prints on the walls, an imitation log fire glowing with red electric bulbs. Even inside, the air felt damp: he had a sudden awareness of thousands of miles of empty ocean only yards away. Nothing but sea between Oregon and Asia.

A ting from some electronic instrument, a metallic voice in a loudspeaker he hadn't noticed, scattered his thoughts.

'Will you please come into the surgery?'

Cartwright was standing in an open doorway across the passage, a blueish-green fluorescent light behind him. He was taller, even slimmer than the stranger had been led to expect. But then the photograph he had studied had been taken some time previously, and in another country. Cartwright had been smiling then, a glass in his hand raised in a long-forgotten toast.

'What can I do for you?' he asked. His face was latticed with a network of wrinkles.

'Filling gone, I think,' said the stranger, and pushed his tongue into his right cheek to show the side.

The nurse was clearing some papers from a desk in the back of the surgery. She went out. They were alone. The chair stood in the far corner, water running into a blue glass cuspidor.

Cartwright put out his right hand to welcome him.

'Please be seated,' he said.

He crossed to a wash-basin, ran the tap, washed his hands, scrubbing the nails with a nylon brush. He began the small chit-chat of his calling.

'My nurse tells me you rang up on your way through. On vacation?'

The stranger lay back in the chair, his head against the leather rest.

'Yeah,' he said, giving nothing away. The less he said, the better.

27

'Now let me have a look.'

The stranger opened his mouth. Cartwright screwed up his eyes, shone a little torch inside. His hands smelled of scented soap.

'Nothing to worry about. Shall I check up on the others?'

'They're all right. Just this one.'

'As you wish.'

He pressed a bell. Both men heard it ring faintly in another room. No-one answered.

'Damn,' said Cartwright, frowning at his watch. 'My nurse must have left. I'll mix the amalgam myself. Staying here long?'

His questions came mechanically. The stranger grunted non-committal replies.

Cartwright put the aspirator tube in the patient's mouth to draw away the saliva, adjusted the blue-lensed bowl lamp above the chair. He worked quickly and efficiently, breathing in through his mouth and out through his nose. This was his last patient.

'Now bite,' he said. 'Gently. On this wad.'

The stranger bit on it sharply. Cartwright removed it with tweezers and tossed it away.

'How does that feel?'

'No pain at all,' said the stranger. 'How much is that?'

'We'll bill you.'

'I'm not staying here. I'd rather pay my debts as I go.'

The stranger turned away, rinsed his mouth with the pink mouth wash, spat it out into the cuspidor. The room was very bright under the fluorescent tubes, and very quiet. The only noise came from the tinkling water jet in the bowl. Cartwright washed his hands again and crossed to the small desk in the back of the room, sat down, and began to write out the bill.

The patient suddenly kicked the chair, making it swing round on its swivel. Instead of lying back, he was sitting upright.

'Nicely balanced things, those,' said Cartwright, not even looking at him.

'This?' asked the stranger, slapping the arm rest with his left hand. 'Or this?'

28

Cartwright looked up, surprised at the tone of voice. He stayed looking, for the man was holding a gun in his right hand, close to his body. Its tiny hole, barely half an inch across, loomed wide as the gateway to eternity.

'Is this a stick-up?' Cartwright asked hoarsely.

His heart began to beat heavily, like an old car engine toiling up a long steep hill on a hot day.

'No.'

'Some kind of joke, then?' Cartwright stood up, his right hand feeling beneath the desk for the hidden button of the alarm bell. But who would answer? The house was empty, and both knew it.

'No.'

'Well, what do you want, then?'

'Your life.'

'But *why*?'

'A contract,' said the stranger.

'I don't know what you're talking about.'

"I don't know the ins and outs of it,' agreed the stranger, as though he was genuinely concerned, as though the whole discussion was a debate, with fine points to be allowed on both sides. 'But I was told to tell you one thing. It concerns a cargo from India. Calcutta or some such place. You would know all about it.'

Cartwright swallowed. His throat had suddenly contracted; he was almost choking. He could see his face in the glass-covered instrument cabinet on the far wall. The flesh was stretched tight as a drum-skin over his cheek-bones. It was as though he was looking at his own death mask.

'It just doesn't make sense. What are you getting for this? I'll double it. I'll phone the bank now.'

The stranger shook his head.

'Too late,' he said, and pressed the trigger twice.

The bullets at such short range blew Cartwright's face to pieces. Shreds of pinkish splintered bone, tufts of thick dark hair clotted with blood spattered the walls. Thick droplets began to slide slowly down the glass front of the instrument case.

Cartwright sagged across his desk like a rubber man. Each beat of his dying heart pumped blood over the white blotting paper and across the elegant red leather gilt-edged top of the desk which he had so admired in the antique shop in Crescent City.

The stranger waited until he was sure Cartwright was dead, then he put away the Walther, lit a cigarette, and glanced at his watch. Six-thirty precisely. He was on time, as he had been on target. He was a professional. This was a matter of pride to him.

The telephone rang. He picked it up.

'Your call from Portugal, sir.'

Foreign voices spoke unpronounceable words, and then a voice he recognized came on the line.

'I have to report I have despatched the parcel,' the stranger said quietly.

'Any complications?'

'None.'

'Thank you,' said the other man.

The line went dead.

The stranger replaced the instrument, wiped it carefully with his handkerchief and walked out of the house, shutting the door carefully behind him.

Two miles out of Waldport, off Highway 101, the stranger stopped his car in a lay-by. He unscrewed the stolen licence plates which he had fitted, walked into the forest, and buried them in the soft earth beneath rhododendron bushes that blazed purple as a Roman emperor's robes. Then he fitted another set of plates he had brought with him, and drove on.

Ten miles farther up the highway, he pulled off the road again, and ripped off the rubber face mask with its red moustache and wig. He carefully wrapped this around his tinted glasses, opened a tin of lighter fuel, soaked the bundle and set light to it in the forest. It flared and burned to dark, brittle plastic dust. He drove on. Nothing to link him now with Cartwright, the motel, with any one.

His headlights bored a wide tunnel through clouds of dancing midges as his car took the hill road in from the coast. The stereo played a new tape.

30

Chapter Three

Jason Love sat under a multi-coloured sun umbrella on the flat roof of his house. Somewhere, out of sight, on the road that led from Luz to Burgau, the air horns of a country bus blared like distant bugles. The rest was heat and silence. He rather liked their brassy tone; he might buy a set for his Cord. He stretched himself lazily on the cane chair and sipped a long glass of fresh orange juice as he thought about this.

It was the morning of his third day on holiday and already the heat and timeless approach of the Algarve had relaxed him. Nothing seemed to matter here. This was lotus-eating country. The sky was a perpetual cerulean. The sight of a cloud, drifting far away towards the North African coast and no larger than a cotton wool swab, was a cause for greater consternation than news of a distant political coup, an armed uprising of insurgents in less summery lands.

One legacy of Love's Presbyterian upbringing was an uneasy feeling of guilt when not actually working. Had he not been told often enough as a boy how Satan would find work for idle hands to do? And had not all his experience of life since proved the truth of this belief? To spend more than a few days without giving a thought to work produced a feeling of guilt that no amount of rational response could entirely eradicate.

The truth was, he liked action: the sudden telephone call to an emergency, the challenge of a case other doctors had abandoned. He missed the lists of patients who had telephoned, of calls to be returned, which his housekeeper, Mrs Hunter, prepared for him. No doubt his locum was coping perfectly. And if he had to so some work here, he could wash and polish his Cord. Yet surely it was absurd to drive 1,800 miles on

31

holiday in a car more than forty years old, just to spend hours cleaning the beast?

A distant sound, imagined almost as much as heard, a faint intruder on the frontier of his consciousness, made him stand up suddenly and glance towards the beach. A speedboat towing two water skiers carved wide and graceful crescents of foam on the surface of the sea. Fishing boats were coming back from Sagres and on the horizon, going in the opposite direction, an old tramp steamer, hull down, was moving so slowly she appeared to be standing still.

But none of these sights of a summer sea had alerted him. Far down the hill on which his house was built, against the shimmering heat, the spikey cactus plants and the fig trees, he saw a sandy cloud approaching. The sunshine heliographed a message from a moving windscreen. Someone was driving up to see him. The car was small and greyish in colour. It seemed unlikely that Ross, who had promised to drive over one morning in his Auburn, would be at the wheel. Perhaps it was some other expatriate, or maybe some diligent Portuguese official eager to read the water-meter of his house, or to ask why the owner had not paid his land-tax? Love considered these possibilities, and found no enthusiasm for them. He knew that he could not be seen from the track where he was, and could think of no reason why he should be seen at all. He would lock the front door and wait in the garage until the unwanted caller had departed. Possibly Hippocrates or Galen or Aesculapius might have frowned on such behaviour, for it was remotely possible that the caller came to seek his professional aid, but this possibility he hoped was so remote that he could totally discount it.

He went down the tiled stairs quickly, crossed the living room and opened the hall door into the garage. It was almost completely dark inside, with the familiar vintage car smell of hot oil and old metal and carnauba wax polish. It was very cool here after the sunshine of the roof top. He picked his way around hazards whose position he remembered; a canoe belonging to one of the house-owner's children, a box of fireworks left over from a birthday party; an open tea chest crammed with items that would not easily fit elsewhere – slings, two skateboards, a table tennis net.

A small window in one wall overlooked the front porch, but the shutters were closed. The heat of previous summers had dried the wood and a knot had obligingly fallen out of its hole. Love applied his right eye to this viewpoint to see who might arrive.

The car came bouncing over the track, past a row of huge cacti that provided a boundary as well as a decoration, and stopped. Dust blew over it and away; the car was a Mini in the grey livery of a self-drive hire company.

The driver climbed out, and locked the door behind him. A cautious, prudent fellow, thought Love. He was tall, broad-shouldered, in a light blue jeans suit. Under his right arm he carried a flat brief-case. He walked towards the door, and Love saw his face. This could be interesting, he thought, recognizing the man, and not as a meter reader or a civil servant. But what the hell was he doing here?

The visitor pressed the bell push and smoothed perspiration off his forehead with his other hand. It was very hot in a small car in the heat of the sun.

Love eased the oiled bolts and opened the window silently. As the man turned away for a moment to look towards the swimming pool that glittered invitingly, Love punched open the shutters.

'Stay right where you are,' he ordered sharply. 'Put your hands on top of your head, and don't turn round.'

The man froze like a statue. His smart brief-case dropped on the tiled patio as he raised his hands.

'Now turn round,' Love ordered him.

The man turned very slowly.

'You bastard,' he said, and his hard face crinkled in a grin.

'I've been called other things,' said Love reprovingly. 'But your description could be nearer the truth.'

'And you a doctor,' said the man, lowering his hands. 'I might have a bad heart.'

33

'I don't think you've a heart of any kind,' Love told him. 'God only gave you a blood pump.'

Love opened the front door and shook the visitor's hand.

'Funny kind of welcome,' said the man.

'It's not meant to be a welcome,' Love replied. 'Just wanted to test your reflexes. A doctor is always on call.'

'You know what I call you.'

'Later,' said Love, and led the way into the sitting room. He opened the drinks cupboard, poured four fingers of The Glenlivet, added some fresh lime juice and a scoop of crushed ice.

'Medicinal purposes only,' he said. 'Good health.'

'I'll always drink to that.'

Years before, more years than Love now cared to recall, Colonel MacGillivray had asked him to undertake what he had assured Love would only be a small and simple task when he was attending a medical conference in Tehran. This minuscule enquiry had in fact ended with Love being lucky to escape with his life, in the snowy emptiness of Canada's North-West Territories, a long way from the architectural incongruities of mosques and skyscrapers of Iran.* But the assignment had provided one bonus, for he had met and worked with Richard Mass Parkington, the professional British agent who now stretched himself out in a wicker armchair. On other assignments which had arisen when MacGillivray had need of Love's services, and could persuade him to co-operate, they had also worked together, with mutual regard and enthusiasm.

Richard Mass Parkington, a heavy drinker, frequently taking a pep pill before hard action, and a sedative afterwards, a man with no relations, no ambitions and even less illusions, was the antithesis of Love, whose training had been to preserve life, to ease pain and not to cause it. Both were professionals. But what part of Parkington's strange profession brought him out to the Algarve, uninvited, unannounced, unexpected – but as Love now admitted to himself – not entirely unwelcome?

'Are you still working for the fruit firm?' he asked. This was

* For this adventure, read *Passport to Oblivion* (Advt).

34

a reference to a Covent Garden company, Sensoby and Ransom, Ltd., ostensibly importers of citrus and other fruit, but in fact a cover address for less publicized Intelligence activities. Under this convenient cloak, men and women of different nationalities and intentions could call at any hour of the day or night without arousing curiosity.

Parkington shook his head.

'When the Market moved south of the river we closed that,' he explained. 'Anyway, I'm on a year's sabbatical.'

'Why? Rumbled at last?'

'Almost. I found I was drinking a bottle of gin a day, and my liver would bark like a dog at the sound of ice in a glass. The doctor MacGillivray uses in such cases told me I had three alternatives. Give up drinking or my job. Or all intention of staying alive. So – I gave up the job.'

'So why are you out here?' asked Love. 'Holiday?'

'No. I leave that to well-heeled country physicians. I can't afford a year without work, so I'm doing a small job for another concern. An insurance company.'

'Don't tell me you've come all this way to sell me a pension policy? I've taken out more policies than you've eaten hot dinners, but I still haven't got my pension. Insurance, so far as I am concerned, is like marriage. You have to die to beat it.

'I'm not selling you anything,' Parkington replied. 'I'm actually offering you a chance of making a little money.'

'How little?'

'Professional fees, whatever they are. Plus reasonable expenses.'

'The operative word is "reasonable", where insurance is involved. Who are you trying to screw?'

'No-one,' said Parkington. 'We want to pay out on a policy – if someone isn't trying to screw us.'

'So how do I come in?'

'Give me another drink and I'll tell you.'

Love poured four more fingers of whisky into each glass. They carried the drinks through to the patio and sat down on

35

cane chairs, their glasses let into specially woven holes in the arms.

'I tried to get through to you in Bishop's Combe,' Parkington went on. 'But you had just left. Mrs Hunter said you were out here, so I took a plane and hired a car to see you. My business is also out here, you see. I trust you can spare a little time for my problem?'

'Which is?'

'I got this job through a friend of MacGillivray. I'm a kind of trouble-shooter for the company. Some fellow insures a barn of hay – or in your line, a vintage car – for what other people think is a bit too much money. And one night the farm is burned down or the car is stolen, and he puts in his claim. Is it an accident – or is it not? My job is to advise the experts.

'Why I'm here concerns some poor devil on the rocks in Luz, drowned and shot. Name of Frank Marshall. Self-made, and said to be proud of his maker. Suicide not likely. So – was his death accident or design?'

'We were both asked to a party, but he never arrived. He met a man with a spear-gun on the way.'

'So you heard about that?'

'Hardly heard about anything else since. Made a lot of gossip out here.'

'Interesting case, doctor. Consider the points. A man with no money problems and apparently no enemies meets someone on the beach – and, after that, neither enemies nor friends can hurt or help him. He was insured by us, the Midland Widows, for £250,000. Payable on death, wife as beneficiary, or failing her, his daughter.'

'And you,' said Love, 'or, rather, the Midland Widows, whoever they may be, don't want to pay out. You want to prove he committed suicide most ingeniously by shooting himself in the guts and then drowning himself. There is always a clause that deals with "notwithstandings" and "here-unto-befores". And under the notepaper crest of friendly handclasps the Midland Widows will have a let-out on a suicide claim. Right?'

'No. Not in this case, at least. I think Marshall was murdered.'

'So does his widow.'

'So why don't the police investigate?'

'Maybe they have or maybe they will, I don't know. I'm not in their confidence. Or maybe they think there's nothing to investigate. No clues. No motive. No witnesses. Englishman on holiday in a rented house, walks along the beach and doesn't walk back. If the police here aren't suspicious, why are the Midland Widows?'

'A good question,' said Parkington approvingly. 'And if you'll refresh my aching epiglottis with a touch more of The Glenlivet, I will endeavour to answer it. And also your slur on my new profession.'

'I'd have said it was one of the oldest,' retorted Love.

The whisky flashed gold in the sun, and then Parkington's glass was empty again. Love refilled it.

'We have an American company associated with us – Western Mutual Nominees,' Parkington began. 'Operates mostly on the west coast, with an office in Portland, Oregon. All large claims for our group are put into a central computer, so I was interested to see yesterday that we had an unusual claim from Oregon. A dentist, name of Cartwright, was shot dead in his surgery in a little town out there. His nurse had left early. She remembered letting in a stranger who had rung up saying he had tooth trouble. Dr Cartwright was able to fit him in.'

'What sort of man was this stranger?' asked Love.

'Her description was of a red-haired man, Caucasian, moustache, sunglasses. He arrived in a Mustang. She remembered that because her boyfriend has one.'

'Who discovered the body?'

'She did. When she came in to work next morning at nine o'clock. And Western Mutual Nominees held half a million dollars cover on Mr Cartwright.'

'Dentists are so much richer than doctors,' sighed Love. 'Who gets the money?'

'His widow.'

'So, like Mrs Marshall, she's going to be a rich widow?'

'Relatively so. And there's a third odd thing. The stranger who presumably shot Cartwright accepted an international telephone call in the dentist's surgery. We have a transcript of it.'

'How?'

'The dentist's wife, now his widow, or, as you would have it, his merry widow, was a jealous lady. Not to put too fine a point on things, she thought her husband was having it off with one of her friends. And on the advice of her lawyers she fitted a simple piece of electronic equipment to monitor his telephone calls.'

'Without his knowledge?'

'Of course.'

'That's the second wife I've heard of in three days who's not sorry her old man has up and died. Makes me think Oscar Wilde had a point about taxing rich bachelors. Said it was unfair that some men should be so much happier than others.'

'Maybe Oscar the wily lad did have a point. But you know the Portuguese proverb about such generalities? They're like the horns of a bull. A point here and a point there – and an awful lot of bull in between! What makes me interested in these cases is that the murderer's call came from the Algarve – from a hotel room. I have checked it out.'

'Who made it?'

'An Englishman who has now left. Name of John Henry Brandon. At least, that is the name he put on the police form visitors have to sign. But I expect it is false. He gave a fake address, of course.'

'Of course,' repeated Love. His experience of life was that most things were not what they seemed, or most people. Where had trust gone? Had honesty also died a violent death?

'What did he look like, this Brandon?'

'Medium height. Generally wore dark blue trousers as opposed to shorts. Heavy smoker.'

'You've checked all the airlines?'

'Certainly. But no-one under that name has booked in or out for a month. And the general description is too vague to be of any use.'

38

'So what do you think?'

'I think he is still here,' said Parkington. 'I also think these killings are involved. Here's the transcript of the call.'

He opened his brief-case and handed a single sheet of typescript to Love.

"I have to report I have despatched the parcel."

'That could mean Mr Cartwright?'

'Obviously.'

"Any complications?" "None." "Thank you."

'Looks like the fellow in Oregon was a hired killer reporting to the man who hired him. Must have been a pro to know he'd finish his job in time to accept a call from six thousand miles away.'

'That's my reading, too,' said Parkington. 'Maybe this fellow Brandon wanted to kill Marshall himself or he *had* to kill him for some reason which wasn't plain when he fixed up to get rid of Cartwright.'

'How can I help?' asked Love.

'Professionally. As I said.'

'As a doctor – or as a kind of undercover snooper?'

'Either or both. The Midland Widows will pay.'

'They'll have to,' said Love. 'I'm on holiday.'

'What about £50 a day, sterling, plus £500 consultation fee? To be doubled if you help materially to solve the problem.'

'And save the Midland Widows £250,000 and the Western Mutual Nominees 500,000 bucks? You are asking for a labour of Hercules, and paying for a labour of Love.'

'What's *your* estimate, then?' asked Parkington.

'A hundred pounds a day,' said Love. 'And a thousand consultation fee. Guaranteed. It's the challenge that interests me, not the money.'

'You could have fooled me,' said Parkington philosophically, and poured himself another drink. 'But even so, you've got yourself a deal. You're hired.'

*   *   *

39

When Dougal Forbes retired from the Royal Air Force as an Air Commodore, he and his wife thought at first they would settle in a small cottage near one of the airfields from which he had flown so many sorties during the war. As with other ex-officers who retired from the services relatively young, Forbes was confident he could carry on some part-time activity, such as growing orchids or asparagus, to augment his pension. Accordingly, he and his wife travelled through Oxfordshire, Suffolk, Lincolnshire and Dorset with lists of properties that estate agents recommended as ideal for their needs.

With high hopes they visited houses about which agents had sent them lyrical descriptions, but gradually their enthusiasm dimmed and finally was completely extinguished. A cottage described as 'quaint, with some most interesting and unique features', proved only to be interesting because the wooden floor was built on earth. The uniqueness of its features included a quaint lack of sanitation, lighting or even locks on its outer doors.

A house claimed to be 'ideal for a country lover' was no more than a hut surrounded by a field of flowering nettles and rancid docks. A dwelling near the coast ('compact and suitable for an artistic person'), had started life as a concrete blockhouse during the war. Cottages artistically photographed in estate agents' advertisements with wells, honeysuckle round the front door and paved patios, were far beyond the pocket of a retired Air Commodore with no resources but his pension. Twice they found something they could adapt to their needs, but each time someone else with what the agent called 'ready cash' stepped in and bought it over their heads. And then something happened that made them decide they must abandon their plans; Mrs Forbes fell ill.

A rare disease was diagnosed; her doctor told Dougal that his wife's life would not be long, and progressive deterioration must be expected. A warm climate was advisable, and soon she would not be able to concentrate sufficiently to help with any business matters. So the Forbeses abandoned their original plan, packed their belongings into their second-hand Ford station wagon and set out to find a house in the sun.

France was too expensive and Italy too exclusive. Spain was not quite to their liking, and this left the last sunlit country in Europe, Portugal. And here, after a leisurely drive south from the Spanish frontier, they decided to settle in the Algarve. The white houses and hot dusty fields brought back memories of outposts where they had served under the British flag in a happier, less complicated world. They had built a house in Monchique, a spa in the hills a few miles inland, within sight of the sea, but unaffected by tourists. Their nearest neighbour, a retired admiral, had set up a telescope on a tripod to watch the shipping lanes. He would list the nationality of passing ships by their flags, and plot the relative decline of traditionally maritime nations against the increase of flags of fiscal convenience. On the other side of the Forbeses', a retired general kept two polished brass cannons by his front door, and on such occasions as the Queen's birthday, St George's Day and the old Empire Day, he would ask friends in for drinks, and, to the consternation of local chickens, fire a royal salute. If requested, he would then fire another and shout: 'To the king across the water, God bless him!' The general never stipulated which king or what water, or why he needed divine blessing, and no-one had ever been heard to ask.

At first Forbes found they could employ a full-time maid and invite friends for drinks on any night of the week, even on his pension. The excellent gin, of course, was extremely cheap and came from a local Bols distillery. The joke was that *agua tonica* was often more expensive than the spirit.

Forbes had little capital, but he owned an old aircraft, a 1938 Tiger Moth, which he had bought very cheaply after the war. He had managed to find space for this on his last three RAF stations, and had actually flown it out himself by easy stages when he decided to emigrate. For the past two years, as living costs increased in Portugal, he had augmented his pension by giving pleasure flights to tourists in the Moth and towing advertising signs above the beaches during the summer, and by spraying crops out of season.

41

He kept the Moth in a hangar on the airstrip in Lagos, the nearest town on the coast. For most of the year Lagos was a quiet, walled town dozing at the mouth of a river, with a well-preserved slave market, a museum containing such oddities as a six-legged cat and a goat with two heads, and ample space for cars to park. During the summer months, it became so packed with visitors that even supermarkets occasionally ran short of supplies. Then Forbes and his wife would take to the air and fly west along the coast to Carrapateira. Here they would have lunch at the Casa Fajara restaurant which another former RAF officer and his wife had created in an old granary. They tried to time their visits for the first Sunday of each month when the dish of the day was a legendary chicken curry with no fewer than twenty-nine side dishes. Afterwards, they would swim in the pool, walk on an invariably almost empty beach that stretched for miles, and then fly back in time for an evening gin.

Recently, Madge Forbes's health had declined rapidly, and she was unable to accompany him. This year she seemed so feeble that Forbes had cabled his daughter Victoria to come out from London. Now he and Victoria were driving towards Lagos *aeroporto*.

'How do you think mother is this morning?' he asked her.

'Worse than when I saw her at Christmas,' she admitted.

'I think so, too. But of course you'd notice any change more than I do. I see her every day.'

Victoria and a woman friend had started a boutique in Chelsea two years previously selling, as a sideline, ornaments and costume jewellery which she made out of sea shells. To her surprise, this soon overtook the sales of dresses and coats, and they began to concentrate entirely on manufacturing such items. Now they sold their designs under licence to manufacturers in other countries. What had been a childhood interest in colouring odd-shaped stones and shells washed up on the beach, became a thriving business. Dougal Forbes secretly marvelled at such unexpected success for a girl just twenty-three. Why, at that age, he was still a flying officer, flying Hengists and Hannibals from Quetta. He was also surprised and pleased because Victoria shared his interest in flying, and had already 200 hours solo in her log-book. Now they planned a flight along the coast together; there was nothing like wind in one's face to put family problems in perspective.

Forbes turned the car off the main road, towards the airfield. The day was hotter than a baker's oven, and the yellow wind sock hung limp as an old man's nightcap. His plane was already outside the hangar. Ramon, a retired Portuguese Air Force fitter, now looked after it as a part-time job, and was waiting for them.

'I have taken off the spraying jets and the tank, senhor,' he explained.

'Why?' asked Forbes surprised. He had an unexpected contract to spray maize crops near Burgau on the following day.

'This morning a gentleman is here who wishes to hire your plane.'

'It's not for hire this morning,' Victoria told him sharply.

'I know, senhorinha, but this man has waited to ask you personally. He is English.'

A man who had been standing in the shade of the hangar now crossed the dusty tarmac. He was tanned and wore a lightweight jacket, a green shirt and well-pressed trousers. He appeared cool despite the heat; a man accustomed to the tropics, Forbes thought with unconscious approval.

'Air Commodore Forbes?' the man asked him.

'The same.'

'My name is Jarrold,' the man went on. 'I am staying in the Penina hotel. I heard you owned a plane, and I wondered if you undertook any charter flights?'

'Sometimes,' Forbes began. 'But . . .'

'I would like to prevail upon you to take me up in your plane,' Jarrold went on, ignoring the older man's hesitation.

'My father and I were flying together,' Victoria said pointedly.

Forbes nodded. Then he and his daughter exchanged glances. She looked suddenly tense, nervous. Perhaps she was annoyed that her father should even consider sacrificing their plan so easily. But money was short. With exchange difficulties and high inflation, fewer people wanted to hire the aircraft, and his wife's medical fees were not cheap.

'It is difficult today,' Forbes said slowly. 'As my daughter says, we were flying together.'

'I quite understand, Air Commodore,' Jarrold replied smoothly. 'And so I would be prepared to pay you highly. For two hours, 5,000 escudos.' Jarrold used the more educated pronunciation, not the local abbreviation, 'scudes'.

'I'll pay you in notes if you wish.'

Forbes looked at his daughter questioningly. This was a lot of money; nearly £65. She nodded, but reluctantly.

'We'll have to make our flight another day,' she told her father.

How far have I sunk? Forbes thought bitterly. I, who held the King's commission, then the Queen's commission, now being offered notes on a shabby airfield from a stranger.

'Good,' said Jarrold briskly, as though he had no doubt whatever over the outcome. 'I am a naturalist, interested in problems of ecology and environment.'

'Where do you want to go?' Victoria asked him.

'Out over the sea. West. Towards Sagres.'

'You will have to keep well out over the water, then,' Forbes told him. 'There are military installations down there the authorities can be touchy about.'

'That doesn't concern me. I am studying the behaviour of dolphins. Whether they follow any specific pattern of tide. You can come down low?'

'To a hundred feet.'

'That would be ideal.'

'Let me fly Mr Jarrold, father,' said Victoria suddenly. 'I haven't flown a Tiger since I was here at Easter.'

'Are you sure?'

Forbes felt relieved. He did not greatly take to this man who was so sure of himself and whose certainty seemed to magnify his own hesitancy. He had been as confident once, but not for

44

years. Events had overtaken him too quickly; rules of etiquette and honour now no longer applied. He was growing old; and since Madge's illness . . .

'I'd *like* to,' Victoria assured him.

'Right, then.'

He turned to Jarrold.

'Have you ever flown in one of these before? If not, I must warn you, they are damned draughty.'

'I could use a draught on a day like this.'

'Climb in, then,' said Forbes.

Forbes folded down the front cockpit's door and helped Jarrold up into the seat.

'Wear this helmet,' he told him, being deliberately brusque to show that, in some areas at least, his authority must be unchallenged.

'Now, this is the Gosport tube. Pull it out to speak. If Victoria has a message, you will hear it in your ear piece.'

He liked giving these instructions, just as he liked the familiar routine of pre-flight checks. Their constancy in a world of swift and kaleidoscopic change was somehow reassuring.

Switch on the fuel, wait while Ramon lifts the right-hand engine cowling and primes the carburettor.

Check both magneto switches are off, and throttle closed.

Wait again while Ramon pulls propeller round 12 times to prime the engine. Then open the throttle and crack and call to Ramon: 'Switches off. Throttle set.'

Give him the thumbs-down signal to show him visually that the switches really are off.

Contact.

Push up front magneto switch. Ramon pulls propeller down and jumps clear as the engine fires.

Flick up rear magneto switch.

Hold the stick back with one elbow to stop the tail lifting off the ground when the engine starts.

Then keep the engine running for exactly four minutes at 1,000 revs to warm the oil.

Check the oil pressure is above 30 p.s.i. Switch both magneto switches off and on quickly to check that both mags are working.

Increase engine revs to 1,600, let the engine settle and then check each magneto to ensure that the drop in revolutions between them does not exceed 50 r.p.m. Check both magnetos are on and throttle back to idle. Then it is hands across the chest, the signal for Ramon to pull away the chocks.

Forbes proudly watched his daughter go through the familiar sequence. He waved to her as the aircraft moved down the runway, weaving from side to side, a zig-zag progress necessary in a Moth on the ground because the angle of the fuselage meant that the nose of the machine completely blocked off the view ahead.

Victoria checked oil pressure and compass again, set the altimeter at zero and tested the movement of the controls to make sure they were working freely. Then she lined up the Moth on the runway and took off.

Her father watched her go, then he thought about her passenger, and remembered his daughter's sudden tenseness. He had seen a similar expression once on a woman's face, years ago, when she pretended not to know a man to whom she was being introduced, although they had actually been to bed together.

As Forbes had fastened Jarrold's Sutton harness his hand had brushed against a hard metallic object in his jacket. Forbes had been in the Services too long not to know what this was. Now, as he drove away from the airfield, he felt unease increase.

If Jarrold was simply, as he said, a naturalist, why did he find it necessary to fly with a gun in the top inner pocket of his jacket? And why did his own daughter pretend not to know him, when Forbes, as her father, felt convinced they had at least met before?

*   *   *

Love heard the drone of the four-cylinder de Havilland engine as he lay on a floating mattress in the swimming pool. The plane came in fairly low overhead, and then turned out

46

towards the sea. He swam to the side of the pool, pulled himself out and followed its progress, surprised that such a vintage aircraft should be so far from home.

Usually, the only aircraft overhead were airliners, either beginning or ending their long climb to or from Faro airport, away to the east. Sometimes, a Portuguese military plane would skim low over the sea, or a holidaymaker, richer than the rest, would arrive in his private Cessna, but this was the only Tiger Moth he had seen. He watched it fly out above the speed-boats, turn over the cargo ship Love had first seen on the previous day. She could barely have covered ten miles in that time. Now she seemed almost stationary. The Moth turned again and flew out towards the horizon, just above the sea. Then she banked and turned once more in a wide circle. It was as though the pilot was looking for something, and not quite sure where to begin to search. Well, that was no concern of his, thought Love thankfully. He pulled a towel around him, and walked across the hot calçada, up the steps to the patio. Here on a cane table, in the shade, the maid had set out a bucket of ice cubes, a bottle of The Glenlivet and some freshly squeezed lime juice. As he stretched out in the chair and poured himself a drink, the Tiger Moth dwindled to a dot in the blueness of the sky.

*   *   *

Twenty odd miles to the west, in an upper room of an hotel near the old fort of Sagres, from which Henry the Navigator had centuries before sent out his sea captains with orders to seek trade routes to the East, another man was also watching the aircraft.

This man was older than Love, with a sallow complexion. His lips were compressed into a thin line; he was not a man who smiled a lot. He wore heavy horn-rimmed glasses, and his chin was blue as steel against the deeper blue of his Sulka shirt. As he raised his elbows, to focus his binoculars on the deck of the stationary cargo ship, a fine gold chain dangled from his right wrist. This bore a slim gold identity disc engraved with his name: Eugene Volkoff.

47

The room was littered with the possessions of a man who travelled widely and always well. A minute stereo radio and an alarm clock were expensively cocooned in a slim case covered with crocodile skin. Half a dozen books high on best-seller lists in London and New York littered the bed. A piece of Indian pottery he had bought in Bombay and carried with him, disregarding excess baggage costs, because he considered it too delicate to send by freight, stood in protective polystyrene packing near the table. Jackets and shirts and trousers were scattered across the bed. Four pairs of Tricker's shoes in trees waited neatly in a line against the wardrobe. Volkoff was a man who had known poverty for long and hardship for even longer. Now he carried with him the visible and unmistakeable signs of success, as men in other countries wear medals and ribbons of orders and awards, evidence of past valour, and others take pride in bearing scars of student duels on their cheeks. All in their different ways are both a badge of virility and a masculine mark of success. They tell others something of their wearer's achievements; and at least as much about the wearer.

Volkoff allowed it to be generally known he had been born in Estonia, now absorbed by Russia, but no-one knew exactly where or when, or who his parents had been or how he could now afford homes in Geneva and Rome. He kept his past to himself, remembering, in the midst of luxury, privations and insults he had endured when he was young and poor, drawing a sour satisfaction from the recollection, as others suck a hollow tooth.

Whatever Volkoff had done, wherever he had been, those times belonged firmly to his past. Every man born of woman was also born to suffer, so his father had frequently told him, and the old man's whole life had been living proof of this melancholy belief. He accepted this as the natural order of things – adding the inescapable truth that the fittest and the fastest and the most cunning and ruthless survive, and whatever else he was, Volkoff prided himself on being a survivor.

He stood now, legs slightly apart to steady the bulk of his body, and his broad shoulders slightly hunched as though ready to repel an attack – or make one. Biceps bulged against the thin expensive silk of his shirt. His lips were pursed and his forehead puckered as he adjusted the glasses. Why the devil was that ship stationary? Surely he of all men had most right to know, for he owned the bloody thing. And, according to his calculations, she should have been past Sagres by now. Instead, she still trembled in a haze of heat, without even a wisp of smoke from her funnel. There must have been a breakdown of some kind in the engine room. If not, surely there would be smoke or steam or *some* sign of life? But even through his Zeiss glasses, which gave a 50 times magnification, he could see no movement on her decks. Were the crew dead? Had some plague or pox struck them down? Could that be the reason for the old-fashioned aircraft circling around and away, diving each time closer to the shabby, old-fashioned superstructure?

And whose plane was this, anyway – an eccentric holiday-maker whose whim was to fly such a machine, or did she belong to some obscure section of the local Portuguese customs or maritime authorities? He had seen two strange old cars in Lagos, an Auburn and a Cord, owned, of course, by Englishmen who found pleasure in old machinery. Perhaps a man who liked old aircraft was indulging his innocent hobby? Questions and answers pursued each other in his mind, always infuriatingly keeping their distance, like painted horses on a fairground swing.

With a gold propelling pencil Volkoff noted the registration number of the plane on an Asprey's pad. The letters meant nothing to him. He wondered who could help him – the manager of the hotel, the local tourist information office? He happened to be travelling on a Dutch passport; perhaps their embassy could help? If not, he had three other passports in the name of Volkoff, in three different nationalities, and one in another name altogether. Surely out of that collection of embassies, *someone* could help him?

He began to thumb through the Portuguese telephone directory, which was divided into sections – Zonas – for different parts of the country, until he came to Lisbon. He noted the numbers he needed – and his eye caught another number on the pad. A number in Waldport, Oregon, in the United States, that he had called earlier that morning. It had been a person-to-person call to Dr Cartwright. He was surprised when the operator had rung him back to say that Dr Cartwright was unable to take any personal calls.

'But I am an old friend,' Volkoff had protested.

'I am sorry, sir,' said the operator politely across 3,000 miles of ocean and even more of land, 'but where Dr Cartwright is right now, no-one can reach him.'

'I have not made myself clear,' said Volkoff, his voice rising in his anxiety to express himself to this unknown alien so far away.

'My name is Volkoff. I am his *oldest* friend. I *must* speak to him.'

'You don't understand me, sir,' she replied patiently. 'Dr Cartwright is dead.'

'*Dead?* How?'

'I cannot help you with any information, sir, but I can put you through to his widow, if you wish.'

'I am a friend of your husband,' Volkoff explained to her, speaking slowly to avoid any possible misunderstanding because of the distance or his accent. 'I am ringing him about a business matter, and I am told that unfortunately he has died.'

'Yes,' replied the widow. 'Day before yesterday.'

There was no trace of sorrow or surprise in her voice. She might have been explaining to a salesman at the door that someone had just sold her a satisfactory vacuum cleaner, and so she did not wish to buy his product.

'But how? In an accident?'

'Murdered.'

'*Murdered?*' Volkoff repeated the word in amazement.

'Yes. Someone came to his surgery just before he finished work, and shot him.'

'What a terrible thing, Mrs Cartwright. I cannot comprehend it. Have you any idea who did this?'

'Of course not. But the nurse saw the caller – before he shot my husband, of course – and gave a description. What is the nature of your business? Can I help you?'

'I met your husband abroad,' said Volkoff carefully, not wishing to become involved. 'In India. He had given my company considerable advice about certain medicinal matters, and I was anxious to contact him on something else arising out of this. But of course, I would not bother you now, madam.'

'Where are you speaking from?'

'I am actually in Portugal now.'

'But there was a call made to my husband's office from Portugal. Was that you?'

'I have never made or received a call from him, madam. I do not think he even knows I am here. Have you the number?'

'Yes, I have. But of course my husband did not speak to the man. The call was taken by his killer. And on my husband's own phone, with his dead body right there in front of him.'

A moment of silence. Static whistled in Volkoff's ear. He imagined the radio waves of their voices crossing Atlantic breakers high as the hills, going on over the coast, above the vast central plains of America, across the Rockies, and down the other side to the bleak shores of Oregon, where another sea beat on another shore.

'Have you a pencil?' Mrs Cartwright asked, breaking into his thoughts.

'Yes, I have, madam.'

'Here it is.' She read out the number to him. He noted it on the pad.

'Thank you, madam. Please accept my deepest sympathies on your bereavement.'

In times of stress, Volkoff fell back on the flowery phraseology he had learned from the professor who had taught him English – how many years ago and in what forgotten university? Had that been when he was reading science at Riga, or philosophy in Warsaw?

'Thank you,' she said. 'And your name, please?'

Volkoff replaced the receiver gently without replying.

Now he pushed the directory to one side. There was nothing to be gained by making a fuss over the plane's registration letters. He would pass this problem on to someone else. He was not so much concerned with the plane, as with the ship. He glanced again towards the vessel, but she was still stationary. He put his binoculars in the brief-case, locked this and placed it in the wardrobe, locked that, and pocketed the key. Then he left the room and walked down the long winding path to the port. At a kiosk, he bought an English newspaper. He liked the crossword as much as the day old news it contained. He hated having a mind inactive and unexercised. That reminded him of years in different prison camps, under Germans and Russians, or as a refugee during that other part of his life which he forced himself to forget.

The brain was like a muscle; if you didn't exercise it regularly, then it became sluggish and feeble. Others sharpened their minds with conversation, but he was essentially a solitary person. If you talked too much, you might give away a part of your personality, maybe part of your plans, and that way could lead to disaster. The jails of every country were filled with lonely men who had talked too soon, too easily, in too much detail.

Volkoff walked into a bar near the harbour. It was a long cool room, hung with ropes of onions and sides of smoked fish. He sat down at a tile-topped table and ordered a Bock beer. While he waited for it to arrive, he glanced through the paper, noting the trivia that seemed so important today and was forgotten within an hour. Then a headline caught his eye: *HOLIDAYMAKER DIES IN PORTUGAL. Frank Marshall, 50, on holiday from his home in Letchworth, Herts, with his wife and daughter, was found dead in curious circumstances on a deserted beach near the seaside resort of Praia da Luz in Portugal's Algarve, last night.*

Marshall, who was half-way through a fortnight's stay, had apparently been shot at close range by a snorkel diver's spear gun. Police are investigating.

My God, thought Volkoff, and lowered the paper. Although

52

the day was hot, he felt suddenly chill. Sweat, nothing to do with the heat, spread like a damp patch of dismay between his shoulders. Cartwright shot in Oregon, and now Marshall – and only a few miles along the coast. What the devil was Marshall doing in Portugal, anyhow? It had been agreed that he would keep well away until everything was finished. The fewer faces that might later be recognized, the fewer people who afterwards could remember anyone, the better. Had he been planning a double-cross? Or had someone double-crossed him?

He sipped his beer, but he did not enjoy it. He felt uneasy, nervous, unsure of himself. He would go to ground until events made it necessary for him to show himself again. Then, if he had to, he would kill. He folded up the newspaper, threw a 50 escudo note on the bar and walked back to his hotel, moving with speed and agility surprising in so large and heavy a man.

As he did so, the man who had been watching Volkoff from an upper window from the moment he left the hotel, picked up the telephone and made a call.

Chapter Four

Five miles east of Sagres, the steamship *Princess Rosael* rolled in the heavy Atlantic swell. The sharp smell of salt that the fierce beating of the sun had released was now overlaid by the dry acridity of hot rust, and the sickly stench of leaking engine oil.

For *Princess Rosael,* 41 years old and displacing 3,742 tons, this unexpected halt was one more delay on her slow last voyage to the breakers. Her seagoing days were all but over. Ahead lay the ultimate dishonour of every old ship: dismemberment under blue flames. For most of her life *Princess Rosael* had carried unromantic cargoes to unexciting destinations. Coal from Newcastle to Tilbury. Wood pulp for paper-making from Oslo to Bristol; spare parts for tanks and tractors; sacks of grain and drums of edible oil to a dozen more distant ports. During the war she had lagged behind in a hundred undistinguished convoys. Sometimes she had carried wounded men on her decks from other ships sunk by U-boat or air attack; once she had been torpedoed but had limped on to Durban for repairs.

After the war, her career had been no less arduous, but even more depressing, flying the flags of countries not renowned for traditional association with the sea: Liberia, Panama, Haiti. Sometimes on these latter voyages, S.S. *Princess Rosael* would be in cargo but her owners would appear more concerned about other ventures. A motor launch with muffled exhausts would approach in the darkness near some unlikely coast – East Africa, the Lebanon, Burma – and disappear discreetly, having embarked or disembarked passengers or cargo that did not appear on the ship's manifest. Sometimes shots had been fired, and on two occasions, both off Mozambíque, there had to be hasty burials at sea with bodies weighted by links of anchor chain.

In the summer of 1967 the *Princess Rosael* was bound from Beirut through the Suez Canal with a cargo of cheap French chemical preparations destined to be relabelled and sold as aphrodisiacs to middle-aged men in Pakistan. Unfortunately, these would-be Lotharios never received this elixir of youth, for the Arab-Israeli war of that year caused the Canal to be closed. All ships unfortunate enough to be caught in the area were refused permission to sail on. For days the crews waited; then for weeks, and then for months. Finally, the owners paid them off and they flew home. A succession of local watchmen took over, careless of maintenance. They spent their time smoking, playing cards. Old paint blistered under a pitiless sun, revealing coats of different colours beneath the uniform grey.

Eventually, holds were sealed and welded shut, and most of the watchmen withdrawn. Several cargoes were sold to enterprising local traders who brought out barges and other craft to carry them away. Items such as heavy machinery, which could not be disposed of because they needed cranes to lift them, rusted in a dozen foetid hulls. At last, after much haggling, and the writing of many letters marked by careful lawyers, 'without prejudice', insurance companies reluctantly paid out on the ships and what they still contained. Then agents there sold both as quickly as possible to other men, without any notable interest in the sea, but who could scent a quick profit somehow – if only in scrap metal if these buyers had what accountants called hot money which could cool conveniently once it was invested in such vessels. There might even be tax losses, so that money on which tax had never been paid would now reap a double dividend. But some ships were more difficult to dispose of, for reasons of uneconomic size or age. Among these were S.S. *Princess Rosael*, and another of similar tonnage.

They were unexpectedly bought by the Associated Assets Inc. of Mayfair, in London. Several distinguished names appeared on the richly embossed notepaper of this concern, but the active partner was Eugene Volkoff. He put in tax claims for many thousands of pounds for refurbishing both vessels. Most of this money was never actually spent on them but on his own yacht lying at Villefranche. There was a small matter of forging bill heads, which, since he owned his own printing press, was simple enough to do. The star of commercial fortune had shone brightly for years on him, and his ventures had prospered in many countries. It was thus only to be expected that after a relatively short delay – during which certain other financial dispositions were made to officials involved – the Egyptian authorities gave permission for the two ships to leave. They were thankful to be rid of them; all other ships in a similar predicament had left literally years before.

A sub-contractor hurriedly engaged a scratch crew, without asking for references: a former captain forced to retire from the French Merchant Navy because of problems of drink; a Scottish engineer of doubtful temper; a Welsh assistant with a jail record; two dozen sailors of Mediterranean appearance, some with stolen British passports, and others who hoped to melt away among thousands of other illegal immigrants once the ship reached Newcastle. The Associated Assets Inc. would then sell the ships as scrap to another company under its control. Bills would be paid in Lichtenstein. Tax losses would accumulate satisfactorily and later be acquired by yet another associated company, for in a world with a declining need for cargo ships, the two ships were like old horses: worth much more dead than alive.

An Egyptian firm of engineers in Alexandria patched up their ancient engines, and they sailed cautiously, with much smoke and smell, into the Mediterranean, and along the rim of the horizon of the holiday beaches. But before this took place, several gentlemen of foreign countenance but Anglo-Saxon names presented engraved calling cards to the captain of the *Princess Rosael* (as the more important of the two) and suggested that for a fee he might be willing to carry certain articles or friends of theirs aboard his vessel, once she had cleared Egyptian customs.

The captain, although a drunk, was a reasonably honest drunk (or not clever enough to consider how he could do this at a safe profit to himself) and had no wish to be used as a carrier of drugs or currency or stolen diamonds, or even international terrorists.

He had therefore declined these proposals, although those who made them steadily increased their offers. Feeling virtuous and incorruptible, he had told his chief engineer, Jock McNab; and McNab, while praising his captain's sense of honour, privately entertained doubts about his sense of commercial values. Thus, when McNab was drinking alone in a bar in Alexandria one evening, and the barman mentioned casually he had a friend with a proposition which might interest him, McNab inclined his head in willingness to listen, and was escorted to an upstairs room where he bent his ear towards this friend. He spoke English well, but obviously he was not English. McNab guessed he was a man made stateless after the war, when his country had been overrun by one side or the other, and no-one had greatly cared because it had not contained mineral or oil deposits or anything else of immediate potential value.

He was a quiet man, as was no doubt fitting for a former citizen of such an unfortunate country, but his quietness had all the confidence of authority. McNab noted that he wore an expensive shirt and a gold Piaget wristwatch, which even at duty-free prices, was not the means by which a poor man counted time. After the customary greetings and solicitous enquiries as to each other's health and the prospects of various sporting teams, and a generous outpouring of whisky, the barman's friend came to the point of his discourse.

'I understand your ship will be sailing soon?'

McNab agreed; this was common knowledge.

'I have something that must be transported back to England. Not drugs, so let me set your mind at rest on that point right away. I know and respect the reluctance of people to become involved with that foul traffic. What I have is something else altogether – part of a set of jewels that once belonged to the

57

regalia of the Royal Family in Albania. I wish – as one who still has relations living in that country – although I am not an Albanian myself, you understand – that these jewels should be returned to their rightful owners.

'It is at present impossible, as you may know, to export jewellery from Egypt without a great deal of bureaucracy. All travellers are searched very carefully for arms or bombs at airports, and so these jewels, which are of some bulk, would easily be discovered and whoever carried them could be placed in a situation of embarrassment. With your ship going to be broken up, however, there will be no customs search as she leaves the Canal.'

'What about when she reaches England?'

'Nothing, my friend. The jewels will be deposited *en route*.'

'We are not stopping anywhere, so far as I know.'

'They could be put over the side in a container and others would pick them up.'

'That would be risky with jewels, surely?'

The barman's friend lifted his shoulders with the air of one who takes the point – but who is not concerned with it.

'Life is risky, my friend,' he assured McNab. 'As we leave this bar, either of us may be knocked down by a taxi, and die in the street like dogs. The drink we are just now enjoying may affect us in an unexpected way. We could be poisoned. Risks are made to be taken, and this is one I am prepared to take. There is, of course, no risk whatever so far as you are concerned.'

'What's in it for me to make me concerned?' asked McNab bluntly, pouring more whisky into his glass. He hated all this convoluted talk; let's get to the bloody point.

'Five thousand American dollars now. Five thousand more on arrival in Newcastle.'

McNab said nothing, but he could feel the whisky pound in his veins with each beat of his heart as he considered this offer.

'Too little,' he said at last, for he was no stranger to transactions in the Middle East. 'I'd be in stook if this was discovered.'

58

'How much do you want, then?'

'Double that. Ten thousand now. Ten thousand on arrival.'

'Too much,' replied the barman's friend quickly. 'Eight now. Eight more on arrival.'

McNab stretched out his hand. He sensed it would be unwise to push his luck too far in a deal like this. And how else could he make 16,000 dollars so easily?

Two mornings later, when the ship was almost deserted, a bum boat bumped against the *Princess Rosael's* hull. In a burnous, with two dark-skinned men similarly dressed, the man approached McNab a second time. He carried a shabby canvas bag with leather handles, and made no sign of recognition. The three men climbed aboard nimbly and spread out wooden carvings on a mat. McNab bought a few trinkets, and was shown what this bag contained: an oblong metal box about a foot long, and six inches wide. All the edges had been carefully soldered to make it completely watertight. There was no label or lettering on the metal. McNab shook it and nothing rattled inside.

'This is the package,' the barman's friend explained. 'And here is something for you.'

He handed an unsealed brown envelope to McNab. It was full of well-thumbed hundred dollar bills.

'You need not count them. I do not make mistakes over money.'

'I hope not,' said McNab. 'When and where do I dump this box?'

'I understand you are keeping in sight of shore all the way?'

'You know more than I do,' said McNab.

The man shrugged, as though denial was pointless, which, of course, it was.

'As you leave the Mediterranean for the Atlantic, you will recognize Sagres, the most westerly town in Europe?'

'I've seen it often enough,' replied McNab.

'Good. Turning north, then, there are cliffs so steep no-one can climb them. As you approach these, watch for a Morse signal – red light at night, mirror if you pass in daylight. The

59

first three letters of the first part of your ship's name – P.R.I. – then the same in reverse, at intervals of five minutes.'

'And then?'

'You are an engineer. So you must weld this box inside a metal drum or some such buoyant container. Then you throw it over the side.'

'In daylight someone might see me.'

'You will wait until dusk if you receive the signal during the day. Do not be concerned. People will be waiting on the shore. They will pick it up.'

'And that is all I have to do?'

'That is all.'

'What about the rest of my fee?'

'When you dock, go to the Royal Turk's Head hotel in Newcastle. You will find an envelope waiting for you at the reception desk in your name. Any more questions?'

'None,' said McNab, although he would have liked to know why royal regalia from Albania should need to be thrown into the sea more than forty years after the late King Zog had left that country. But somehow he sensed this was not the moment to ask. Had it been considered necessary for him to know, no doubt he would have been told.

The barman's friend salaamed, as though he was indeed a humble Arab trader grateful for European custom. McNab waved him away. The bum boat moved slowly back to shore.

Now McNab, awoken from sleep by a telephone call from his deputy, the Welshman, was down in his engine room as the ship rocked, dipped and rolled sluggishly like a broken-backed whale. He was thinking about this meeting. He had tried to open the box, of course, but it had been expertly welded and he could not melt the joins without the risk of damage to the contents. Were they jewels? It was possible, but he could not be sure. Whatever was inside must be of considerable value if he could be paid $16,000 simply for transporting it through the Med.

He had also wondered about the identity of the barman's friend, each time he felt the dollars heavy against his stomach, for he had crammed the bills into the moneybelt next to his skin. Maybe they would meet again, and there would be other missions for even greater fees?

Under the throbbing electric bulbs in their screened cases on the bulkheads, the ship's engine gleamed and glittered; McNab was a conscientious engineer. The engine room smelled strongly of oil, and metal plates creaked wearily against each other as the ship rolled. McNab checked the dials and gauges. Why the devil had the engine stopped? He walked around its huge shining bulk, and gave an exclamation of surprise. A copper feed-pipe had been nipped with a pair of pincers. The engine was being starved of fuel – deliberately. What the devil did that mean? He was examining the break when he heard footsteps behind him, the faint squeak of rubber-soled shoes on a metal catwalk. He turned.

His deputy, the Welshman Terry Hood, stood behind him.

'Bloody pipe's been nipped,' began McNab, perplexed.

'I know,' said Hood. 'I did it.'

'*You* did it? What the hell for?'

'I had to stop the engine.'

'Had to stop the engine?' McNab repeated. 'But why?'

'Because you are carrying something aboard this ship that I want.'

'What the hell are you talking about?'

'Don't give me that crap,' said Hood shortly. 'You know what I mean.'

McNab stared at Hood, unease spreading through him. How could this Welsh bastard have discovered about the tin box? Had he overheard something – or had the barman's friend told him? Sixteen thousand dollars was a lot of money – and obviously only a fraction of the value of whatever that box contained. He would have to play this carefully; Hood was younger, bigger and tougher than he was. But not, he judged, a brighter man.

'I don't know what you are talking about,' McNab said flatly.

'Then this may help you to understand – quickly.'

61

Hood took an open-ended spanner from the back pocket of his jeans and smashed the knuckles of McNab's hand as he gripped the rail.

'You bastard!' cried McNab. 'It's bloody mutiny.'

'It'll be bloody murder if you don't tell me. Where is the packet you're carrying?'

For a moment, McNab stood, stroking his injured hand, looking at Hood with what he hoped was bewilderment. The floor of the engine room moved slowly with the turning tide. Somewhere, a transistor radio was playing. He heard the drip, drip of fluid from a leaking gland.

'The bridge will be on the blower to ask why the engine's stopped,' he said. He was playing for time, hoping to get his hands on a spanner or a marlin spike, anything to beat down this lunatic. But even in a ship bound for the scrapyard, the engine room was as tidy as he could keep it. All tools were neatly clipped in racks on bulkheads. He could not reach them in time.

'I have reported a fuel-line break to the bridge and said I'm repairing it,' Hood replied smugly.

'So you've worked this out then?'

'Since we left port, I've been looking for what you smuggled aboard. And you're going to tell me where you've hidden it. *Now!*'

Hood hit McNab again, this time below the left knee. McNab was not expecting the blow, and he staggered and slipped on the metal floor, winding himself.

'All right,' he admitted sullenly, as he crawled to his feet. 'I'll tell you. I *was* given a box. But I don't know what's inside it.'

'Where is it?'

'I've welded it inside an oil drum.'

'There are a dozen drums here,' said Hood. 'Which is it? Hurry, man.' He raised the spanner again threateningly. McNab jerked his head towards a row of identical black metal oil drums, lashed by a rope to a bulkhead.

'Third from this end,' he said shortly.

Hood crossed the floor, untied the rope and rolled the drum for a few paces. Then he shook it. Both men heard a splash of liquid and something heavy and metallic boomed against the side.

'How do I know it's in there?'

'You can hear it, can't you? And look at the top of the drum where I've welded it.'

Hood examined the scars of metal which McNab had roughly concealed with black paint.

'Well?' asked McNab. 'Satisfied?'

'I have to be,' said Hood. 'But if you are playing tricks with me, you'll get it, mate, good and hard. That'll be your lot.'

'Tell me one thing,' said McNab. 'How did you know?'

'Ah, that would be telling, wouldn't it? Let's just say that you're not the only one who wants to make a bit on the side.'

'I see.'

'What's the juice in the drum?'

'Petrol. So it will float. But don't open it down here. We may start a fire.'

'I don't intend to open it at all,' Hood replied.

McNab bowed his head wearily as though abject in defeat. Hood looked at him with all the contempt of youth for age. He put the spanner back into his pocket and picked up the drum. It was heavy and awkward to carry. He struggled up the companionway, cursing its weight. McNab waited until he had reached the next deck, and then limped across the engine room and went out by a side door. He ran to his cabin, opened the second drawer in the chest next to his bunk and took a ·38 Smith & Wesson revolver which he kept in a waterproof pouch under his shirts. He checked that it was loaded, crammed the weapon in his belt and went up on deck, forward.

To starboard, the land lay like a long dark crouching animal. Lights glittered faintly as cars drove along the coast road. The sea was choppy, flecked with breaking waves. The wind blew salt spray in his face. His gashed knuckles ached and throbbed. He sucked the wound as he crept along the deck.

Hood was up towards the stern, glancing around to make

63

sure no-one was in sight. McNab waited in the shadows. Hood raised the heavy drum and threw it out as far as he could away from the ship. It landed with a splash, and bumped once, twice, against the metal hull with the deep boom of a giant gong. Then the tide took it.

Hood stood, leaning over the rail, hands pressed on the wood, eyes straining in the darkness to watch its progress. He did not hear McNab come up behind him; and when he did hear him it was too late.

McNab gave him a heavy rabbit punch on the back of the head with the butt of his revolver, and as Hood reeled, legs sagging, McNab heaved him up and over the side. Hood gave a scream as he hit the water, then disappeared in a froth of bubbles. He surfaced and began to choke and shout frantically, waving his arms.

McNab fired. His first bullet went wide. The second hit Hood in the shoulder. He jerked in the water like a marionette, and gave a shrill cry of pain and alarm. Then he saw McNab aim again and dived to swim out of range. McNab watched him surface near the drum. Then he lost them both in the darkness. McNab broke his revolver, threw the empty cartridge cases into the sea and returned to his cabin.

He cleaned the revolver carefully, replaced it in the drawer and poured himself four fingers from one of the half dozen bottles of whisky he had bought in the bar in Alex. Only then did he return to the engine room to deal with the nipped fuel pipe.

The bridge telephone tinkled. He picked it up.

'How much longer with that repair?' the first officer asked him gruffly.

'We're both working on it, sir,' replied McNab smartly. 'It's not just a fault in the line, as Hood reported. There are complications.'

'Well, do your best with them.'

That's just what I am doing, thought McNab, as he replaced the receiver. He smiled at his reflection in a sliver of mirror pegged against the bulkhead. And it's just what I'll go on doing until I've got the rest of that cash.

Chapter Five

The Algarve was a country long before it became a province of Portugal. Its name comes from the Arabic *El Gharb*, west of 'The land beyond', and Algarve still bears the legacy of five centuries of Moorish rule – in the dark faces of the locals as much as in the white cube-like architecture of their houses, and the graceful minarets that disguise humble chimneys.

Until 1910, when Portugal became a republic, the Algarve – 80 miles of coast by 30 miles of land – was Europe's smallest kingdom. Its rulers had held the title of 'Kings of Portugal and the Algarve', from the days when the Crusaders captured the ancient city of Silves, about nine miles from the coast, and drove the Moors over the sea to North Africa.

The Algarve's climate and vegetation owe more to Africa than to Europe; and Western civilization owes more than most imagine to the Algarve.

From Lagos, a fleet set out on a July day in 1415, to capture the great Arab port of Ceuta, opposite Gibraltar. The commander of this force, which involved 50,000 troops, was Dom Joao, whose son, the Infante Dom Henrique (half-English, because John of Gaunt was his grandfather), later became governor of the Algarve. At Sagres, Europe's most westerly port, and thirty miles from Lagos, Dom Henrique – known also as Henry the Navigator – established a school with cartographers and geographers to instruct his sea captains in the arts of navigation. Then, in caravels little larger than the fishing boats their descendants use today, these mariners sailed west, to the Azores and Brazil, south towards the Cape of Good Hope, east to India and China. Without these men and their vessels, without Henry the Navigator to teach and inspire them, without their upbringing in the Algarve, these great pioneering voyages of discovery would have been delayed for generations. But while Sagres was the port of departure for their ships, Lagos was where the ships were built, and so holds a special importance in the conquest of the seas.

Love was thinking about this as he sat now at an open-air café in Lagos. He was wondering what these old captains would say if they could see all the foreign tourists in shorts and jeans and bikinis (according to age, sex and inclination) walking up and down the streets. Was it for this shrinking of the world into terms of plastic souvenirs and package tours that they had sailed into the vast unknown?

A shadow darkened his table. Love looked up. Ross was standing behind a chair, smiling.

'A drink?' Love asked him.

'Delighted,' said Ross. 'A Sagres beer.'

He took a seat beneath the striped umbrella.

'Mrs Marshall has seen the consul,' he went on with the importance of one with serious information to pass on. 'Her husband's body is being flown back to England tomorrow.'

'She's going with it?'

'No, she is leaving later. I don't know when, exactly. I think she is bearing up very well.'

'Remarkably so,' agreed Love. He thought, but did not add, that Mrs Marshall would doubtless be even more upborne when the Midland Widows came across with their £250,000.

'I would be very pleased if you and your wife would come up for a drink with me tonight,' he continued. 'In your Auburn. It would be fun to take a photograph of the two old cars together. A friend of mine, Dick Parkington, is going to drop in. Maybe we could all go on somewhere for dinner, like the other night?'

'We'd love to,' said Ross, 'but tonight we are already booked for drinks. Tomorrow, perhaps? By the way, I'd like you to meet an old friend out here, name of Forbes. He was in the RAF and flies a Tiger Moth. Has a pretty daughter staying with him. I saw him yesterday on his way back from the air-

66

strip. I've told him of your interest in old cars, and he'd like you to drop in. I'll give you his address. Unfortunately, his wife is a semi-invalid. Forbes doesn't like leaving her alone at night, in case she has a turn or something.'

'What's wrong with her?'

'Goodness knows. Something that seems to be getting worse all the time. And she used to be so active.'

Love nodded sympathetically.

'You know what I think?' he said.

'What?'

'The good do die young. That's why people like you and me are left to grow old.'

'There's not a lot of choice, really, is there? If you don't grow old, then you die young.'

'For that observation,' said Love severely, 'You can buy *me* another beer.'

* * *

It was that hour of evening when a man, lacking other company, can be alone with his thoughts; when many who are not alone wish they were, and some who are, yearn for laughter and the comfortable conversation of old friends.

Forbes, wearing well-pressed but slightly old-fashioned white-duck trousers and highly polished shoes, a dark shirt and a loosely tied cravat around his throat, sat on his patio looking towards the sea. His neat appearance gave away his age and upbringing. He was not a casual man; he had lived his life, as he liked to say, by the book. And now that there seemed so few rules of conduct and behaviour, he still stuck to the old ways.

He was thinking about other balconies, other verandahs, other patios where he had sat in hot countries, sometimes alone but generally with Madge, watching the evening sun slide down the sky. Most often, he remembered her in a cane chair, knitting or reading a letter from Victoria that had taken days or even weeks to come from England.

Those other houses had been of wood or stone or concrete, designed and built without concern for fashion by the local Public Works Department. They had been in Malaya, India, Ceylon, and then gradually, as the British Empire had shrunk, these houses – and the service bases they surrounded – had all moved closer to Britain, and become smaller and less solidly built with each move.

It was almost as though their architecture mirrored the political uncertainty of the future. Once, everything had been built to last. Then its life expectancy was cut to ten years, to five, then to one. Finally, that flag on which the sun had formerly never been allowed to set, was coming down everywhere. The sun had at last set, not only on the flag but also on the faith of those who had served it for so long and so well. It was scarcely worth making new friends when you would only be in a station for a matter of months; it was hardly worth unpacking.

Suddenly, that old life was over, finished, done with, something as remote as the Greek and Roman empires, and Forbes was prematurely retired. Not really old, he would tell himself, if you counted age in years only, but not young, if you did: in either case, beyond the hope of making a new career.

He glanced at his watch. Dr Love and Mr Parkington were due to have drinks with him at eight. The evening was chill; that damned sirocco or levant wind would be springing up soon; he knew the signs.

He walked into the living room. Photographs of squadrons long since disbanded, with their mascots – a bulldog in Penang, a tortoise in Kandy, a goat in the Sudan – hung on the walls. Young men with strangely innocent faces and cheerful expressions and short hair looked on as he busied himself with his drinks in the same methodical way he always went through pre-flight checks. Two bottles of Bols gin, one full, one half full. A full bottle each of Negrita rum, sherry, Martell Cordon Bleu brandy and some excellent port. After all, you'd expect that in Portugal, and yet the British had invented the drink, not the Portuguese. In the days of the first Duke of

68

Marlborough, when Britain was at war with France, the British government of the day understandably gave Portuguese wines preference over French. But not all Portuguese wines were agreeable; those from the mountainous wine-growing area of the Douro in the north seemed especially harsh and dry. So to make them more palatable, brandy was added – and port was discovered.

He was a bit short on *agua tonica,* and had tried to telephone the local supermarket to ask them to send another case, but the phone was out of order. This was not infrequent in the summer months, when all lines seemed overbooked, but Forbes found it symptomatic of the times, another offence against order and efficiency.

Forbes went in to see his wife, with an iced orange juice. She was sitting up in bed, reading. He noticed how thin her hands were, and how they trembled as though she was holding a great weight, and not just a magazine.

'I have two guests tonight, my dear,' he told her. 'One is an English doctor, keen on old cars, apparently. He's bringing a friend. Do you want me to introduce them?'

'Please,' she said. 'I am always glad to see anyone new. We have so few visitors now. Not like the old days is it, darling?'

Their eyes met, and Forbes put his strong brown hand over her frail fist. He was thinking of other parties when they were young: the fun, the laughter, the practical jokes. And what had happened to all their friends in the squadron photographs? Dead or scattered, living on pensions, and in the past. For all of them, the play was almost over, the curtain about to come down.

The flutter of a car engine outside the house made him turn. 'Here they are.'

The bell rang. Forbes closed the bedroom door, crossed the hall and opened the front door. Three men stood in the porch. They were taller than he was, more powerfully built, and half his age. They were dressed alike in white short-sleeved cotton shirts, and well-pressed khaki trousers. Behind them was a blue Skoda with foreign number plates. They looked like campers.

Several new camping sites were thriving now on the coast.

'Mr Forbes?' asked the first man with a slight accent that Forbes could not identify.

'Yes,' he said. 'What do you want? Who are you?'

Something about the men disturbed him. Without appearing to move, they somehow seemed to be closer to him, almost ringing him in. Once, in the 1930s, in India, he had been detailed – as the only British officer available – to accompany an Indian magistrate to a violent demonstration in Amritsar. They had both suddenly been surrounded by a mob of strangely silent people. He had felt an animal reaction of panic then, quickly stamped down, and he felt the same instinctive reaction now. These men were dangerous.

'I wonder if we could have a word with you?' asked the man in the centre.

'What about?'

Instead of answering, they all suddenly moved forward, pushing Forbes back, so that they were inside the house. One of them closed the door behind them, drew a flick knife from his pocket, and bent down to cut the two wires that connected the bell push to its battery.

'What the hell are you doing?' asked Forbes, annoyance driving out alarm.

'A private word, Mr Forbes. In some room where we can speak undisturbed.'

Forbes heard his wife call.

'What's the matter, Dougal?'

'Nothing, dear,' he assured her. 'Nothing at all. Not the people we were expecting. I'll be right with you.'

He led them into the sitting room and closed the door. His heart was beating fast, as though he had been running a long way uphill. He had heard of burglaries and violence against foreigners in lonely, isolated places, but he had never experienced it himself. In any case, there was nothing here to steal.

'What do you want?' he asked again.

'We understand you run an aircraft, Mr Forbes?'

'That is true. A Tiger Moth.'

'And you – or someone else – took a person up in it very recently?'

'What business is that of yours?'

'Only that we would like to hire it ourselves.'

'I see.'

Relief flooded through Forbes. How foolish to be alarmed over nothing! The fact was that so many young men nowadays looked so frightening, simply because their clothes, the length of their hair and their whole attitudes were alien to him. He was growing old, that was the reason. How Madge would laugh at his fears! And then he remembered the knife on the bell wires and his confidence vanished.

'Where do you wish to go?' he asked, hoping his unease did not sound in his voice.

'Where did this other person fly?'

'Along the coast. Then out over the sea.'

'Why?'

'Why? Because he wanted to, that's why. He was a naturalist.'

'What is his name?'

'What has all this to do with you?' asked Forbes. 'It is my affair entirely, if I choose to hire out my plane for a couple of hours.'

'He is a friend of ours. We are trying to trace him.'

'I cannot help you.'

'Didn't he give you his name?'

'He was a Mr Jarrold.'

'What did he look like?'

'Why, if he is your friend, do you want to know what he looked like?'

'We would like to surprise him. He does not know we are here.'

'Well, I cannot help you any more,' said Forbes briskly. 'And as regards hiring my plane, it is already booked for the next two days. Crop-spraying. Perhaps you could ring me after that?'

He took out a card with his address and telephone number and handed it to the man. He slipped it into his pocket and

71

then moved so quickly that Forbes sensed rather than saw his fist. The pain of the jab to his stomach swelled and spread and engulfed his body. He sank down on his knees, sobbing with the unexpected agony. One of the men trod on his hand on the floor. Another pulled the curtain across the glass door to the patio.

'Who's the woman in the other room?'

Forbes found his voice, or a voice that did not sound like his.

'My wife,' he gasped. 'She's an invalid.'

Even as he spoke, he could have bitten out his tongue.

'In that case, Mr Forbes, perhaps we should deal with her and not with you?'

'What do you want? I have no money here. There is nothing to steal.'

'We want the true name of your passenger. The man who hired your plane. And what he really wanted.'

Forbes crawled up, steadying himself on the edge of the settee. A brass ashtray that hung on a strip of canvas across one of the arms had fallen on the floor and he thought: Madge wouldn't like that. They had bought it in Benares on their first tour in India, just after their marriage. A different life, then, a totally different world.

'I tell you, I don't know any more. He said he was a naturalist. He wanted to study the movement of dolphins.'

'Did you fly over a ship?'

'I didn't even fly the man. My daughter did.'

'Where is she?'

'I have no idea.'

'Did he signal to a ship?'

'I tell you, I wasn't there. I don't know what you are talking about.'

Forbes began to struggle to his feet. The man hit him again. He went down heavily and stayed on the floor.

*   *   *

'Where's his house?' Love asked Parkington.

They were in the Cord, trundling up the long, winding road to Monchique. Pine trees drenched the air with scent. Far beneath, spread out like a toy landscape, villages and fields stretched to the distant shimmering sea. There was little other traffic. Here and there a car had pulled off the road so that someone could photograph the view.

They came along the high street where stalls displayed horn-handled knives and such unlikely items as wooden-soled shoes for shepherds and inner tubes for cycle tyres. They passed the general's house with his polished cannon, and further on the house of the admiral, who was at his telescope on its tripod.

'Here we are,' said Parkington. 'Looks like the party's started.'

Another car stood in the gateway; Parkington noted its East German number plates. Love drove past the gate and parked his Cord on a grass verge off the road. They walked back and up the short drive. He pressed the bell-push, and they stood looking at each other in the way of the English everywhere when on someone else's doorstep; like actors off-stage awaiting their entrance. But this time there was no cue; the bell did not ring. The door had neither knocker, nor letterbox to peer through. They stood for a moment, irresolute. Bougainvillaea and hibiscus blazed on either side of the porch. The blue trumpet flowers of morning glory gave a garland to the garden wall. Then both heard a despairing cry from inside the house, the voice of a man driven to the edge of endurance.

'I tell you, I know *nothing*! Nothing!'

Love glanced enquiringly at Parkington.

'Let's go round the back way, and have a butcher's,' said Parkington. 'May just be an English-language play on the box.'

They moved swiftly and silently along the wall of the house. The first window opened into an empty room. They passed frosted glass panes in a bathroom window, and then a french window with the curtain carelessly drawn across it.

Love turned the handle cautiously. The door opened slightly. There was no wind. The curtain did not move. He moved the edge half an inch and looked inside. Three men were gathered around a much older man who was down on the ground on his hands and knees. As Love watched, one of them kicked him in his kidneys. The older man collapsed, breathless.

'I think you are lying, Mr Forbes,' said the man who had kicked him.

'And I think you've had it,' said Love.

The three men turned at his voice. Love picked up a brass door-stop and flung it at the nearest. It hit the side of his head. He reeled and, as he staggered, Love ripped away the curtain and threw this like a gladiator's net over his head and shoulders. Then he and Parkington were through the door. A fast left to the man's stomach, a knee in his groin, and he fell.

The other two jumped at Love. The nearest pulled an automatic from his pocket and jammed it in Love's navel. Love pivoted to his right, elbows in, and knocked the muzzle to one side. Then he seized the man's wrist with his left hand, brought up his right knee into the East German's stomach and for good measure rammed the knuckles of his right hand into his eyes. He collapsed. Love kicked the automatic across the floor. As he did so, the third man leaped towards Love, foot out to aim a killing blow. But he had signalled this by drawing back his leg slightly, and Love was ready: message received and understood.

He swung to his right and whipped his left forearm under the man's knee. At the same time, he seized his ankle and kicked him hard in the crotch. The man crumpled like a deflated rubber toy. How often had Love demonstrated this technique to the judo class of the local Royal British Legion branch in his Somerset village! Now he felt pleased and relieved surprise that the motions through which he had gone so slowly and thoroughly on these occasions worked just as he had always assured his class they would – perfectly.

'A bit more like that,' said Parkington approvingly, 'and they'll give you a black belt.'

'They already have,' replied Love.

He helped Forbes to his feet. The older man leaned weakly

against a chair for support, shaking his head as though to drive from his mind the horror of the previous few minutes.

'Who are *you*?' he asked at last.

'Your guests, Mr Forbes. Jason Love and Richard Mass Parkington.'

'Oh, yes. Of course.'

'What happened?'

'These fellows forced their way in. Cut the bell wires and I think cut the phone wires, too. I couldn't get a call out.'

'What did they want? Money?'

'No. They kept quizzing me about a man my daughter took up in my plane.'

'What did they want to know?'

'Exactly where they'd flown. Had they gone over some ship or other. Why they went. What they saw. I couldn't tell them anything – and if I could, I wouldn't, not the way they went on. Swine.'

There was silence in the room except for a faint moaning from one of the men on the floor, nursing a broken arm. Through the thin wall of the room, Mrs Forbes called: 'What's the matter? Are you all right, Dougal?'

'My wife,' Forbes explained to Love. 'Thank God you came when you did. They were threatening to hurt her. She's not at all well.'

'Shouldn't think this would improve your health, either,' said Parkington drily.

Forbes moved slowly and painfully to the drinks cabinet and poured out three huge brandies.

'Here,' he said. 'I'll just tell Madge there's nothing to worry about.'

Parkington and Love drank the Martell Cordon Bleu with relish.

'What about these?' Parkington asked, turning over one of the men with his foot.

'What about them?' repeated Love. 'It's not worth involving the police. Any amount of form-filling and horsing about. Let's get them on their way.'

'You think they'll come back and have another go at Forbes or his wife?'

'Would you, after this reception?'

Parkington shook his head.

'That guy you threw has a broken arm.'

'Easier to mend than a broken heart.'

At that moment, the whole house trembled as though it would collapse. The roar of an explosion deafened them. Love and Parkington were facing the french windows and the force of the blast flung them back against the sideboard, knocking the glasses from their hands. Window panes splintered into a thousand dagger blades. The photographs of Forbes' old squadrons crashed down, as the ceiling split and buckled, and plaster rained down. The room was suddenly full of dust, thick as a fog. Love's ears rang like church bells. The sideboard was covered with smashed bottles that leaked rum, gin, brandy.

He shook dust from his eyes and saw the three strangers climbing through the open french window. Parkington was unconscious; a brass vase had struck him on the head. Love ran through the debris out on to the patio, still dazed, unable to comprehend what had happened and why. He steadied himself against the wall. The men reached the Skoda. The one with the broken arm crouched in the back, his face contorted with pain. One man jumped behind the wheel and started the engine. The little car reversed into the road and was away.

Love turned back towards the house. A girl was standing in the far doorway of the shattered room, her face a mask of horror and disbelief.

'Who are you?' he asked her, not really caring, his mind still numb by shock.

'Victoria Forbes.'

'I am Dr Jason Love.'

'What's happened? My bedroom's blown up. As though a bomb went off.'

'A bomb did go off,' said Love grimly. He knelt by Parkington, feeling his pulse.

'If there's any brandy left, give him some,' he told her. She

76

poured three fingers of Martell Cordon Bleu from a broken bottle into a dusty glass and Love held it to Parkington's lips.

'What happened?' asked Parkington weakly.

'That's what we're going to find out.'

Forbes came into the room. His eyes took in the extent of the disaster: broken windows, smashed ornaments, the ceiling hanging down, spilled drink staining the carpets.

'My God,' he said slowly. 'It's like an air-raid.'

'My room's even worse,' his daughter told him. 'The explosion took place there. Are you sure you're all right, Daddy?'

'I think so,' Forbes replied shakily. 'I think so.'

Love introduced Parkington, who was now on his feet, feeling the back of his head tenderly with one hand as he poured himself a second brandy with the other.

'Is mother all right?' Victoria asked her father.

They went into her bedroom. Glass in her windows had cracked and plaster dust lay like powder across her eiderdown, but otherwise there was little damage. Madge Forbes sat up in bed, looking at them enquiringly, a woman who had once been pretty but whose face was now sunken and pale with illness. Only her eyes remained bright and alert.

'What on earth has happened?' she asked. 'Was it the boiler? I told your father we needed a new gas cylinder. I am sure that old one was leaking.'

'It wasn't that, darling,' replied Forbes gently.

'What was it, then?'

'Nothing to worry about. And it doesn't matter so long as you are all right. Nothing matters, apart from that, my dear.'

When they were outside the bedroom, Forbes turned to his daughter.

'Did those men get away?' he asked her.

'Yes. They had a car.'

'They'll be miles away by now,' said Love.

'Let's help you clear up this mess. And if you have your insurance policy handy, let my friend here have a look at it. He's in that line of country.'

'What company are you insured with?' asked Parkington.

'The Midland Widows.'

'I knew it,' said Parkington. 'That's the third claim I've been involved with this week.'

And I wonder, thought Love, I just wonder, whether they could all be connected.

Chapter Six

Volkoff stood at his bedroom window in Sagres, all lights out and the curtains pulled well back, focusing his night glasses on the moonlit horizon. To the left of his vision, three local fishing boats lay at anchor. Floodlights suspended from spars blazed into the water to dazzle the fish. Volkoff used these lights as stationary markers to gauge the progress of the ship in which he was interested – *Princess Rosael*.

She had also been stationary, but now she had started to move, very slowly admittedly, but gradually the distance between her and the fishing boats was increasing. He put her speed at no more than three knots. Had there been another breakdown in the ancient engine? This explanation was so simple that he naturally distrusted it. In any departure from an agreed plan or procedure, Volkoff invariably saw treachery and danger to himself. Usually, he was right.

He lowered the glasses and switched on the bedroom light. Then he sat down at a dressing table, took out a pocket calculator and began to work out how long *Princess Rosael,* at the rate of three knots, would take to round Cape St Vincent and begin to beat north. She was running behind schedule, and as a punctual man, this worried him.

A knock at the door, a rat-tat-tat, in a special way repeated twice, disturbed his thoughts. He crossed the room, unlocked the door and opened it. A young man came inside. He wore a short-sleeved white shirt and khaki trousers. The shirt was torn and stained with blood. He had a bruise and deep cut above his left eye. He sat down thankfully in an armchair.

'What's the matter, Heinz?' asked Volkoff anxiously. 'What's happened?'

'I went with Kurt and Jan to see the old Englisman who owns the plane. We tried to find why he was flying over the ship. It turned out his daughter was the pilot. And she wasn't there. He claimed that the man who hired it was a naturalist.'

'Did you find out this man's name?'

'Yes. As you thought. Jarrold.'

'And?'

'And then two of the old man's friends arrived. One he said was a doctor. I don't know who the other man was. They took us on.'

'And beat you?' finished Volkoff sarcastically. 'You're lucky they didn't call the police.'

'They couldn't. We'd cut the line. And then there was an explosion somewhere else in the house – or just outside it. We got away under cover of that – just as Forbes' daughter arrived.'

'What caused this explosion?'

Heinz shrugged.

'No idea. It just happened, and we took advantage of it. Jan has taken Kurt on to hospital. He's broken his arm, by the way. Or rather the doctor broke it for him. Jan pulled a gun, and the doctor was too quick.'

'Bloody fools, all of you. Why not handle the visit with tact? Offer the old man Forbes money instead of beating him up?'

Heinz said nothing. He sat sullenly in the chair, head down. Volkoff regarded him with disfavour. The trouble with so many young people you had to employ now, in East and West alike, they had never known real hardship, such as he and his generation had known. They simply could not imagine how many ways there were of doing a deal or killing a dog. They lacked patience, finesse, judgment. Thank God, he would soon be through with all of them. He glanced instinctively towards the window. The distance between the *Princess Rosael* and the fishing boats was still increasing.

'She's moving at last,' he said thankfully, almost to himself. 'But why so slowly?'

'What about it?' asked Heinz irritably. He had expected sympathy, more interest in his predicament. But this cold character was only interested in himself.

'I don't like it, that's what's about it. So I am going to take steps to cover my investment – *our* investment. You and the others will be on the beach with the motor-boat at four o'clock tomorrow morning.'

'Kurt won't be much good with only one arm.'

'That oaf's not much good with two. But get him there. Full tank of petrol, torches, and a length of rope. We're going to take a cruise around the bay.'

'Not be able to see much at that hour.'

'Which, my friend, has two distinct advantages. No-one will be able to see us. and if we find anything in the water, we can remove it before anyone else sees it is there.'

*   *   *

Hood lay stretched across the oil drum, so still and pale he might have been dead.

Only a faint movement of his head, as he lifted it in a feeble attempt to avoid a breaking wave, showed he was still alive. At first he had shouted and whistled and screamed, but no-one heard him, and soon *Princess Rosael* began to move away from him, and the tide bore him steadily out to sea. All the while, the drum rolled and spun like a wheel with each blow from the waves, and he had clawed and grabbed at its shining sides, fearful of losing it and what it contained, and also desperate for its buoyancy to keep himself afloat. Now he just gripped it as best he could, with elbows and fingers, and when the sea revolved it within his grasp he let it turn. The water was far colder than he had imagined. He had no feeling in his legs; his feet were totally numb, and his watch had stopped. He had no idea how long he had been in the sea.

At first he had tried to propel himself to the shore, but the tide defeated him. The wound where McNab had shot him had bled a lot and he felt weak and lightheaded. Once he found

81

himself on his back with the drum slipping from his gasp and he knew he had fainted. To faint a second time could be fatal, so he lay across the barrel, head to one side, oblivious of the waves and the rocking motion, forcing himself to stay conscious.

I have to hold on, Hood kept telling himself. *They are picking up the drum, so they will find me. Once ashore, all will be well.*

He must have slept or fainted again because suddenly he was aware that the sky was a shade lighter. Dawn could not be far away. As waves lifted the drum he caught brief glimpses of the dark rim of the coast. He was still possibly a mile out. They must pick him up so long as he could hold on. Surely they would? He dozed again, butted by the heaving motion of the waves.

This time the faint noise of an engine, the putt-putt of an outboard, awoke him. A small rubber inflatable boat with three men in it was coming out from shore, heading to his right. He raised his left arm, wincing with the pain. In his anxiety to be rescued he had forgotten about the wound. The drum slipped from under his other arm, and he floundered and choked with sea-water, and was lucky to regain his balance. The noise of the engine increased. They were circling around him about 300 yards away. He saw a man in the boat point towards him.

'There's a drum,' said someone excitedly.

'Go down current against it,' ordered someone else.

'My God, there's a man hanging on to it.'

Hood could smell the engine's exhaust now, they were so close. Strong dry hands reached out and gripped his shirt.

'My arm,' he gasped painfully. 'I am wounded. Shot.'

They dragged him in as carefully as they could. He collapsed thankfully in the rubber-smelling bottom of the boat. Then the drum came in, booming with whatever it contained.

The three men in the motor boat exchanged glances.

'Who shot you?' Volkoff asked Hood.

Hood shook his head wearily; no names, no trouble.

'What's inside that?'

'Petrol,' replied Hood quickly. 'And a box. I fell in the water when I was carrying it.'

Even as he spoke, he realized how strange this must sound. How could he fall over a ship's rail when he was carrying a metal drum this size? But he felt weak and sick with reaction; it was the only excuse he could think of.

'What ship?'

'*Princess Rosael*. Bound for Newcastle from Alex.'

'And no-one raised the alarm?'

'I don't know, do I? No-one picked me up, that's for sure. Thought I was a goner.'

'What's your name?'

'Hood. Terry Hood.'

'You are English?'

'Welsh.'

They were going now towards the shore. The day was almost light. The bows of the little boat whacked up and down on the running tide, bending amidships as rubber craft do. The motion, the smell of petrol and exhaust fumes made Hood feel dizzy and sick.

'But why should anyone throw a drum of petrol after you, Mr Hood?'

Hood heard the question as from a great distance, as though someone was calling from down a well, and the voice echoed and re-echoed in his exhausted mind: 'Why? Why? Why?' Then he was falling down the well-shaft himself, at a great speed, past empty, rushing darkness. The voice diminished and was still.

Heinz opened the throttle as fully as he dared. The rubber snout of the boat hammered the waves furiously. Spray drenched the three men as they crouched, gripping rope handles on the black sausage-shaped sides. The beach raced towards them. Heinz cut the throttle and pulled the engine out of the water, so he would not damage the propeller on the long sweep of sand. He leaped out as they grounded, and pulled the boat up the beach. Volkoff and Jan carried Hood across the damp sand. They had landed in a cove, with an expanse of

83

open marshland to their left and, beyond this, buildings on the edge of Sagres. Lights were coming in the staff rooms of an hotel crouched on the cliffs. Several fishing boats were sailing in line back to harbour. To their right sprouted a huge rock outcrop. Ahead of them was a restaurant. A dog stood on an otherwise deserted verandah, ready to bark or wag its tail, according to their reaction. Volkoff snapped his fingers and patted his right thigh. The dog wagged its tail, satisfied they were friendly.

To one side of the building a few cars were parked, windows streaked with early morning dew. They belonged to campers and to guests in a motel, a long, single-storey building looking in the half light like a huge railway carriage.

Volkoff and Jan carried Hood past the cars and along a tarmac track. Fifty yards farther on, a grey V.W. Caravette was parked in a clump of cactus. Heinz unlocked the side door and slid it open. They climbed inside and closed the door carefully behind them. Heinz put the oil drum on the floor. It smelled disagreeably of seaweed and petrol that had begun to seep out around the cap.

The blue canvas of a tent pitched outside one window darkened the interior of the vehicle. Even with the swiftly growing daylight, the men might have been sitting beneath the surface of a summer sea.

Volkoff and Jan laid Hood on the floor; the carpet was ingrained with sand that rasped their fingers. Kurt poured out some brandy into a mug and tried to persuade Hood to drink it while the others supported him, but he did not open his mouth.

His face was greenish, with deep mauve shadows beneath his eyes. A thin rope of saliva trickled from the corner of his mouth. Volkoff felt his pulse.

'He's bad,' he said. 'His heart's scarcely beating.'

'Let's get him into Sagres to hospital,' said Jan nervously.

'Try some brandy down him,' suggested Heinz.

Again they lifted him, but now Hood's body seemed heavier, as though his muscles lacked all control.

84

'Drink this,' Volkoff commanded Hood, but the brandy just trickled down his chin. His head rolled to one side like a doll's head as they lowered him again. Volkoff raised one of Hood's eyelids as he felt his pulse.

'Let's get him to a doctor,' urged Jan anxiously.

'Too late. He needs an undertaker.'

'You mean . . .?' Jan could not speak the words.

'Yes. He's dead.'

*   *   *

Love opened the french doors and walked out on to the patio in his pyjamas and dressing gown. Above the sea the sky blazed blue without a single cloud. The only sound was the faint approaching hum of an aircraft. He shaded his eyes against the morning sun. The Tiger Moth's wings waggled as it turned, made one circle of the house and landed in the field behind him. Dust from the parched earth ruffled the air. Love went into the kitchen to make coffee. Through the window he saw Victoria walking towards the house, swinging her leather flying helmet from one hand. She stopped at the fig tree by the front door and picked herself a fig.

'If I'd known you were coming, I would have dressed,' he told her.

'Not a very flattering way to greet any girl,' she replied. 'But at this time in the morning I don't usually expect compliments.'

'What do you expect?' Love asked her. 'Usually?'

'Black coffee, for a start.'

He carried a tray of coffee and rolls out on to the patio. They sat down in cane chairs in the shade of the arches. The sun danced off the swimming pool.

'I am flying out over Sagres, and my father wondered if you would care to come along?'

'Delighted. How are your parents this morning?'

'So-so. My father is staying in with mother. He had a bad shock last night with those fellows. Why on earth should they want to know who had hired his plane?'

Love shrugged.

'What sort of man was he?'

'Middle-aged. Nothing special about him.'

'Where did you fly him, exactly?'

'Along the coast and then a few miles out to sea. He had a camera and binoculars. He photographed a shoal of dolphins we saw, and we crossed over an old cargo ship going very slowly.'

'Was he particularly interested in that?'

'Not really. But he did ask me to come down so he could read the name on the stern.'

'Which was?'

'*Princess Rosael.*'

'Nothing else?'

'Nothing at all. He paid me when we got back.'

'He gave you his name?'

'Yes. Jarrold. Staying at the Penina Hotel outside Portimao.'

Love stood up and, shading his eyes again, scanned the horizon. The ship was still there, but had sailed appreciably farther west. Some way behind it, also travelling slowly, was a second ship, low down in the water and putting out a lot of smoke.

'Why the devil are they going so slowly?'

'They're old. Bound for the breaker's yard,' Victoria explained. 'Our neighbour is a retired admiral. Watching ships is his hobby. He says they are old boats that were locked in the Suez Canal for about ten years after one of the Arab-Israeli wars. Most were released some time ago. But two of them at least have only just reached here. They daren't put on speed in case they burst their engines.'

As they finished their coffee, the maid arrived with her usual cheerful greeting: 'Bom Dia!' Love and Victoria walked out towards the plane. She had parked it out of the sun, behind a huge fig tree, with two stones set against the wheels as chocks. Victoria explained how he was to swing the propeller. After two or three cautious attempts, the engine fired. Love kicked away the stones and climbed into the narrow cockpit. He had

86

never flown in a Moth before and was surprised at the crudity and fragility of the machine. The cockpit flap was secured by a bolt that might have come from a bathroom cupboard of the nineteen thirties. Control wires moved on either side of him.

The front cockpit had its own set of controls, and the second joy-stick moved like a huge admonishing finger between his legs. He kept his feet carefully placed on strengthened parts of the floor, and out of the way of the rudder controls which also moved as Victoria steered the plane across the field. Forward visibility scarcely existed. He had to peer out to one side to see the junipers and fig trees and the open flat land ahead. As Victoria opened the throttle and the plane surged forward and then took off, white needles trembled on dials with single figures quaintly lettered 'Tens of miles per hour' and 'Hundreds of revs. per minute'.

'You all right, Jason?' her voice asked metallically in his ear through the Gosport tube.

'Fine.'

He glanced around the cockpit and saw a lever that seemed alien to the air; a rod set to move a valve in a thick pipe against a heavy spring.

'What's that?' he asked.

'For controlling the sprayer. My father's spraying rough land with paraffin this afternoon to burn up the weeds. Don't touch it – or anything else.'

'I won't,' Love assured her.

Once airborne, the curiously old-fashioned machine took on a grace and elegance Love would not have imagined possible. He could instantly understand the attraction of vintage aircraft. The feeling was of a closeness with the element for which they had been designed: man and machine were part of a trinity of which the air was the third member.

Within minutes they were out over the sea, the roar of the engine muted by the flying helmet Victoria had given him. Through his goggles Love saw his house disappear like a vanishing toy, than the long sweep of sand and rocks, and a few speedboats pulling tracks of foam. They flew down over the two ships, both making slow progress against the tide. They circled once and were off again, over deeper, darker water. They flew to Sagres, around the lighthouse at Cape St Vincent, and the sheer cliffs that sheltered the harbour.

Victoria spoke into the Gosport mouthpiece.

'According to the map, we are approaching Carrapateira.'

Love looked to the right through his goggles: a swimming pool gleamed like a square of lapis lazuli near a house on the edge of fields, with a pagoda-like building in the distance. A wind sock hung limply on a mast. The world fell away at an angle and they came over the beach, flying low, their shadow pursuing them across the white empty sand like a following cross.

In the lee of the rocks, Love saw half a dozen parked cars and Volkswagen Caravettes with bright blue and orange tents and canvas rooms. Smoke rose from camp fires. People were still cooking breakfast. Some waved to him; he waved back.

Victoria brought the plane down to land on the runway. Love helped her button down tonneau covers over the two cockpits. They chocked the wheels with stones and walked across the dry baking ground, past the swimming pool, to the house. This had been turned into a guest house and restaurant, the Casa Fajara; the original hall was now the bar. They ordered two iced Sumols, and sat in the shady room looking out at the flat expanse of fields.

Nothing moved, not even the dry leaves of sweet corn. Then something caught Love's eye, because it was so out of keeping with the lethargy of the morning. A man was running along the track from the beach.

That he was unmistakably British, Love could tell from his too-long shorts, his blue cellular shirt, which would have been ideal at Margate but not for Portugal; from the triangular patch of red, sun-scorched skin at his throat. He wore National Health spectacles, misted with sweat, and his hair grew short on his skull. Love had seen his type often, small of head, narrow of shoulders, peeping myopically between the rim of a steering wheel and the base of the windscreen as they drove through

Bishops Combe in cars piled high with luggage on the roof. Now Love watched his approach with disfavour; such a courier could only bring bad news.

'Do you speak English?' the man asked him.

'I should do. I am English.'

The lenses of the man's glasses magnified his eyes so they appeared twice life-size, flecked with the relish of describing a tragedy involving someone else.

'A body has been washed up,' he announced importantly. 'Fell off the cliffs. Badly battered, face bashed in. Fish have eaten out his eyes.'

'It's a man, then?' asked Love.

'Was. Where is the nearest doctor?'

'Here,' said Love.

'You a doctor?' He peered at Love in disbelief. 'I must say, you don't look like one.'

'But I can act like one,' Love answered him. 'If the poor fellow's in the condition you describe maybe he needs an undertaker rather than a physician?'

'Or even an insurance man,' said a suave voice behind him. 'In which case I can possibly be of assistance.'

Love turned. Parkington had appeared on the verandah, a glass in one hand, a cigar in the other. He bowed to Victoria.

'You're selling insurance then?' asked the man.

'Not actually selling,' Parkington corrected him. 'Shall we say, discussing? Let us see what we can do to help anyhow. I have a car here.'

They went down the steps, climbed into Parkington's hired Mini, and bumped along the track towards the beach. A crowd of holidaymakers had gathered on the edge of the sea, staring with fascinated horror at what the tide had deposited at their feet. Some parents held children up in their arms for a better look. In the midst of life, thought Love, we are always in death.

'Make way for a doctor,' said Parkington curtly.

The crowd moved reluctantly aside. Love knelt by the dead man, going through the motions of investigation. His face was terribly mauled, either by a fish or from being battered against the rocks. His clothes had not lost their dye and he saw no bloating of the body, so he must have died fairly recently. Instinctively, Love's hand went to his left wrist. The watch had stopped at 10.30 – but would that be night or morning, and, again, which night or morning? Love unbuttoned the man's shirt and saw a fine gold chain with an engraved medallion: *Terence Richard Hood. Blood group A.* Well, that was of no use now. Terence Richard Hood was beyond help of all transfusions.

'What happened?' Love asked. 'Anyone speak English?'

'I do,' said a man who was obviously not English. 'I can help you a little, doctor. I saw this person some hours ago. I thought he was going fishing.'

'Was he carrying a rod?'

'Seemed to be carrying something,' agreed the man. 'Something wrapped up.'

'Fellow fell off there only last month, so they told us at the pub,' said a middle-aged Englishman in the front row, clicking his false teeth. 'Went up the top and had a look-see myself. Wouldn't go too near, rocks aren't safe.'

Love looked down at Hood's corpse. He saw the nick that McNab's bullet had made in his shirt, and examined the wound from which the sea had rinsed away all blood. Who would shoot a fisherman on that cliff? Had he drowned or was he dead before he entered the water? That would take a post-mortem to discover, and who would carry that out?

'We'd better go for the police,' said Love, standing up. 'There is nothing I can do for him.'

'I'll contact them,' said Parkington. 'I'll go to the nearest town, Vila do Bispo, and ring a colleague in Lagos. That will be quicker than trying to contact the police ourselves. We don't even know their number.'

'I'll wait here,' said Love. He turned to Victoria.

'I think you had better fly back on your own. Parkington can give me a lift home, for I'll probably be around for some time yet. It's one of the snags of being a doctor.'

'I suppose so,' she said. 'I had never really thought about it.'

Her face was strained. Love thought, she has probably never seen a dead person before, and violent death was never a pretty sight.

Someone brought a tent flap and Love spread this over Hood's body. Already greedy flies were buzzing round the open mouth and nostrils and the raw scars.

One by one, people drifted away. Love took Victoria's arm. He could feel her warmth, young and appealing through the thin stuff of her shirt. Her face was tense and pale.

'Walk back with me to the plane,' she asked him suddenly. 'I can't start the engine on my own.'

They walked in silence across the hot sand towards the brown dry grass and rough stunted bushes that lay between the beach and the road. Cactus plants spread spiked leaves encrusted with snails. A tethered donkey waited, head down, dozing in the shade of a hut. Victoria shivered. Love looked at her in surprise.

'What's the matter?' he asked.

'I'm scared,' she said in a small voice.

'What of? A dead man?'

'No. A live one. He was standing at the back of the crowd. Didn't you recognize him?'

'No. I don't know what you're talking about.'

'Well, I do. He was one of the three men who came to our house to beat up my father.'

*   *   *

Love watched the Tiger Moth rise into the air and head back towards Lagos. Then he strolled down to the beach to wait for Parkington. New arrivals, not knowing what had happened, did not give the canvas-covered hump near the sea a second glance. He sat down on a rock, lit a cheroot, and waited.

Voices grew louder and he looked up, divorcing himself from his thoughts. Parkington was approaching with two policemen. They wore grey uniforms, peaked caps with black polished leather riding boots that squeaked with every step in the soft sand. The man who had discovered the body now appeared to tell his story.

He had seen what he had thought was a bundle of clothes against some rocks, and waded towards them to investigate – and found this body.

'You will have to repeat it again at the police station,' said Love. 'I don't think they speak much English. Looks like you will be there for some time.'

'What will my wife say?' asked the man, glancing towards a severe woman who sat in a large straw hat and mirror-faced sunglasses, watching the group with disapproval.

'I don't know,' admitted Parkington. 'But I'm sure you will soon find out.'

Love wrote down his address and telephone number in Luz for the police, should they wish to contact him, and then he and Parkington walked slowly up the beach and climbed into Parkington's hired car.

'Penny for them?' said Parkington.

'They are worth more,' Love told him.

'A drink, then?'

'Agreed.'

They crossed the road and drove along the track between dwarf palms to the restaurant, reached from this side by a stone staircase. To one side of this a rattan roof had been set up on poles where cars could park in the shade. Parkington drove in here and opened his door. Love did not move.

'What's the matter?' Parkington asked him. 'What are you waiting for?'

'The answers to some questions.'

'Like what questions?'

'First, I think you have given me a load of rubbish about your involvement with the Midland Widows and the Western Mutual Nominees. Right?'

'How do you mean, rubbish?' countered Parkington.

'The leopard doesn't easily change his spots nor the Ethiop

his skin, and that also goes for the spy and his trade. Once in business, always in business. I believe you are still working for the old firm under whatever name it may be now. Perhaps it *is* Midland Widows?'

'What makes you think that?'

'A doctor becomes like a policeman or an egg-sexer. He can spot a bad 'un by instinct. He knows at once when something is not quite right, for he's heard too many half truths in his surgery to be fooled any longer. And your story is as sound as that corny old excuse about catching pox from a lavatory seat. It just ain't so. Before I become any more involved, I want to know more. And not more bull – more facts.'

Parkington sat for a moment, stroking his chin.

'All right,' he said at last. 'I *am* working for the old firm, but the Midland Widows don't know. For I am also genuinely working for them. I became involved because one of our people who had been in the East – a naturalized American, actually born in Romford – was murdered.'

'Name of Cartwright? In Oregon?' asked Love.

'Yes. He was very much on a part-time basis like you, and had gone back to the States. He told us that something of potentially great value to the West was about to be smuggled out of India.'

'What sort of thing?'

'I don't know, and he was too cautious to be specific,' replied Parkington. 'But something that would be at least as valuable to the other side – or to any countries or terrorist groups who needed a lever.'

'Why was Cartwright so vague?'

'Because, in our view, he thought of us as potential buyers. And if he gave away too much too soon he feared we might cut him out.'

'So he was double-crossing the old firm?'

'Not really. Just being careful. I have the feeling he was probably in deeper with the smugglers than he let on. Maybe he intended to do a private deal on his own and cut *them* out. Or maybe he just needed money – fast. His wife knew that

93

another woman was involved, and she was the sort of person who'd lean on him – hard. She'd leave him with his prick to pee with, but not a lot more.'

'Even that's more than he has now, though,' Love pointed out. 'Was Marshall also in all this?'

'I think so. Cartwright gave us a description of one man that tallied with Marshall. We had nothing on him in the big league, but he had been involved in a number of shady deals. Right back from the days fortunes were being made and lost in army surplus stores – tanks, trucks, anything. I wouldn't think mourners will crowd out the ceremony at his funeral.'

'What about the men who came to beat up Forbes? Are they involved?'

'I just don't know. They – or someone who sent them – obviously wanted to know who flew over that cargo ship – and why.'

'Victoria has just told me she saw one of the men on the beach, near Hood's body.'

'She didn't tell me.'

'You weren't there,' Love pointed out.

'So why didn't you do anything about it?'

'I didn't see him, and she told me too late – when he'd gone.'

Parkington reached into his shirt pocket and pulled out a piece of paper, damp with sweat.

'I called at your house this morning and the maid told me you had flown up here, so I followed. But while I was there I had a telephone call. From London. Your old firm.'

'You mean, yours,' Love corrected him. 'What did they want?'

'To give me a message, through you.'

'Which was?'

'Mrs Cartwright also took a telephone call from Portugal a matter of hours ago.'

'Who from?'

'No name was given. All we have is a number.'

'The hotel Penina?'

'No. Another one. In Sagres.'

'We are only five miles away from Sagres now,' said Love. 'Let's go on over.'

'Long, long ago, when I was in the army,' replied Parkington, 'I was taught that time spent in reconnaissance is seldom wasted. So let us discover who put the call through before we visit the hotel. That might save questions to the manager, which could warn the caller. It would be of even greater use if we could get a key to the person's room.'

'That's asking a bit, isn't it?'

'Ask,' replied Parkington enigmatically, 'and thou shalt receive. Don't ask and you'll get bugger-all. Now, I owe you at least one beer.'

'At least one,' replied Love. They went up the steps to the Fajara.

*   *   *

Senhor Manuel Jones Diaz was a thin man with a small black beard and a parchment-coloured skin. Everything about him was precise; some said he was like a well-pressed manikin. *Dapper* was how he described himself, showing off his knowledge of English. His manner of dress accentuated this effect. He wore amber pointed shoes, fawn lightweight suits and invariably a snake-skin belt with a buckle in the form of a large 'D'. He was fingering this buckle as he sat behind his desk in an upper room of a house overlooking the old slave market in Lagos. He did not cross his legs in case this damaged the sharp creases in his trousers.

Senhor Diaz was a bachelor, and as such, in middle life, could indulge his pleasures and tastes. Fortunately, these were modest, because he was not a man of great means. He described himself as a critic and a student of politics, and wrote a weekly article about literature and political trends which was syndicated to several weekly newspapers in South America.

Diaz had also published (at his own expense) a book on the Marquis Marialva, one of Portugal's great noblemen of the eighteenth century. Marialva developed the technique of bull

95

fighting by mounted men, and lived in such style that when he sat down to dine in his splendid house, his servants placed a silver basin on either side of him. This was to allow him to vomit between courses in order that he could eat more.

The sales of Senhor Diaz's book did not justify such a life style for him, but his literary activities did attract the attention of a quiet Scotsman who, some years earlier, before the Algarve had become fashionable, entered into an agreement with him. This Scotsman, one Douglas MacGillivray, explained that he represented a British features syndicate, the West European Press Alliance, with offices in Salisbury Court, off Fleet Street. He and his colleagues had the highest regard for the literary skills of Senhor Diaz and were prepared to pay him a regular monthly retainer for a carbon copy of every article he wrote. This money was paid from a bank in Geneva, and deposited each month into Senhor Diaz's account at the Banco Portugues do Atlantico in Lagos.

Sometimes, the Alliance would seek the Senhor's help with other enquiries, for all of which he was paid promptly and generously. Once or twice, men of indefinite nationality, but carrying British passports and obviously not holidaymakers, had sought his advice on matters that only the most liberal could associate with literary journalism. One, for example, needed help in leaving Portugal over the Spanish frontier at a remote spot unknown to police and other officials. A second, shot in one arm, and bleeding badly, required the services of a surgeon who would not report the nature of the injury. All claimed to be writers, however, and whatever Diaz's own thoughts might be about their real professions, he remembered his monthly retainer and gave them every assistance.

Now he sat, the thin tips of his fingers pressed spatulate together, regarding Richard Mass Parkington with barely concealed disfavour. Parkington sat in the only other chair the little room possessed. Outside, the sun blazed on the stone yard where, centuries before, shackled slaves from the other Lagos in West Africa had waited for others to decide their future.

Thoughts like this induced in Diaz what the Portuguese

called *saudade* – a feeling difficult to translate, but meaning a vague state of longing, a sense of loss, a yearning for things past and times gone. To this natural melancholy of his mind was added unease at the request the large Englishman had just made.

'You are a writer?' Diaz asked hopefully, trying to salve his own conscience as, many years ago, some slave-dealers had perhaps assured themselves that the transfers were really in the best interests of the slaves, who would no doubt be far happier working hard in the New World than running buck-arse naked in the Old.

'Yes,' replied Parkington at once. 'I am writing about a large number of people and places, and I need your help.'

'But how does your work require that I should obtain a facsimile of a key of a room in an hotel in Sagres? Surely this is more the work of, shall I say, a burglar than a writer?'

'A writer *is* very much like a burglar,' retorted Parkington. 'The novelist steals parts of other men's lives and decisions – and then presents them as his own.'

'I had not thought of my work in that light before,' said Diaz stiffly.

'And nor does anyone else, senhor, for you are a true creative artist, a writer of honour and sensitivity. But for the work I have in mind, it is essential I gain access to this room to satisfy in my mind what an intruder feels. As a seeker after truth, Senhor Diaz, you must sympathize with me? A writer should experience life at first hand, would you not agree?'

'Of course, Mr Parkington. But it could be embarrassing if you were discovered. Then you might also experience our jails at first-hand.'

'That is something I would have to bear. But my skin is thick, my shoulders are broad. Spare no sympathy for me in my search for truth.'

'Then you might please spare some for me,' said Senhor Diaz nervously. 'I do not know where I can find a key.'

'I am sure you have friends or relations of friends who could help?'

'It is true I do have contacts in many places. Assuming that I *am* able to help you, which room do you wish to open?'

'I have no idea,' replied Parkington. 'That is another problem for you to solve, senhor.'

'For *me*, Mr Parkington? But how can I possibly know which room it is? The hotel has fifty or sixty rooms and all are certain to have different keys.'

'You are a great researcher for your articles, are you not?' said Parkington.

Diaz inclined his head gracefully.

'People have been kind enough to compliment me on my ability to unearth hidden facts.'

'Then I hope I can also compliment you on your ability to unearth this particular hidden fact. Someone in that hotel made a telephone call to a number in the town of Waldport in Oregon, on the west coast of the United States. I want a key to that person's room, and his name as well.'

'These are difficult assignments, Mr Parkington,' said Diaz gravely.

'That is why I came to you, senhor,' replied Parkington. 'I knew, of all people, I could rely on you.'

Their eyes met. Diaz looked away first. Parkington had not mentioned that this was the first request MacGillivray's department had given to Diaz for two years. But Diaz knew that he knew, and he needed the money. He swallowed and spread his hands flat on the top of his desk.

'I will do my best, senhor,' he promised.

'I know that, senhor. You have always helped with every request the West European Press Alliance have asked of you. My chief, Mr MacGillivray, is full of your praise.'

'He is still the senior editor there?'

'He is still in charge,' agreed Parkington enigmatically.

'Please give him my regards.'

'I certainly will,' said Parkington. 'And I will also ask that he reviews the salary, which I understand you have been receiving from us for the past few years. And of course this service for me will merit an extra fee.'

98

'I am very grateful,' Senhor Diaz told him. 'Inflation here is far worse than with you.'

'But then you are a single man. You have no other mouths to feed,' said Parkington.

'That is true, but my one mouth takes some feeding. Well, well. We have talked enough. I will do what I can.'

'When?' asked Parkington, standing up.

Mr Diaz also stood up. Parkington towered over him by a head.

'This time tomorrow, here in my office?'

'Agreed.'

'I will have certain disbursements to make, Mr Parkington. Expenses of a confidential nature. Could I therefore ask for an advance of expenses. Say 10,000 escudos?'

Parkington took out his wallet and peeled off ten notes, handed them to the smaller man.

'I am in your hands, Mr Diaz,' he declared. 'And I know that your hands will bear me up as Aeneas bore the old Anchyses from the ruins of Troy.'

'You speak like a writer, Mr Parkington.'

'Now perhaps you will believe I am one?'

Diaz nodded, but not in agreement. He watched Parkington walk past the slave market, towards the statue of Henry the Navigator, on its peculiar pavement designed to give the impression of waves curling. Then he opened his desk, took out a small book bound in black snake-skin, and wetting the tip of his finger in his mouth, began to turn the pages for the name and number he needed.

*   *   *

The little cow bells on the metal door of Mrs Marshall's rented house tinkled as Love lifted the latch and began to climb the stairs. Mrs Marshall was sitting on a sun-lounger under a raffia screen. She wore a swim suit and a pair of dark glasses. As Love approached, she took off the glasses.

'Hullo, doctor,' she said in surprise. 'Professional or social call?'

'I'll leave that for you to decide,' he replied.

She motioned him to sit by her in the shade. A transistor radio was tuned to a North African station; Arabian music wailed like a dirge. Love saw the half-empty bottle of Silvertop gin, the lime juice, the bowl of crushed ice and the large empty glass on the floor beside her. She intercepted his glance.

'Drink?' she asked him.

'A bit early for me.'

'Well, what brings you here?'

'As a doctor and an acquaintance, I felt I should tell you something.'

'About what?' she asked. Her voice was very calm, her face unlined and unconcerned. She watched him with expressionless eyes.

'About your husband's death. A friend of mine, Dick Parkington, as you probably know, represents an insurance company with whom your husband held a large policy. He has been telling me some rather disturbing things about the background to his death.'

'Would they disturb me?' she asked.

'I remember that you corrected me when I said it had been an accident. You said your husband was murdered.'

'That is so.'

'If that is indeed so, Mrs Marshall, then have you considered that the person or persons who killed your husband might not be content to let the matter rest there?'

'You mean, they might kill me?'

She sat up now, moving quickly with a feline speed and grace. For the first time, Love saw concern on her spoiled soft face. He had seen similar women with similar expressions across his desk in the surgery when they had complained about their husbands or their in-laws; of inconsiderate behaviour by their children, as though they had no share of responsibility for whatever might currently be irritating them.

'I do not wish to be dramatic, but Parkington thinks your husband's death is tied up with another murder that took place only hours earlier on the west coast of the United States.'

'But how can it possibly be? I don't understand.'

'I don't understand myself,' admitted Love. 'But tell me one thing. Why didn't your husband want to leave this house? Why didn't he want to come here at all?'

'If I knew, I would tell you. But I have no idea.'

Love calculated she was speaking the truth.

'He said he would take me to the Seychelles, Bermuda, Barbados, *anywhere* but here. But *I* wanted to come here.'

'So you came?'

'Of course.'

'Why did you choose this particular house?'

'We looked at half a dozen others first. He wouldn't stay in an hotel, and none of the other houses had this view of the sea.'

'So you think that was important to him?'

'I don't quite understand what you're getting at, doctor. How could I know? I am simply stating a fact. This house has a superb view of the sea.'

'If he didn't want to leave the house, why did he suddenly walk across the beach alone? Or go to the Rosses' party. Or want to take you out to dinner?'

She thought for a minute.

'He seemed to relax his attitude that afternoon,' she said slowly, thinking back.

'Because it was his birthday?'

'No. I don't think so. He used to watch the horizon with a pair of binoculars. On the afternoon he died he was out here nearly an hour, watching one ship. Then he put the binoculars in their case and he seemed relaxed, almost at ease.'

'Did you see the ship?'

'Only without the glasses. It was an old tramp steamer, going very slowly. In fact, I thought it had stopped.'

'I saw it, too,' said Love. 'You think there was some connection?'

She leaned over, poured herself four fingers of gin, added lime juice and two ice cubes.

'I have no idea. It doesn't seem possible. I am simply trying to answer your questions. We were going out to dinner after

101

the Rosses' party. For his birthday. Before this, he had refused all previous invitations.'

'What line of business was he in?'

'He had a knack of meeting people who wanted, say, a hundred second-hand Land Rovers, and he'd supply them. Then maybe someone else had a warehouse full of bankrupt stock from a run-down company, and he would get rid of it. He travelled a lot. He was in India only weeks ago.'

'How did he begin?'

'In the used-car trade,' she said. 'Worked from a bombed site. Then someone suggested he should buy the site and build on it. Borrowed some money from the bank – and put up a 17-storey building. He sold this and used the capital for other deals.'

'What was he buying and selling here?'

'I don't know,' she said. 'He never told me. And I never asked him. So long as there was enough money coming in, that was all I was concerned with.'

'You know he was insured?'

'Yes,' she said. 'Your friend Mr Parkington has already been to see me about that.'

'Well, Mrs Marshall, thank you. I had better get back.'

'Wait,' she said. 'I have answered your questions. Now answer mine. Do you really think my life is in danger?'

'Whoever killed your husband may think you know more about his business than you appear to. If you ask my advice, then I must tell you, I would leave – now.'

'The planes from Faro are all booked. It is the height of the season.'

'Then hire a car. Drive to Lisbon. If you can't get a plane there, go by train.'

'But that will take days to get back to London.'

'Better be a few days late in this world, Mrs Marshall, than perhaps twenty or thirty years too soon in the next.'

Chapter Seven

Dusk dropped its curtain over the sea with the speed of a tired innkeeper calling time. Shadows spread from almond and fig trees to the junipers that surrounded Love's house, and then across the fields. The reds and pinks and yellows of the flowers dimmed to a universal indigo and disappeared.

Love sat at the wheel of his Cord, its hood down and its long white bonnet facing the road. Down nearer to the sea, some lights gleamed in holiday houses and a record-player boomed cheerful music for a barbecue. Love lit a cheroot from the dashboard lighter, and as its glow reflected in the engine-turned panel that surrounded the dials, his thoughts turned to the peculiar attraction the old car possessed. There must be something psychological in this. Perhaps it was because he had seen his first Cord at an impressionable age; perhaps because when the car was built everything about it was a challenge to accepted principles and a triumph for improvisation and individuality. And in a world of careful conformity, when the cars of all countries looked depressingly alike, this made it unique. There were also lessons to be learned from the improvisations that necessity had forced on its makers.

On the prototype, for example, the brakes overheated badly, so the factory experimental department bored large holes in the wheels. These solved the cooling problem and the designer, Gordon Buehrig, liked their appearance so much that they were adopted for production. Within months, such wheels became fashionable on many other makes of car.

Again, Buehrig wanted the Cord to be instantly recognizable after dark from the rear – the bonnet was already distinctive. At that time, most cars had only one small red rear light that also illuminated the number plate. Buehrig set the rear number plate in the centre of the body, with its own light, and fitted two back lights, each of 4¾-inch diameter at the bottom of the boot lid. This was revolutionary then – and again became standard on most other cars within a year. Why were the lights exactly 4¾ inches across? Because these were the only ready-made lights he could find. Shortage of funds and time had produced unexpectedly successful results. As Le Corbusier said, form follows function.

And what sort of form, what sort of pattern, Love wondered, was emerging from the two murders Parkington had reported? Had a shortage of money – and therefore a need for quick profits – been the motives? Could two insurance policies be the only link between the victims? Or could there be other implications, other complications?

Love turned over possibilities in his mind, instantly rejecting some, recycling others, relishing the pungency of cheroot smoke against the scented wind from the eucalyptus trees.

He saw the lights of a car move along the rough track between the clumps of trees, and turn towards his house. He stubbed out his cheroot.

Parkington switched off his headlights, crossed over to Love, and climbed into the Cord beside him.

'Did your fellow come up with anything?' Love asked him. Parkington handed him a flat metal key. It glowed silver in the dim lights of the dash.

'He tells me that this is a copy of the master key. It's soft metal, so we will have to be careful using it in case it bends.'

'You mean, *I* will,' replied Love. 'Because I am going in.'

'In that case, it will help to know what room it opens – Number 013.'

'Who's inside? A lovely woman, I hope?'

'No, a middle-aged man, travelling on a Dutch passport. Name of Volkoff.'

'Who exactly is he?'

Parkington shrugged.

'If I knew, you wouldn't have to go into his room and find

out. My contact says he has received several male visitors, apparently mostly East German campers.'

'I wonder if one of them has a broken arm?' Love asked him.

'Let's go and find out.'

The heavy car moved slowly down the rough track with a woffle from its dual exhausts like a motor-boat putting out to sea. Night moths danced in the tunnels of amber light from its headlamps. Love accelerated away on the main road, his tyres squealing on tarmac still warm from the afternoon's sun.

The smell of herbs hung like honey on the night air. Two donkeys laden with cork trudged along ahead of them, a man walking alongside, his head bowed. A country bus swung towards him ablaze with lights like a galleon, and then there was little except the regular red and white milestones, until they were running down into Sagres. Love parked the car off the road where it would be screened from the headlights of other passing vehicles.

'If someone sees that,' said Parkington as they started to walk into town, 'we may as well post a letter and say we are coming.'

'But who knows who we are?' Love asked him.

Parkington grunted.

'You speak for yourself,' he said.

The hotel perched on the edge of the cliffs. Far beneath it, the ocean moved like a shifting shining floor. Half a dozen cars were parked in the driveway, beneath palm trees whose leaves rattled in the wind.

Three middle-aged women tourists stood in the entrance hall, taking their time about selecting coloured post cards from a rack to send back to friends at home with bright holiday insincerities: 'Wish you were here. Having a wonderful time,' and so on. A clerk with a Castro moustache worked a mechanical adding machine behind a desk. No-one looked at Love and Parkington as they walked through the lounge, and on into the bar. Here, piped music played, the barman polished a glass, candle flames trembled in glass jars on half a dozen small and empty tables. The main stairs lay at the back of the bar. They went through swing doors into a corridor. The

105

barman replaced the glass on a shelf and picked up another.

'You go back into the bar and wait,' said Love.

'That's no hardship. But what if anything goes wrong?'

'Then your name is Smith,' Love told him. 'Don't ring me, I'll ring you.'

'And if you can't?'

'Give me ten minutes, and then come up. Knock on the door. Say you're a waiter with a message.'

'They also serve,' said Parkington, and turned back to the bar. Love went on up the staircase to the second floor. The corridor was carpeted; fluorescent lights flickered in the long stuccoed ceiling. Behind ventilating louvres in a service door, a refrigerator hummed softly. Love took out Parkington's key, cautiously tested it for strength between his hands, and tapped with it on the door of Room 013. There was no answer.

He put the key in the lock, turned it slowly, opened the door and closed it behind him. He stood for a moment in the tiny entrance hall of the bedroom suite. The air was warm, as though the windows had been closed for too long. The bedroom door stood open. A red neon sign outside painted everything the colour of blood. Beyond lay the infinite darkness of the sea. Love stood, listening. Someone flushed a water closet in the room next door, and there was a faint rattle of hooks as a curtain was drawn. The walls must be very thin; he would have to be extremely quiet.

He put on a pair of rubber surgical gloves, went into the bathroom and shut the door behind him, turned on the light and searched the room methodically from left to right, top to bottom, as MacGillivray's men had taught him how to search a room. Nothing was concealed in the flush tank, or taped behind the swan-neck of the lavatory pan. He did not know what he was looking for or what he might find, but it was still disappointing to find nothing.

He switched off the light and went into the bedroom. He felt it was too risky to turn on the main light so he used a pencil torch, the sort he often shone down the throats of patients when examining their tonsils.

106

As he opened each drawer in turn, ran his fingers beneath the silk shirts and folded sweaters, he wondered what these patients would say if they could see their physician in a stranger's bedroom going through his possessions. He opened the cupboards, shone his torch on three expensive pairs of shoes in trees, and two lightweight suits on hangers. The tailors' names had been removed. He opened the drawer of the writing desk: two packets of Cintra cigarettes, Zeiss binoculars with especially powerful lenses, a silver lighter, a pocket calculator. He closed the drawer and shone his torch over the chairs, the bed, the bedside table.

Something was wrong.

He sensed this rather than saw it in the tiny beam. He shone the torch on the bedlight, the telephone, the built-in radio in the wall – and again on the bedside table. Two Gideon Bibles lay on it, and in every hotel room where he had stayed there was only one.

He crossed the floor and opened the nearest Bible. Then he opened the second. After the Book of Deuteronomy, the pages had been skilfully hollowed out. An automatic with twelve rounds lay padded in foam rubber. As he looked at this, Love tensed, adrenalin raced in his blood. A key was turning in the lock of the main door.

He looked round for somewhere to hide, but there was nowhere. The cupboards were too narrow; the bed was blocked in beneath the mattress. He scooped up the automatic and three rounds and crossed the room in two giant strides to stand on the far side of the doorway. He grabbed a blue and red ashtray on his way and held his breath and waited.

The door opened very slowly and carefully. A triangle of light from the corridor spread across the hall carpet and narrowed and died as the door closed just as quietly. This, he guessed, was not Volkoff coming in; this must be someone else, and not a hotel maid. Only someone who had no business to be in the room would enter so cautiously.

Love could not attempt to load the weapon because of the noise. Instead, he rolled the ashtray like a wheel across the

107

carpet. As it hit the skirting, three shots cracked like twigs snapping. So the visitor was armed with a silenced gun. The smell of cordite was suddenly very sharp and strong. The door opened and closed again in a hurry. The carpeted corridor soaked up the receding sound of feet.

Love waited for two minutes by his watch and then shone his torch on the shattered ashtray. Whoever had come in was a good marksman, and might be waiting for him outside. He picked up the telephone and dialled the bar. The barman answered.

'I would like to speak to Mr Smith,' Love told him. 'He has a drink for me.'

Parkington came on the line.

'Come up carefully,' said Love. 'There's a Humphrey around outside. Or the local equivalent.'

Love replaced the receiver and waited. Minutes later, he heard a discreet tap on the door and Parkington called: 'Your drink is ready, sir.'

'So am I,' said Love, and opened the door. He locked it behind Parkington.

'What's the trouble?'

'Someone came in very carefully – too carefully. He didn't switch on the light. I rolled an ashtray at him, to see what he'd do. He fired three shots and pushed off. A silenced gun, by the way.'

'So we are not the only ones interested in Volkoff,' said Parkington. 'Let's have a gander around his pad while we're here.'

Parkington pulled on a pair of lightweight gloves, drew the curtains and switched on the bedside light. He went from bedside table, to drawers, to the desk.

'This gun was in the Gideon Bible,' said Love. 'I took it out in case I had to use it.' He replaced the automatic as Parkington began to feel behind the curtains, moving his fingers expertly into the folds, up on the top of the pelmet, under neatly folded silk shirts in the chest of drawers. But he found no clues to the identity, the character or the business of the occupant.

108

Above the built-in cupboards was a space for suitcases. To one side lay a T.A.P. airline bag, and next to this a soft-leather suitcase flung carelessly on its side. The case had four small round knobs on the bottom, so that it could stand on any surface without scratching the leather. Something drew Love's eyes to these small metal bumps. It took him a few seconds to realize what it was. Only three were metal, slightly scuffed where they had stood on pavements. The fourth was glass. He pointed this out to Parkington.

'Thought there'd be something somewhere,' said Parkington triumphantly. He stood on a chair and gently lifted down the case. Inside was a tape recorder, with an attachment that made it start at the sound of a human voice. Alongside this, and taped with its lens behind the glass knob, was a camera. Parkington opened it and removed the film.

'Infra red,' he said. He took out the cassette from the recorder, searched in the side pocket of the suitcase for a new one, inserted this and carefully put the case back in its position. Then they went down the back stairs, out into the grounds and walked in silence to the Cord.

'What do you make of that?' asked Love as he climbed behind the wheel.

'Well, our absent friend Volkoff is a professional,' replied Parkington.

'But what is his profession?'

'I wouldn't say it's one of the learned professions.'

'That's what worries me.'

Love started the engine, let in the clutch.

In an upper bedroom of a house across the road, the watcher who had observed Volkoff return to his hotel with the newspapers earlier in the day, now watched Love turn the Cord and drive back up the road. He made a note on a memo pad, checked the time with his watch, and reached for the telephone.

*   *   *

As Victoria let herself into the front door she heard her

mother's voice calling in the querulous, resigned voice of the permanent invalid: 'Who is that?'

'Me,' she replied brightly, as she always did, and went into her mother's bedroom. Mrs Forbes lay propped upon pillows, a thermos flask of iced orange juice on the bedside table. A silk curtain held at bay the brash glare of the sun, but the filtered light only accentuated the pallor of her mother's face, the violet shadows beneath her eyes, her sunken cheeks and pale lips.

'How are you feeling?' Victoria asked her.

'Much the same. Mustn't grumble. I have a lot to be thankful for – you coming to stay with us, for one thing. There's a letter for you, by the way, Victoria. It came with one for your father about his pension.'

Victoria went into the sitting room. The Air Commodore was sitting at his writing desk adding up some figures on a piece of notepaper. The paper was covered with small calculations and crossings out.

'These pension wallahs have got it all wrong,' he said irritably. 'Taking off tax they are not entitled to. I'll have to write to them again. Not that they ever read the damn letters. There's a letter for you, Victoria, by the way. From India, according to the postmark. Wonder what things are like out there now?'

Victoria opened the envelope and began to read. Then she sat down in an easy chair with the letter in her lap, her hands trembling slightly.

'Feeling all right?' her father asked her anxiously.

She nodded, not answering.

'Bad news?' he went on. He pushed aside his calculations and sat down on the arm of her chair, one hand round her shoulders.

'Yes. When I was in Calcutta, I used to visit an old retired Middle-European professor, a stateless person, I suppose, who lived out there very quietly, just glad to be alive and away from persecution. I knew he had T.B. but there wasn't much I could do to help him. Now his daughter has written to say that some anonymous kind-hearted person paid for him to have the best possible treatment in the most expensive private clinic out there. But it was too late. He has died. If *I* had money, that's how I would spend it – helping other people. And not leaving it until they're past helping.'

'Always easy to say when you haven't any,' replied her father drily. 'My bet is you would spend it like everyone else who has any – enjoying yourself. But why so sad? Surely it's not because some old fellow has finally gone to his long home, eh?'

'I *was* expecting another letter,' she admitted. 'Or at least some different news in this one – about someone else. But there's nothing.'

Her father looked at his daughter thoughtfully. How quickly had the little tomboy girl disappeared and a young woman with a life of her own taken her place, involved with people he had never heard of. She was presumably worrying over some man who hadn't written, some affair that had meant more to her than to him. He sighed, thinking back to girls he had known in faraway outposts; girls he had loved briefly and to whom he had promised to write but to whom he had never written. Where were they all now? Did they think of him as seldom as he thought of them? There was only one way Forbes could suggest to cheer up his daughter, and himself; a specific for all ailments of mind, heart and body in every hot country.

'Have a drink,' he said.

Victoria shook her head.

'No, thank you,' she said dully. 'There's something else.'

'Yes.'

'I'm afraid.'

'*Afraid?* What of?'

'On the beach at Carrapateira this morning I saw one of the men who tried to beat you up.'

'You were alone? Did he threaten you?'

'No. I was with Dr Love and his friend, Dick Parkington. This man was in a crowd. Apparently someone had fallen off the cliffs and drowned. The body was on the beach, and Dr Love was called. This man was watching.'

111

'Did he recognize you?'

'Yes. He cleared off very quickly.'

'Did you tell Love?'

'Only afterwards. When the man had gone.'

'What did Love say?'

She shrugged.

'There was nothing he could do then.'

'I suppose not. Well, don't let it worry you. They were probably only roughs wanting money. They must realize by now we've little enough for our needs, let alone theirs. Cheer up, my dear. Tell me about this professor in Calcutta. You've never mentioned him before.'

'There's not much to tell. He was a Serb – and very proud of it. He'd been at Budapest University for nearly thirty years. When the Communists came he was denounced, first as a reactionary, then as a deviationist. Somehow he managed to escape. His wife was dead. He had only one daughter. I came to know him through her.'

'How did he get to India?'

'I don't know exactly. He was in Cairo for some years. Then he lectured at Aligarh University in India. He liked it. But the job folded and he settled in Calcutta. I think he did some research and translation work to make ends meet.'

*   *   *

Professor Borda had lived in shabby rooms off Park Street in a block of flats due for demolition before the war. Now, trees several feet high sprouted in the gutters, down-pipes were stained green with mossy slime, and the drains stank. Slats were missing from faded shutters pinned back like ears across the cracked stucco walls because they were now too fragile to close. This crumbling building was home to a number of people who had known better times, but who had long since abandoned hope of such times returning. For them it was sufficient that they could survive without persecution. Families lived in single rooms, sharing bathrooms. Most of the lavatories were blocked

112

and beyond repair, so they used privies on the ground floor.

Victoria had been in Calcutta for six months, working as a volunteer helper in a medical complex run by a Quaker charity. She worked under an American dentist, Eric Cartwright, to whom the professor had come for treatment. After a difficult extraction the old man had looked so frail and ill that Victoria had taken him home in a taxi.

Victoria remembered the first time she had seen the squalid apartment, with a string of washing stretched from corner-to-corner of the main room. Yellowing photographs of college groups, most long since dead, standing in front of buildings demolished years ago, were tacked to the walls. Their sepia, strangely innocent faces reminded her of the squadron photographs at home, and her heart warmed to the old man. She had visited him about once a week thereafter and became friendly with his daughter, Judith.

Cartwright had a dry sense of humour, and a compassion for people, curiously at variance with his anguish to be rich.

'I emigrated to the States because, in my profession, that's where the money lies,' he admitted to her shortly after she started to work for him. 'You can earn a lot of cash there as a dentist. But to be really rich, you don't *earn* money. You have to *make* it. One day I'll get that break and I'll be away. Think of me then, Victoria. I'll send you a postcard from the Bahamas.'

'Maybe I'll be there with you?'

'You might be at that.'

That night, they'd had dinner together, and danced together in the Grand Hotel, and then gone to bed together. It had seemed the most natural thing in the world. She knew he was married, but his wife was thousands of miles away, and anyhow, what did it matter? They would only be in Calcutta for six months, and after that their association would end. Or – would it? Within a week, Victoria had moved into Cartwright's flat at Alipore, and so began the happiest time in her life.

She had been brought up in a Service family, where life ran to a regimented routine. Meals were at set hours, expenditure must always be watched carefully because money was perpetually short. There could never be any scandal, or any hint of anything shocking, because this might rebound on father's reputation, and hence on his chances of promotion, which had dwindled as successive governments had cut back on the size of the R.A.F. Now she found herself with a man in his late thirties who had plenty of money to spend and who believed in spending. Cartwright possessed a talent for enjoyment and an appetite for fun which opened golden doors to new and unimagined horizons of laughter, and what she began to believe was love.

One morning she arrived late at the surgery and found him examining some X-ray plates. His face was serious as he passed them over to her. She held them up to the light. They were not of teeth, as she had expected, but of a man's rib cage.

'Professor Borda,' he explained. 'I dropped in to see him the other night with a bottle of whisky – purely for medicinal purposes, poor old boy – and he was running a temperature. I had him X-rayed. This is the result. Not a lot of hope for him, I'm sorry to say. Advanced T.B. And at his age, with his weakened constitution, there is usually a fairly quick ending. Unless he could get specialized treatment now.'

'Does he know how bad it is?'

'He knows he's ill, of course, but he appears stoical. Says he has lived long enough, all the tragedies he has seen, and so on. But he is worried about Judith. She has only a temporary job.'

'She tells me her father is writing a book. Would that make them any money?'

Cartwright shook his head.

'Academic books bring in very little,' he replied. 'But he has shown me some scientific papers he brought out of Hungary which might bring in a bit. The sort of stuff a new and well-endowed American or Arab university might – just might – buy for their libraries.

'What are they about?'

'Mostly above my head, actually. I can make out some of the

equations, and follow several of the theories, which are extra-ordinary – if they work. What we need is an expert to advise us.'

'Not much hope of that in Calcutta, is there?'

'There could be. I've one lead, that fellow who came in for a crown on his upper right seven the other day. He's staying at the Great Eastern. Fellow called Volkoff.'

'He's a scientist?'

'So he told me. Riga University, in Russia. Goodness knows what he's done since then. I could ask him. Even if he can't help us, maybe he'll know someone who can.'

Cartwright put the X-ray negatives in a folder.

'Just one thing before we see our first patient.'

'What's that?' she asked.

'This,' he said. He pulled her roughly towards him, and pressed her back into the chair . . .

'A drink now?' Forbes was asking her, pouring himself more gin.

'No, thanks. Sorry. I was miles away.'

'Any idea who's paid the bill for this old professor of yours?'

'No,' she said. 'None at all.'

But she thought: I wonder if it was Eric Cartwright? It's the sort of thing you would do. Dear Eric. Oh, why haven't I heard from you?

*   *   *

Volkoff stood in his hotel bedroom in Sagres, head slightly on one side, sniffing the air carefully like a gun dog. He had been close to many bullets in his life; some he had despatched, some he had nearly received. The smell of cordite was as unmistakable as the scent of danger.

He noted that the curtains had been drawn, and the bedside light lit. Perhaps the room maid had done this, for he had left the room in daylight. Or maybe whoever had been in the room, and had fired the shots, had also drawn the curtains. He looked around the skirting boards until he found what he sought: three bullet holes in the wood. He prised out one of the slugs with a penknife and examined it through an eyeglass. A heavy calibre ·38, the gun of a man who meant business, not someone who simply carried a toy automatic to frighten a sneak-thief or a mugger. This was the weapon of a professional, and as such should be regarded with respect.

He opened the Gideon Bible. His own automatic was still there, and unused. He pulled his suitcase down from the top of his cupboard and examined the camera and tape recorder. He sensed now he was dealing with an adversary as careful as himself. But who could this intruder be? And why should he fire three shots into the woodwork? Could two people have arrived – perhaps at different times, and one found the other already in the room? The idea was plausible, but led him nowhere.

If he moved from the hotel, which was his immediate reaction, then this professional would doubtless follow him. He must have followed him here, so it was reasonable to suppose he would still be watching him. To run now would be to ask for pursuit; he would stay where he was, but bring forward his whole programme so that he could leave Portugal before he had planned to go.

He checked the time on his watch. Ten-thirty. He turned out the light, opened the curtains wide, and looked out towards the sea. The ship had gone. But that did not mean that it would be more than a few miles along the coast. It might not even have passed the cliffs at Sagres. He had never seen this fellow Hood before he picked him out of the sea, had never even heard of him. Obviously, something had gone badly wrong. But – what? Maybe McNab was injured; he could even be dead.

The only way to find out what was happening was to speak to him and, if that proved impossible, then to someone else who could at least tell him why the ship had been stationary for so long, and why Hood had been shot and jumped – or been pushed overboard.

He slipped the automatic from the Bible into his back pocket, went out and down the stairs, to his rented car. He drove along almost deserted roads towards Carrapatiera. On either side, eucalyptus trees and cork forests stretched into an infinity of darkness. Once or twice, ahead of him, he saw a country cart moving slowly and creakily along the side of the road, the only illumination from a hurricane lamp tied to its axle. He turned off towards the beach, and stopped near several parked cars and mobile caravans. Lamps glowed inside blue and orange tents. A transistor played tunes of the fifties. The air smelled of damp salt, and the pound of the sea beat like a giant pulse. He tapped lightly on the door of the second Caravette in line.

'Who is it?'

'Me,' replied Volkoff quietly.

The door opened. Heinz, Jan and Kurt were sitting round a little table under the pale light of a fluorescent ceiling lamp, playing cards. Several tins of beer were on the table, and empty tins lay on their sides on the floor. A little pyramid of grey ash and cigarette stubs grew in a saucer. The room smelled of stale smoke and sweat.

'I had a visitor in the hotel tonight,' Volkoff began. 'He fired three shots into my room – when I wasn't there.'

'Who was it?'

'I don't know. But someone who must be on to us. We will have to move more quickly.'

'How much more quickly?'

'I am going to persuade McNab ashore,' Volkoff replied. 'I must find out what's gone wrong.'

'Why not ask him on the radio telephone?'

'Because he probably could not tell us. But if we get him ashore on some pretext he can bring the stuff with him easily enough. Four o'clock tomorrow morning, then. In this vehicle. In position.'

The others nodded. Heinz opened another can of beer; he did not offer Volkoff a drink. They picked up their cards. Volkoff went out and walked back to his car. For a moment he stood, looking towards the white breaking rim of the waves. The beach was deserted. From Cape St Vincent the lighthouse, the most powerful in all Europe, spread its white beam across sixty miles of sea. The sailors of Henry the Navigator's days

117

had called this Cape *O fim do mundo*, the end of the world, for it stood at the tip of Western Europe, facing the whole force of the wild and unknown Atlantic. Volkoff did not like the name; it sounded morbid, defeatist.

He had a feeling of immense solitude and emptiness, of being alone in a damp, hostile world of darkness and the sea. He shuddered. He wanted to be back in the safe familiar warmth of lights and people, without this feeling someone was stalking him, hunting him. If he were not extremely careful, this hunter could kill him. Three men had already died; Marshall and Hood on the beach, and Cartwright in Oregon. He had no intention of being the fourth.

As he drove back to his hotel, deliberately keeping in the middle of the empty road because he felt that this minimized the chance of any attack from the side, he thought back to his first meeting with Cartwright. Volkoff had been in Calcutta on what he had loosely described on his airport disembarkation card as 'business'. This was not a description with which all would have agreed, but certainly his business was always profitable and, for Volkoff, profit was not only the name of the game, it was the game.

For this particular enterprise that had taken him to Calcutta, he had registered the business name, Associated Assets Inc. in Mayfair, and at the same time had letterheads printed for the Second National Bank of Iowa at the same address. Among the list of directors he had chosen the names of several distinguished senators taken from *Who's Who in America,* without, of course, either their knowledge or involvement.

Using this notepaper he then typed a letter as from one of these directors to a credit card company, explaining that Mr Volkoff, a senior director, would shortly be approaching them for membership, and would require £5,000 limit to his credit to cover international travel expenses. With this card, he bought an air ticket to Johannesburg, where he gave an interview to an airport reporter, and explained he was interested in buying diamonds. He tipped lavishly and without discrimination in taxis, restaurants, and his hotel. Within two days, several diamond dealers approached Volkoff. Some, for political reasons, wanted money out of South Africa and were willing to accept a considerable discount for their diamonds. Others wished to do business on behalf of un-named clients. All were impressed by the obvious extent of Volkoff's credit, as shown by his prodigal hospitality, and the fact that he received frequent calls from well-known banks and companies in the City of London.

Two dealers agreed to supply him with half-a-million dollars worth of diamonds every month for one year. They did not know that the telephone calls emanated from an associate of Volkoff's in several previous financial transactions, Frank Marshall. He had rented a single room in a London hotel, which had facilities for dialling Johannesburg direct.

Volkoff flew back to London, presented the letters of intent from the diamond merchants to one of the smaller banks, and on their security negotiated a short-term loan of £100,000. This money he deposited in Bangkok, to which city he flew, again using his credit card to pay for the ticket.

Here, Volkoff bought an 8,000 ton cargo ship, which would otherwise have been scrapped, and insured it for £1,500,000, including a full cargo of wood pulp. He hired a scratch crew and sailed this old freighter down the Chao Praya River, and headed for the open sea. Soon, a lifeboat, with Volkoff and the three others of his crew, headed back to shore. The ship had unfortunately developed engine trouble. Then plates began to leak, her pumps inexplicably failed, and within an hour she had sunk without trace.

Fortunately, there had been time for the crew to escape, and from the lifeboat Volkoff had been able to take photographs of this ship as she settled and finally went down. These photographs clearly showed the name on her stern, which Volkoff did not feel the need to explain to the insurance company's representatives that he had repainted, so that the lettering would stand out clearly, even in a bad light.

After some haggling, the insurers paid the claim. The money was transferred to the safety of a bank in Vaduz, Lichtenstein, and Volkoff set out for London by easy stages to prepare for the next foray into the realms of finance.

The first stage of this journey took him to Calcutta, a city which excited him. Although it was crowded with poor and wretched people, to him they had everything his own early life in Estonia had made him value: vigorous optimism and an unquestionable determination to survive. He decided to utilize the poverty to his own profit and telephoned Marshall in London to register a charity for helping Indian children who were made orphans in famine. Sooner or later, usually sooner, famine strikes somewhere in the Indian sub-continent, and here was a ready-made opportunity to appeal to millions of good-hearted people in the Western world, and touch their pockets through their consciences.

Not all the money they subscribed would actually help the children. Most would help Volkoff to buy other ships which he had discovered in inlets and creeks along the coast of India. Some had been there for years, scabby with rust, long since looted of everything that could be carried away. Others were only hulls rusting on muddy bottoms of silted rivers, lacking funnels or masts, but still recognizable as ships.

Not all these ancient vessels had been removed from the Register at Lloyds. Some on paper appeared to be in good shape and plying about their business. His interest in shipping brought him other offers. He heard of ships lying in creeks south of Bombay; in the Suez Canal; half submerged in swamps off the East Coast of Africa. Some, Volkoff bought outright; on others he took long options to purchase.

One evening in Calcutta, while eating a prawn curry, he broke an upper back tooth on a grain of grit contained in the rice. A guest in the hotel recommended him to Cartwright who crowned the tooth, and then came to ask his advice on a bundle of scientific papers. At first Volkoff was not greatly interested; it was many years since he had studied science.

They sat together in one of the downstairs lounges, as he looked through the closely written pages. The handwriting was faded, and the paper had turned yellow, but he had only to skim through half a dozen pages to realize that here was a treasure that could make the profits of his shipping deals seem like small change – and with little risk.

'You think they could be worth anything?' asked Cartwright, watching Volkoff's face closely. 'They're not mine, you understand. I'm trying to help a friend, Professor Borda, who is ill and without money.'

'The Eastern bloc would pay highly for these, and so would the West,' Volkoff replied. 'Or one of the international terrorist groups that has the funds.'

'How much would you say they would pay?'

'It is my experience, Mr Cartwright, that nothing has any real value until someone else wants it. We could stimulate interest by introducing several potential buyers to bid against each other.'

'Can you handle this?' Cartwright asked him bluntly.

'With pleasure, Mr Cartwright.'

'Should we not have a letter of agreement?'

'The most expensive contract, Mr Cartwright, is without value – unless there is goodwill,' replied Volkoff chidingly.

'And there is goodwill here?'

'The best,' Volkoff assured him. 'Absolutely the best. But I cannot handle this on my own. I need to involve two people who have helped me in other negotiations in the past. We have to approach several parties who might be interested. We have to be diplomatic – or these people might simply seize the papers by force and pay us nothing.'

'You speak as though this were some sort of underhand business, Mr Volkoff.'

'When stakes are high, Mr Cartwright, most businesses can become, as you say, underhand.'

'And you are sure these papers are worth so much money?'

'Nothing is sure or certain in this life, Mr Cartwright, except that one day we shall all be required to leave it. You have asked my advice and I have given it to you. If you do not wish to take it, then, of course, that is your prerogative.'

'No, no, Mr Volkoff. I want you to handle this for my friend.

121

It is just that I am surprised how these old papers could be so valuable.'

Volkoff shrugged. Cartwright's surprise was of no concern to him.

'Well, that is agreed, then,' he said. 'Now, as to my two colleagues. The first is a Mr Jarrold, whose contacts are very high-level in the areas in which we will have to negotiate. The second is a Mr Marshall whose qualifications are also essential for our success. I suggest we split all profits equally between you and me. I will pay my expenses and you pay yours, whatever they are.'

'Out of my share, I will pay the professor?'

'Whatever you wish. Give him the whole lot if you like. Out of my share, of course, I have to come to an arrangement with my colleagues.'

'What do you think these papers will fetch? Five hundred pounds? A thousand?'

'I would hope for rather more, but any estimate would be only conjecture. Let us put the matter to the test as soon as possible.'

Later that night, Volkoff flew to Bombay where he booked into the Taj under the name of Blake, chosen at random because he saw a paperback at the airport describing the experiences of George Blake, the Soviet spy who escaped from Wormwood Scrubs. He telephoned Jarrold and Marshall in London and urged them to fly out now, rather than later, as they had intended, in connection with his charity. They met in his room on the morning of their arrival. He explained about the professor's papers. They heard him out in silence.

'You are certain about their value?' asked Marshall.

'As positive as I can be.'

Volkoff turned to Jarrold.

'I'll give you a list of what *some* of the papers contain, and you try them on your contacts. But don't say we have the papers here, in case they try to get them without paying.'

'It may take time,' Jarrold pointed out. 'This isn't the sort of thing I can set up in a day.'

'You have as long as you need.'

So Jarrold went about his shadowy business: a guarded telephone call to one man, a meeting with a second, a message from a third. Finally, after further negotiations, a car came to his hotel and he was driven for several miles out of Bombay. The driver stopped near a double-storeyed house surrounded by an unusually high wall. In this house, a middle-aged Indian wearing blue-lensed spectacles looked through the documents, cluck-clucking now and then with surprise and admiration. He sat on a silk cushion on a carpeted floor, and Jarrold had to crouch beside him because there were no chairs in the room.

'These papers could be as valuable as your friend believes,' said the Indian at last. He spoke in quiet educated tones devoid of any accent, but there was a hardness in his voice that commanded Jarrold's respect. As the Indian handed back the documents, Jarrold caught a faint whiff of expensive perfume. The room was filled with wood carvings and brass statues of ancient gods. Scented sticks burned in a holder in front of an effigy with many hands. Jarrold did not like the room or the man.

'What would you bid?' he asked bluntly.

'It is not for me to engage in matters of money, Mr Jarrold, the Indian replied gently, 'I can only assess the value of the equations.'

He paused.

These bloody Indians went round and round, thought Jarrold irritably. Why couldn't they name a sum, *any* sum to start the bidding?

'But if I were in the market, Mr Jarrold, I think they might be worth at least the equivalent of five million sterling.'

'As much as that?'

Jarrold had not altogether believed Volkoff's assessment of their worth.

'You will tell your people of this value?'

'I will inform my principals,' the Indian agreed. 'Now, perhaps you will join me in some mint tea?'

Volkoff and Marshall were waiting for him, white faced,

123

outside their hotel. They led him past old horse-drawn carriages whose drivers pleaded for the privilege of their custom.

'What's the matter?' Jarrold asked Volkoff. He was eager to tell him what the Indian had said. But Volkoff was in no mood to listen; he had news of his own.

'Our rooms have been ransacked,' he said tersely. 'Mattresses ripped up. Even the lining is torn out of our jackets in the cupboard.'

'Why?'

'Why do *you* think?' retorted Marshall. 'Because of these bloody papers.'

'If I hadn't been carrying them round with me, they'd have gone. They must have worked fast,' said Jarrold. 'But then my contact tells me they are worth five million sterling, so that isn't surprising.'

'If he says that, then they are probably worth more,' said Volkoff soberly.

'If they know we are in the hotel, they'll know where we are now,' Jarrold pointed out. 'We can't keep walking about with these papers any longer. We daren't. And the danger is, we don't know exactly who is against us. Whether they are Eastern bloc agents or terrorists. The people I've contacted deal with both groups.'

'I have booked us out,' said Marshall. 'We are in a little hotel near Victoria Terminus. And we are on the first direct flight out of Bombay to London at six tomorrow morning. So we have only one night to keep out of their way, whoever they are.'

They hired a taxi and drove to a Chinese restaurant on the edge of town. They waited until the restaurant closed, and then took another cab to a late-night cinema. They felt safer in crowded places. At five o'clock in the morning they drove out to the airport by a roundabout route in case they were being followed. Marshall gave the two others their tickets, and went to the check-in counter first. Ten minutes later, Volkoff followed, and Jarrold five minutes after him. They joined different queues to go through Customs. Volkoff kept the papers in his brief-case under his arm. To his surprise, all the queues were stationary. Ahead of them stretched a line of passengers, standing by their luggage, with that air of droop-shoulder weariness and resignation that characterizes air-line travellers facing yet another inexplicable and unadvertised delay.

'What's the trouble?' Volkoff asked an Indian official.

'We have heard that some foreign people are trying to smuggle out something without Government permission,' he replied importantly.

'What do you mean, smuggle *out*? I thought you people were more concerned with smuggling things *in*?'

'So we are, sir. But not when it comes to ancient documents of value to the State. All luggage is being searched minutely.'

'I see,' said Volkoff. He exchanged glances with Marshall in the next queue, who in turn looked to his right and stroked his chin. Jarrold nodded almost imperceptibly. The three men left their queues, and by different exits, walked out of the building. They met on the edge of the vast car park. Ahead, the lights of the airport's Centaur hotel glowed weakly in the early morning sun.

'It's too risky,' said Jarrold. 'Someone has tipped them off. Ten to one these Customs wallahs don't know what they are looking for. But if they see a mass of papers they will seize them. And once the opposition have sight of them, we're done.'

'So what do you suggest?'

'Cancel the tickets,' said Marshall instantly. 'Fly to Delhi instead. There is no customs check on internal flights. Then we can try our luck from there with a direct flight out to Zurich or Rome. But not London.'

'*Don't* cancel the tickets,' said Volkoff. 'That's asking for trouble. But I agree with the rest.'

By evening they were in Delhi. Volkoff was in his air-conditioned hotel-room when the telephone rang. Jarrold was on the line, his voice tense with fear.

'Have you heard the radio?' he asked.

'No,' said Volkoff. 'What's happening?'

125

'That plane we should have caught from Bombay. It blew up in mid-air. A bomb.'

'My God! You think they believe we were on it?'

'I don't know, but we've got to be a bloody sight more clever than we've been so far, or we'll lose everything.'

'Including our lives,' said Volkoff . . .

Now, driving along the empty road to Sagres, Volkoff remembered his reply. He shivered. The little car sped on.

* * *

McNab lay snoring in his bunk, mouth open, face glazed with a patina of sweat. He had been reading, and had fallen asleep with the light on. Now, as he heard the beating on the outside of his cabin door, he started up, heart racing, mouth dry, eyes blinking.

'What's the matter?' he called thickly.

'Radio telephone for you,' replied the ship's radio operator.

'For *me*?'

'Yes. About your daughter.'

'My daughter? Caroline?'

'So he says. Hurry.'

'What's happened?'

'I don't know what's happened. Bloke's on the blower for you. That's all I know.'

'What bloke?'

By now, McNab was at the door, a fuddled figure in pyjamas, his hair tousled.

'Come *on*,' said the operator. 'He won't hang on for ever.'

McNab grabbed his uniform jacket, put his feet into slippers and followed the man up to the radio room. He picked up the telephone. An impersonal voice asked, 'Is that the chief engineer, Mr Rob McNab?'

'Speaking. Who is that?'

'One moment, please.'

The ship rolled and creaked. Black needles on hair springs danced across white-faced dials. A spurt of static wheezed from a wall loudspeaker. McNab caught a sight of himself in a mirror on the far wall, pale, worried, tense, old.

'This is Lagos General Hospital,' said another male voice, again in English, but equally not English. 'Can you hear me clearly, Mr McNab?'

'Yes. I hear you.'

'Mr. McNab, we have admitted a young girl and a young man as patients to our casualty department. They have been in a motor accident. Her name, according to her passport, is Caroline McNab. A British subject. Her profession is a school teacher. I understand you are her next of kin?'

'Yes. I am. She's my daughter. What's happened? How is she?'

'She was travelling in a car in collision with a truck on the road to Lagos from Lisbon. Her friend was driving.'

'Is she all right?'

'I cannot give medical details over the telephone, Mr McNab, but she is asking for you. I would suggest you should visit her, because your presence could be a comfort to her.'

'But how can I leave my ship? I am the chief engineer.'

'We can send a launch from Sagres to pick you up if you can give us your position. You can rejoin your ship at Lisbon.'

McNab felt numb with shock. The last he had heard, Caroline was planning to travel with this boy friend in his wretched car through France. They must have gone on south to Spain and so to Portugal.

'How bad is she?' he asked.

'She is seriously ill, Mr McNab. That is all I can say. Shall we send a launch for you?'

'Wait one minute, please.'

McNab held a hand over the mouthpiece.

'Where's the captain?'

'Asleep. Or drunk. Or both,' said the radio operator shortly. He owed the captain no loyalty. He had served too often with scratch crews in worn-out empty tankers and ruined cargo ships due to be laid up or cut in pieces, to owe loyalty to anyone; even to himself.

127

'Shall I find out?' he asked.

'No,' said McNab. His mind was made up. He removed his hand from the telephone.

'I'll meet your launch,' he told the caller. 'If you can guarantee to get me back to Lisbon.'

'That should present no difficulty, Mr McNab. It is barely five hours drive by car or train from Lagos,' the man assured him. 'Let me have your bearings, please.'

McNab gave them.

'We should be past Cape St Vincent at first light.'

'A launch will come out for you at five o'clock, Mr McNab.' The line went dead.

McNab put down the receiver and turned to the telegraphist.

'My daughter is in hospital. She's had a car accident,' he explained. 'Will the captain be awake by five o'clock?'

'Never has been so far.'

'Well, wake him now. Tell him I'm leaving the ship then in a launch for the hospital people.'

'You do your own dirty work, mate.'

'I'll only be away for a couple of days. The engines will be OK for that long. I'll rejoin off Lisbon.'

The radio operator shrugged.

'Your affair, mate,' he said.

McNab woke the captain to explain the situation. The captain had been drinking heavily. His eyes were red and raw. His head beat like a drum.

'You woke me up just to tell me that?' he grumbled. 'Of course you must go and see your daughter. We are putting into Lisbon anyhow for provisions. Join us there. We are due on the seventh. That will give you two days, if necessary. If there are any other developments, cable me care of the agents there. If you miss us we'll take on a substitute. Now, bugger off and let me get some kip.'

The captain had been dreaming of ships in which he had once served in various junior capacities; ships with fresh, newly painted white superstructures and polished brass work, and decks scrubbed every morning; ships of a type and style

128

and class he had once hoped to command. He had worn a freshly pressed uniform then, he had dined with rich passengers and exchanged Christmas cards with famous people. But somehow the ships had grown steadily shabbier and smaller, and soon there were fewer of them, or maybe it was just because his addiction for the bottle had grown with his failure to pass the exams for his master's certificate. And finally, when he had managed to do so, he was down to commanding this floating scabby iron bath held together by flakes of rust, pounding her way uselessly to her own graveyard.

And that bloody fool McNab had woken him and destroyed his dreams, and hauled him back to the bitterness of reality. He staggered to the lavatory and relieved himself, and rolled back into his bed between the sweaty sheets. Then he remembered something, and stretched out his hand for the bottle of rum in his locker drawer. He poured three fingers into his tooth glass, drank greedily, and he fell back; to sleep, but not to dream.

Chapter Eight

The building was a skyscraper, modest by today's heights, but built in the early 1960s, when anything above eight storeys was considered to be adventurous architecture.

Each floor was given over to separate offices. The top-floor office had a brass plate let into the door opposite the lift: Inter-Dominion Exports Ltd. Visitors would arrive and leave at all hours of the day or night, which was understandable in such a business, and the office block was half-way between the M3 and M4 Motorways and so usefully close to London Airport.

Not all these visitors realized that a concealed closed-circuit TV camera and microphone were built into the wall, and actuated by the opening of the lift doors. The face and conversation of everyone who opened or closed these doors was faithfully recorded.

This camera was considered necessary, for the office was one of several used by the British Secret Intelligence Service throughout London. There was a rooming house in Balham, flats in blocks in Bloomsbury and St John's Wood, and other covers, such as a travel agency, a tailor's shop, even a delicatessen elsewhere in the suburbs. These might be used for weeks or months, or sometimes not at all, depending whether the opposition discovered their whereabouts and could home in on discussions with long-range microphones and infra-red cameras. Many Londoners – and probably most taxi drivers – knew the whereabouts of SIS's official headquarters, but very few knew of these outposts.

This particular office was decorated in modern, uncluttered style. Behind the wallpaper were sheets of aluminium, and other metal foil was woven into curtains and venetian blinds to frustrate unofficial attempts to listen electronically from a distance – perhaps in a parked van or from a room in another building.

There were also some devices not usually found in commercial offices: electronic locks on all doors, which also had bullet-proof steel plates built into them, and a number of alarm devices actuated not by pressing a button but simply by raising the voice to a certain pitch, and, of course, shredders in place of a wastepaper basket in rooms used by secretaries.

Through double-glazed and bullet-proof windows, the main room overlooked a suburb of semi-detached houses built in the 1930s when fields had surrounded them. It contained a desk, a couple of armchairs, a bookcase with some reference books and a few pictures on the walls on loan from the Department of the Environment. As with most rooms used by the SIS, it had an air of impersonal impermanence; it could be empty tomorrow and no trace of its former occupants, no hint of their characters or identities, would remain.

Colonel Douglas MacGillivray sat with his elbows on the desk, cleaning his pipe. The desk top was bare except for a blotter (with black paper to reduce the risk of any unofficial eyes reading in a mirror what they were not meant to see), a buff-coloured folder, and two telephones, one green with a scrambler button. The other was an ordinary outside line. Its proximity reminded MacGillivray that he must ring his wife soon and explain he would be late for dinner.

'Again?' she would ask, and he would reply, 'Yes, I'm sorry. Again.'

There would be no explanation asked for and none offered, for MacGillivray could never give the real explanations, and he regarded false excuses as an insult. One day the reasons might appear in the memoirs of a retired Cabinet Minister, but that was not his concern. He had enough to contend with now. Silence and discretion were as much part of his profession as official insistence that his department did not exist.

MacGillivray wore a Squire's houndstooth tweed jacket with

131

leather pads on the elbows, and well-polished Tricker's brogues. His face was reddish and looked as though he had shaved but minutes before. He might have been the managing director of a large public company, with his black Silver Shadow waiting outside the main office, chauffeur already at the wheel, engine running, a white frond of condensation at the exhaust. Or again he might have just come in from a day's deer-stalking in the Sidlaws. He rather cultivated this appearance; it appealed to the actor in him. To a psychologist, it would be instant evidence of a deep wish for another way of life, an escape from the tensions and intrigue with which his job abounded. For MacGillivray was deputy head of British Secret Intelligence Service.

He lived modestly in an old-fashioned flat off the Brompton Road on an overdraft from an obliging bank manager and a civil servant's salary. Their only hope, he would tell his wife, half-truthfully, was that eventually he would receive an index-linked pension.

'Only if you live that long, dear,' she would reply drily, and he would grimace, for his job so often seemed impossibly frustrating, with changes in official policy, ineptitudes and ignorance in official policy, and, all too often, no official policy whatever.

How could he persuade agents in the field – MacGillivray always smiled ironically at that analogy with Victorian missionaries – to risk their lives obtaining information for the good of their country when too often the information they gathered at such cost was disbelieved, not acted upon, not even read?

And for how long would such agents be needed in an increasingly automated and electronic world? Soon, he had been told by one of the professors of science he employed on a retainer basis, one silicon chip would accomplish what a dozen spies – perhaps a hundred – had been required to achieve in simpler, less demanding times.

Day and night, aircraft of East and West now encircled the world, carefully and tirelessly photographing it, country by country, ocean by ocean, metre by metre. And above them, out in the silence of space, satellites kept their perpetual listening watch. A camera twenty or thirty miles up in the heavens would provide him with a picture of a city street so clear that he could not only read shop signs – but also the number plates of individual cars in that street.

Instead of studying a file on some suspect or some potentially dangerous trend, he fed in questions to a computer which spewed out answers within seconds. He was required to locate a bald-headed man with bad eyesight who played the violin and drove a yellow Cortina? Within the time it took to phrase the question he had a list of all known subjects with these attributes. But yet, although such electronic wizardry was impressive, MacGillivray always pointed out to younger members of his staff that a human being was still required to ask the essential questions, to push the buttons that activated the electronic brains of silicon and quartz and goodness knows what else. And it was imperative that such men and women should ask the correct questions, for the best and most complex machine was only as good as the human brain that still controlled it.

But sometimes human beings, being human, asked the wrong question – and not of the machine, but, worse, of the wrong person. And when they did that, unpleasant results, sometimes fatal results, inevitably resulted. Maybe that was why Cartwright had been killed? He did not know; probably he never would know. But it seemed a possible reason, for whatever Cartwright's qualifications might have been as a dentist, as an agent he was strictly part-time, and so both vulnerable and instantly expendable.

In MacGillivray's profession one had always to look for the fact that did not fit into the accepted pattern: the guard dog that didn't bark, the wife who passed her best friend in a crowded street – not because she had not seen her, but because she had. Maybe Cartwright had not noticed the danger signals that a more experienced operator would have instantly recognized.

Well, dead men told no tales, and the living were not always

133

over-communicative, either. MacGillivray lit his pipe and began to thumb through the folder of signals in front of him. At the back of his mind he knew he was looking for something, some link, maybe one word that would immediately trigger off a whole chain reaction. He did not know what this might be, but he trusted his intuition and the antennae of curiosity; and with the eighth signal his faith was rewarded.

Calcutta.

Of course. Cartwright had been there, practising as a dentist, and MacGillivray had been in Calcutta long before that. For a moment he thought back across the years to names that then had been as familiar to him as stations on the District line on his way home: Chowringhee, Alipore, Ballygunge.

He read through the signal again. There must be a link between Cartwright and the brief bare facts the message reported. This was where the human brain could still score over the computer. MacGillivray sat puffing at his pipe, smoothing the flimsy sheet of paper with both hands. Then he smiled. Of course, the link was obvious, like a name concealed in an anagram, the final clue in a crossword. He closed the folder and pressed a bell for his secretary.

*   *   *

Jason Love gave one last glance around the room. The small candle bulbs glowed warmly in their polished brass lanterns around the wall. Lights outside the patio lit the garden so that the bougainvillaea blazed with a noon-day brilliance and the scent of the huge pendulous blossoms of senhora da noche hung sweet as honey in the room.

Love was expecting a guest to dinner, and the Portuguese maid had excelled herself with a local speciality, lulas recheadas. Lulas are small squid that can be served in a dozen different ways. The way she had chosen was to put chopped garlic into a pan of hot olive oil and, as the oil turned golden, she added onions cut into pieces and tentacles of the lulas. She then added herbs, chilli, salt and breadcrumbs and packed this mixture into the hollow sac of each squid and sealed the end

134

with a wooden skewer. The lulas then simmered for about half an hour in a thick aromatic sauce. As a second course, she had prepared another local dish, an egg custard flavoured with vintage port and covered with caramel. Love had consulted Ross as to the best local wine to accompany such a meal; they would start with Bucellas, which Ross recommended to him. This wine came from an area North of Lisbon and was delightfully fresh and dry.

After this they would drink Setubal, from Moscatel de Setubal, south of the capital. This, Ross had assured him, was a fine muscat dessert wine and, having tasted it, Love agreed. The grape skins were steeped in the wine to increase the fragrant scent. After this, they would eat figos recheados, large dried figs stuffed with grated chocolate and ground roasted almonds, and drink port and Medronho, a liqueur distilled from the small arbutus berries grown on mountain slopes, and sweetened with honey. After that, well, who knew what might follow?

Love put an L.P. of the Pasadena Roof Orchestra on the record player and lit a cheroot. Muted trumpets and trombones stroked the night with music. He sat down in a cane chair looking out towards the dark sea, thinking about life and death; two deaths in particular, the unexpected mortalities of Marshall and Cartwright. If, as Parkington had said, time spent in reconnaissance is seldom wasted, time spent thinking never was. Two lights grew larger along the track. He went to the front door. A car stopped; the lights went out; the driver's door opened.

'Hullo,' said Parkington brightly from the darkness.

'And goodbye,' replied Love without enthusiasm. 'I am expecting a lady.'

'Then I won't stay long. But I have something to tell you first. Something important.'

Love closed the door behind Parkington, poured him a gin, added ice and lemon.

'What's so important you have to tell me about it now? Can't it wait until tomorrow?'

'Possibly. But I can't. I have just decoded a message from MacGillivray in London. He says there is a lot of activity among the opposition in Calcutta and Bombay.'

'Who are the opposition, exactly?'

'Those who are not with us are against us, as the Good Book says.'

'What's that got to do with me?' asked Love.

'I'll leave you to judge,' said Parkington. 'But hear me out before you do. First, an emigre Serbian professor in Calcutta was kidnapped. He was apparently seriously ill with T.B. One day an ambulance calls to take him to an expensive private clinic for treatment. He was told this was being paid for by benefactors.'

'Was he cured?'

'In the way all diseases are finally cured. By death. His body was found in a canal.'

'But how does this possibly concern us?'

'He lived with his daughter, and she says that when he was trying to raise money for medical treatment, he produced a bundle of old papers. He showed these to an American dentist who was doing a year's stint on some do-good scheme in Calcutta. He hoped an American University might be interested in them.'

'Could that dentist just be the late Mr Cartwright?'

'Check. Anyhow, Cartwright seems to have done his best to help. He took the papers to a visiting scientist who'd come to him for dental treatment. Name of Volkoff.'

'I am beginning to see why you called,' said Love.

'Great. And there's more to come. The Customs in Bombay were alerted that priceless documents relating to Shah Jehan, the seventeenth-century Emperor in Delhi, were being taken out of the country illegally to sell abroad. They carried out the most stringent check on all passengers on overseas flights, but found nothing.'

'So what effect did that have?'

'Quite an effect on the lives of the 100 or so people who caught the most likely flight. Their plane blew up 500 miles out over the sea.'

136

'I read about that,' said Love. 'A terrible thing.'

'At the same time, three European passengers did not turn up for the plane, although they'd booked on it.'

'Have I ever heard of any of them?'

'I don't know,' said Parkington. 'One gave his name as Blake, another Pole, and the third, Reade. I'd say they are pretty obviously false names. But one last thing. Three single rooms in the Taj hotel in Bombay occupied by men with these names were literally torn to pieces, totally vandalized. Even their suits were ripped up. Someone was looking for something in a hurry.'

'The professor's papers?'

'I think so. Yet this is hardly behaviour you'd expect from university librarians.'

'My guess is they didn't find them.'

'Is it only a guess?'

'Yes, but based on possibilities. That cargo ship the three Germans were so interested in, sailed from Suez. Your three men, whoever they are, were in India. It is unlikely they would go farther east, so the only alternative is that they would come west. Suez is mid-way. Tell me, how would *you* leave India against the clock if Bombay airport was blocked?'

'I'd go inland,' replied Parkington at once. 'Delhi or Calcutta and try from there.'

'Calcutta would be too risky – especially if you'd had anything to do with knocking off the old professor.'

'So it's possible they would leave from Delhi or even Madras?'

'Right,' said Love. 'And if you are carrying something of value, something people would kill for, blow up a whole plane for, it is reasonable to suggest these characters would also make the same deduction — and be waiting for you whenever you arrived in Britain.'

'I take your point,' agreed Parkington. 'Now take one from me. If whoever is after these papers, blows up an aircraft because they think they are aboard, what do they gain? The papers would all be lost with the aircraft.'

137

'Probably a last-ditch plan. *They* mightn't get the papers, agreed, but at least it would stop any rival having them. Which means that the papers have very high international value. Politically, not just commercially.'

'Let's pay another visit to Mr Volkoff.'

'No,' said Love. 'Going back would be like returning to an old affair. It wouldn't work.'

'But what other leads have we got?'

'I am reminded of Napoleon's reply when the relations of his future wife asked: "Who are his ancestors?" Napoleon retorted: "I am my own ancestor." Here, we have no leads, so we will make some now. Do you ever read the Bible?'

'Too rarely,' admitted Parkington.

'Then I recommend to you the gospel according to St Luke, Chapter 12, Verse 34. He was a physician, so naturally I choose him first. But Matthew 6, verse 21, has the same message.'

'Which is?'

' "Where your treasure is, there will your heart be also." My guess is that Volkoff's treasure is aboard that boat. His heart is certainly there, with his binoculars in a room that overlooks the sea. Just as Marshall's was. He had one of the best views of the sea along the whole coast.'

'So what do you suggest? We go aboard on some pretext and search the ship?'

'No. We haven't any pretext and we're not certain what we are looking for. But Volkoff is. Let him do the dirty work.'

'You think there will be dirty work?'

'Positive.'

Two headlights flared through the darkness, turned and died outside the house. The wind was rising now, rustling leaves and making doors that had shrunk in the sun rattle impatiently against their locks. The front door bell pealed.

'My guest,' said Love.

'Then I'll leave,' said Parkington.

'Not yet. Join us in another drink.'

He opened the door to Victoria. Her eyes regarded the room with approval, and registered the fact that while only two

138

places were laid for dinner, three people were in the room.

Love poured a gin for her. She sat down listlessly, turning the glass round and round in both her hands, making a brave attempt to appear cheerful. Love could see that her eyes were suspiciously puffy and red-rimmed. She had been crying. But why? He busied himself with talk, trying to row the conversation along like a man in a heavy boat against a running tide. Victoria smiled at his efforts.

'Sorry I am a bit down,' she said at last. 'But I have had some bad news.'

'Not about your mother, I hope?'

'No, about an old man I knew in Calcutta, an emigre professor. He was very ill with T.B. Then some unknown benefactor paid his medical expenses, but it was too late. He died.'

'I didn't know you had been in India. What were you doing there?'

'Dental nurse. One of these volunteer things. I was getting over an affair and thought I'd do some good for the world.'

'Self interest,' said Parkington pontifically and tactlessly, 'is the basis of most good deeds. It is far safer to make a friend than an enemy.'

'And a whole lot harder,' added Love. 'Who were you working with?'

'Various dentists,' replied Victoria. 'I ended up with an American, Eric Cartwright, who had actually been born in England. Professor Borda had brought some old documents out of Hungary or somewhere. They were the only marketable things he possessed. Eric tried to get some money for them. He thought a university might be interested. Maybe the buyer paid the old man's bills. I don't know. Pity it was all too late.'

'What happened to the dentist?'

'He went home. As a matter of fact, he is getting a divorce. We may get married when he's free.'

'Did he tell you who he's shown the papers to?'

'Yes. A patient who'd been to a Russian university. A man named Volkoff.'

'Did you meet him?' asked Parkington.

'No. He came to the surgery on my day off. But I did meet a colleague of his – after Eric went back to the States. Fellow called Tom Jarrold. I was in Bombay, on my way home – thought I might see a bit of India before I left – and he rang me. He knew all about the professor and wanted to help. I gave him my address in London, but told him I might be coming down here to see my parents. He was most interested when I said I had a private pilot's licence.'

'I suppose he was the man you took up in the plane?'

'Yes. He telephoned me in London, and said he was in the Algarve and something was going wrong which only I could help put right. One of his colleagues was trying to swing things his way, which meant that Eric and the professor would get little, or maybe even nothing. Eric was back home and too far away to do anything so I said, right, I'd do what I could. Tom told me he would explain why later, but he had booked into an hotel as Mr Brandon. He might use that name or his own when we met, but I wasn't to let on we had met before.'

'Did he give reasons for this?'

'Said they were political. He mightn't be welcome here. Eric and I thought that these papers could be worth a few hundred pounds, and now Tom was talking in terms of a fortune. My father suspected I knew him, when we met in Lagos, although, of course, I pretended I didn't.'

'Why did he ask you to fly him over the sea?'

'He wanted to go round and round an old cargo ship. It's very difficult to see much from the front seat of a Moth unless you circle. You can't see forward because of the angle of the fuselage and you have to lean over the side.'

'Was that the first time you saw him out here?'

'No,' she said. 'I've seen him since at the hotel where he was staying – the Penina. He explained that finding the right buyer for the professor's papers was proving difficult. In order to arouse interest, he had to tell potential buyers more than he wanted about the contents. And as soon as he'd done that, they either tried to cut him out or even steal the papers outright.

140

Someone involved in the negotiations had turned up in Portugal. He should have been in England, making arrangements to sell them, but instead he was in Luz. His name was Frank Marshall, and I was to keep an eye on him. That was quite easy. I just ogled him a bit and he started to follow me about.'

'You spoke to him?'

'Only once. He helped me pick up some shells.'

'Almost at the place where he was killed?'

'Yes. That frightened me. It made me realize that the papers could, after all, be worth a lot of money. It seemed to shake Tom, too. After that, he lay low. I rang the Penina but they told me he'd left. I've not seen him since.'

'Have you ever seen the professor's papers?'

'Never.'

'What about those three men who tried to beat up your father? And the explosion in your room?'

'I can't think of any reason why *anyone* should do such things.'

'Well, there must be a reason and we intend to find it,' said Love grimly. 'Dick Parkington is working for an insurance company, investigating what seems like a pretty big fraud. He thinks that the men who were going to sell the professor's papers are also involved. Two's company and three's none, so one of the three has been taken out of the game.'

'But how could any papers be worth so much?' asked Victoria in a puzzled voice. 'Flying here from Calcutta and staying in a big hotel must run into hundreds already?'

'We are not talking in hundreds, but in very large sums of money.'

'Just how large?'

Love turned to Parkington for his estimate.

'Millions,' said Parkington at once. 'Millions.'

*　　*　　*

The sharp bows of Volkoff's hired launch sliced like a butter knife through the incoming Atlantic rollers.

The little craft shuddered, and the propeller screamed in protest as it briefly came out of the water and then plunged back beneath the spuming waves. Volkoff sat in the stern. The hired skipper was at the wheel in the cuddy. Heinz and Jan sat on either side of him to balance the boat. They all wore dark blue trousers and shirts and peaked jockey caps. Volkoff considered they looked vaguely nautical, as though this really was a launch on official business.

Waves, which from the shore looked like tiny white horses, now loomed gigantically when viewed from only a few feet away. The little boat would hesitate and teeter on the crest of one and then plunge down into the green foaming trough. *Princess Rosael*'s stern rose and fell, but steadily they were growing nearer. As they came alongside, a gangway was already down. Volkoff raised his glasses and scanned the decks. A crew member, leaning over the rail, watched them without interest; the wind blew his long hair behind him like a horse's mane. Another man began to climb down the gangway before Volkoff could pick up the loud-hailer. He wore khaki trousers, blue open-necked shirt, an alpaca jacket. Volkoff focussed on his face. McNab. He moved into the cuddy so that the Scotsman would not see him until they were well away from the ship. Heinz gave a mock naval salute towards McNab.

'Engineer officer McNab?' he asked.

'Yes,' said McNab. 'You are from Lagos?'

'The same.'

'How is my daughter? Have you any news?'

'Last report was that she was rallying well. Very pleased you are coming to see her. The doctors think she will be all right.'

'Thank God.'

Heinz steadied the bucking launch with a boat hook. The captain turned his wheel. A gap of sea grew suddenly between the two vessels.

'The sea's a wee bit choppy this morning,' said McNab, rubbing his hands. He came forward into the cuddy. Volkoff was looking through the salt-streaked windshield, seeing the horizon move and the *Princess Rosael* drop to one side. Ahead

142

lay the distant rim of the coast under a lightening sky. The skipper pushed forward the throttle, the launch trembled and then steadily drew away. When there were 200 yards between them and the cargo ship, Volkoff turned to McNab.

'My God!' cried McNab in amazement. '*You!*'

'Yes, me.'

McNab stared at Volkoff; the last time they had met he had come aboard *Princess Rosael* disguised as an Arab.

'But why get me off the ship? What about my daughter? Is she ill?'

'So far as I know, she's all right. But I have never set eyes on her.'

'You mean, it's all a fake, this accident?'

'It was a reason to get you off your ship without any questions being asked.'

Relief and anger showed on McNab's face, then his eyes narrowed questioningly.

'But why? What's happened? Who *are* you?'

'We'll discuss it when we are on shore.'

They put into the quay at Sagres, and walked up the steeply sloping slipway into the town. Early morning sun was already drying streaks of overnight dew on the windscreens of parked cars.

'Get in,' said Volkoff. He nudged McNab into the back of the Caravette. Heinz drove. No-one spoke until they were out through Vila do Bospo. An old woman in black was drawing water from a well. On either side of the road, fields stretched into the distance; small white houses perched high on hillsides.

Heinz slowed, waved on a small car that had come up behind them, and turned off to the left, along a rough track, between cork trees and pines. Great flakes of cork had already been removed, and the peeled trunks gleamed smooth as elephant tusks.

Dust billowed around them in a moving cloud. There were no markers, no fences. The road climbed and fell again, twisting like a sandy rope across the folded hills. In the distance, the sea gleamed. The road suddenly ended on a cliff-

143

top near an empty, shuttered house surrounded by a high wall. A chain secured a metal gate. Heinz turned the Caravette, switched off the engine. The roar of the sea was like the shouting of a distant angry crowd. McNab felt uneasy.

'Why come here?' he asked.

'Because we want to ask you some questions,' said Volkoff. 'Quietly.'

'Let's have 'em, then,' said McNab.

'Why did the ship stop?'

'Engine trouble. Fellow deliberately cut one of the fuel feed pipes. I had to find the break, mend it, bleed the line and start again. It took about an hour and a half.'

'Who did that?'

'Man called Hood. We had a row. He fell over the side.'

'I picked him up,' said Volkoff.

'You did, eh? Where is he now?'

'On a mortuary slab in Lagos.'

'He wasn't dead, surely?'

'Not when we took him out of the water. But he died on the beach. Loss of blood. Exposure. Must have been in that sea for hours. Cold enough, if you are in for minutes. He would have drowned, of course, if he hadn't managed to hang on to an oil drum.'

'You opened it?' asked McNab.

'Yes. It contained some petrol, and a sealed tin with a lot of old magazines. What's that all about?'

'You mean you took me off my ship just to ask me that?'

'We took you off because I *had* to find out what was happening. Is the package safe? Who was Hood?'

'We are a scratch crew, as you can imagine. Hood was my number two. Not a bad engineer, but a surly bugger. Chip on his shoulder big as a bag of coal. Said he knew I was carrying something secret and there was money in it. He tried to beat me up to find out what it was, but I'd been around a bit longer than him. He got the worst of it.'

'What made him suspect there was something?'

'He wouldn't say.'

144

'What about the package?'

'What about it?' asked McNab belligerently. 'I put a dummy in the drum just in case anyone on the ship *did* get on to the fact I was carrying something. It's not very hard for the engineer to cut open a metal drum and weld it up.'

'But where is the real package?'

'That's my affair,' retorted McNab. 'You'll get it when we dock – so long as I am aboard, that is.'

'You believe him?' asked Heinz.

Volkoff looked at McNab, trying to read the man's thoughts behind his bleary eyes.

'You know what happens if you double-cross me?' he asked him quietly.

'No, but I can guess. And I won't. Now, have you finished? If so, you might get me back somewhere where I can hire a car or catch a train for Lisbon. I have to rejoin my ship there.'

'A train's easiest. But there is no railway station at Sagres. The nearest is Lagos.'

'Well, take me to Lagos. How many trains a day from there to Lisbon?'

'Two. Morning and afternoon.'

The sun was coming up fast now. Heat hit the metal of the Caravette like a fist. They sat sweating on the plastic seats.

'Any idea of the times?'

'No. You'll have to find out at the station.'

Heinz started the engine. They drove back along the dusty track to the main road. A little more traffic was about now; a bus, some holiday cars with foreign number plates and luggage on roof racks. At Vila do Bospo the road branched left to Lagos, and right to Sagres. Fields, dusty and brown, dotted with green fig trees the shape of giant bee-hives, stretched to the skyline on either side. Here and there an abandoned house showed the wooden ribs of its roof to the sun. No-one noticed the nondescript car parked behind a fig tree off the road.

Diaz, who had followed them out from Sagres and noted where they left the road, watched the Caravette accelerate away and followed 300 yards behind it. Two miles along the road he turned off between whitewashed gate posts and drove along a track to a farmhouse. Chickens clucked in the straw of a barn. A dog growled on a chain, half stood up and then lay down as it recognized the visitor. Diaz walked up to the side door. His brother came out to meet him.

'If I could use your 'phone, Fernandes?' asked Diaz.

'Feel free,' said his brother. 'And if you are not in too much of a hurry, stay and have a chat. Haven't seen much of you lately.'

'Business first, pleasure later,' said Diaz primly, and began to dial a number.

Chapter Nine

Parkington was sitting, his mind switched off, in a cane arm-chair on the patio of Love's house, a glass of iced Bock beer in the hole that the makers of the chair had thoughtfully incorporated, Eastern fashion, in its right arm.

The telephone pealed imperiously in the hall. He thought it interesting that the telephone system in every country had its own distinctive and peculiar style of seeking attention. In Britain, there are two rings close together and then a space of silence. In the States, there is a single long burr, and then silence. Here, the bell pealed like a carillon for several moments and then stopped. Maybe this was an original discovery, or maybe he had just been drinking too much beer too early in the day. He walked to the hall, and picked up the instrument.

Diaz said, 'I am trying to contact someone who could help me with a problem of rose-growing in the Algarve.'

'A rose by any other name would smell as sweet. And cost twice as much,' replied Parkington, using that week's recognition phrase.

'I am speaking on behalf of the West European Press Alliance,' Diaz went on.

'So I should hope,' Parkington told him. 'What's news?'

'On your instructions, I saw a man come ashore from the ship. His name is McNab. I felt it prudent not to interview him. Three friends met him. They stopped near Carrapateira, off the road, for twenty-five minutes. I still could not see my way to interviewing him in person.'

'Where is he now?'

'On the road past your house, heading for Lagos. To the

147

station. He's going to catch a train to Lisbon to rejoin his ship.'

'How do you know this if you haven't spoken to him?'

Parkington was aware that many agents on surveillance used electronic equipment which would register the minute shock waves of the human voice against a window pane and translate these into sound. But a part-timer like Diaz would not have access to such a sophisticated piece of gear; and MI6, always short of funds, would be unlikely to have provided any other equipment for him.

'I can lip-read, and used binoculars,' Diaz explained simply.

'Good for you. I'll be at the station within half an hour. Is there any way of keeping him there until then?'

'That will not be necessary. He has to wait a long time if he wants to catch a train. He will not make the seven-thirty. And the next one leaves at ten past five this afternoon.'

'Where are you ringing from?'

'A relative's house. Near Vila do Bospo.'

'Do one more thing for me, then,' said Parkington. 'No, two. Go into Sagres and hire two speedboats with a range of at least sixty miles. See they are full of petrol. I may want one to take our friend back to his ship. And one for another trip. Have aboard the one I will use a folding leather or plastic bag the size of an airline bag, but stronger.'

'I'll wait for you on the quay, senhor,' Diaz promised him. 'What is the other thing?'

'You have an answering service when you are not at home?'

'It is necessary, senhor.'

'Of course it is. So when you get home you will find a message that a Miss Victoria Forbes has telephoned. Please do exactly as she asks. She needs your help.'

'She is a writer, too, senhor?'

'Of the very best kind,' Parkington assured him and replaced the receiver. He felt uneasy for a brief moment. He was acting on Love's suggestion, not his own, and the outcome could be risky. He paused, then shrugged. What the hell, he thought. Life's risky. I risk being poisoned every time I drink a glass of

148

water – which is why I so rarely do. He poured himself another Bock. Love called to him from the patio.

'Who was that?'

'Our local man,' explained Parkington. 'Someone called McNab has come off the ship. He's at Lagos railway station, of all places. But first, I want to speak to Victoria.'

He picked up the telephone and began to dial.

Love put on his sunglasses and peaked cap and went out to the Cord. He had parked it in the shade of the house. Parkington climbed in beside him, and they set off down the hill, through Luz, out on the main road and into Lagos. Then along the boulevard by the river bank, and right over the bridge to the station.

To their right was a boatyard. Workmen tapped away with mallets and chisels, fashioning a fishing boat much as their ancestors had built the caravels for Henry the Navigator hundreds of years earlier. The sweet distinctive smell of raw wood shavings drifted in the sun towards the station booking-hall. The ticket window was closed. A few passengers, mostly old men in rough suits and black felt hats, dozed patiently on benches waiting for it to open. The station had been built many years previously, and the ticket hall was beautifully tiled with old-fashioned ceramics. An attempt to modernize the building had begun half-heartedly and abandoned. This appeared to consist of little more than removing the original elegant ceiling lights and replacing them with fluorescent tubes.

McNab walked impatiently up and down the single platform, keeping out of the sun, mopping his red face with a handkerchief. The rails burned brightly in the morning heat. His train would start from Lagos and would stay in its siding for hours yet. He decided to walk into town to a bar; anything to pass the hours he would have to wait. On the way through the booking hall, two tall men approached him.

'Excuse me,' Love began. 'But you are Mr McNab?'

'Aye. I am. Who are you?'

'A doctor on holiday here. I heard you'd come ashore and were waiting for a train to Lisbon to rejoin your ship. A friend

149

keeps a speedboat in Sagres. We are going out in it and could easily catch up your ship in an hour or two instead of you having to hang about here until five o'clock – and then have goodness knows how long in a railway compartment.'

'But I've bought a ticket,' said McNab cautiously. 'And how do you know anything about me?'

'A friend saw you come ashore,' Parkington explained disarmingly.

'But I don't know you.'

'That is our misfortune.'

A warning bell rang in McNab's mind. These two strangers could not possibly know he had come from a ship and was hoping to join it at Lisbon, unless someone who knew him had told them. Who was this friend they spoke about? Could he be the same man who had told Hood he was carrying something of great value?

'Thank you for your offer,' he said carefully. 'But I will stick to my own arrangements.'

'And we have arranged otherwise,' said Parkington quietly.

'Who the hell are you?'

McNab glanced sharply at his face. There was something compelling in his tone of voice. Then McNab's gaze dropped. Three inches from his stomach, partly concealed by a red silk handkerchief in Parkington's right hand, the round blued barrel of a ·38 stared at his belt.

'Is that real?' asked McNab hoarsely.

'I'm too old to play with toys,' said Parkington. 'Now, keep walking.'

They approached the Cord. Love climbed in behind the wheel. McNab got in on the other side, and Parkington squeezed in after him. He handed a pair of sunglasses and a blue jockey cap to McNab.

'Put these on,' he told him. 'Just in case someone thought they recognized you.'

They drove in silence back through the town, on through Luz, and up to Love's house.

Parkington left the car first and frisked McNab. He was

150

unarmed. Parkington motioned him into the house. It felt cold as a wine cellar after the harsh blaze of morning sun in the open car. Love went to the refrigerator, took out three bottles of Sagres beer, opened them and put them with glasses on the table. They sat down. Parkington put the revolver in his pocket.

'Now let us talk,' said Love. 'You are from the *Princess Rosael*?'

'That is so. Chief engineer. And who are you?'

'A doctor of medicine, as I have already told you. Why did you come ashore?'

'What's that to do with you? What do you mean, holding me up with a gun and bringing me here?'

'We mean to solve a mystery,' Love replied. 'And in so doing, possibly save your life. After all, as a doctor, my profession is to save lives.'

'I don't know what you're talking about.'

'Then let us discuss something within your knowledge, Mr McNab. Why did you come ashore?'

'I had a radio telephone call saying my daughter was critically ill in hospital here after a car crash. A launch came out and brought me ashore.'

'And your daughter? How is she?'

'I am told she is well.'

'So you haven't seen her?'

'No.'

'What did the doctors say?'

'I – er.'

He paused.

'Mr McNab,' said Love. 'You are not being entirely frank with us. You have not seen any doctor, have you?'

McNab said nothing. Fear flickered in his eyes. His face grew pale.

'You were brought ashore for other reasons. Someone wanted to know why a man was shot and jumped – or was thrown – overboard. And the whereabouts of a certain package you were given to carry to England. Am I right?'

151

McNab still said nothing. There was no need for him to speak; his expression replied for him. When he finally spoke, his voice sounded thin and fearful.

'Who is this man with the gun?' he asked Love.

'He is employed by the government.'

'Which one?'

'Ours. The British.'

Parkington flicked a Ministry of Defence pass across to McNab. He recognized the plastic card in its celluloid case; he had seen similar ones often enough in dockyards.

'What do you want with me?' he asked, some confidence returning. 'I'm supposed to be joining my ship at Lisbon. I'm an engineer, not a smuggler or a crook.'

'As an engineer, you may be the best, but otherwise you don't rate so highly. You are not a smuggler yet, either. Only a potential makee-learnee smuggler. More a courier, really. You *are* taking a package to England?'

'An Englishman gave me something to carry, yes,' said McNab. 'But he promised it was not drugs. I took his word. There is no reason why I shouldn't carry this package.'

'When you arrive, you will be paid for your services?'

'I have been paid half already,' said McNab proudly.

'And that is all you will get,' replied Parkington grimly. 'If you knew what that package contained you would also know that anyone involved with transporting it simply could not afford to risk having a whisky-drinking Scots engineer telling the story of what he smuggled in and how much he had been paid. The police would be on to you in days, if not hours. So you would not live to tell that tale at all. Most likely, you would be found dead in a ditch. Or knocked down outside a pub after closing time by a hit-and-run driver.'

'Balls,' retorted McNab with spirit. 'Why bring me here at gun point to tell me this?'

'Because we want to know who gave you that package and where it is.'

'Ah, so it all comes back to that, eh?'

'Yes. Everything,' agreed Parkington. 'Which is why

152

they won't allow you to live in case you talk too much about it.'

'Listen,' said Love earnestly. 'As a doctor, I have sometimes had to tell people they are suffering from a disease for which there is no known cure. Maybe they only have a few months to live. Maybe only a few weeks. If you go on to Lisbon and rejoin your ship, you'll have even less. Once you deliver that package, you're a dead man.'

McNab sipped his beer. In the cool room his forehead glistened with sweat. He remembered the friend of the barman in Alex; he was aware of the thickness of 8,000 dollars in notes around his waist: he recalled Hood's scream as he fired at him in the sea. He felt suddenly sick and old and afraid.

'So what do you propose, doctor?' he asked. 'You seem so sure of my demise if I do what I was doing – running the engine room of an old cargo ship and carrying a parcel. So what is your alternative?'

'Hole up here for a while,' replied Love.

'No-one knows you are here,' Parkington added.

'We have to go out for maybe an hour, but we will be back with a new set of clothes for you and a new passport.'

'Stay here until we return. You will be quite safe. You'll find food and beer in the fridge. But do yourself one favour. Do not open the door to *anyone*. Do not answer the telephone. We have the only door key, so anyone else who comes is a visitor.'

'What's to stop me leaving as soon as you have gone?'

'Nothing,' said Love, 'except what I have told you. You walk out of here, and you go home in a coffin. Wait for us to get back and we can help you.'

'Why the hell are you doing this? Not for me, is it?'

'No. It's because we don't want what is in that package to fall into the wrong hands,' said Love.

'Personally,' added Parkington, 'I don't give a fish's tit whether *you* fall into the wrong hands or the wrong feet either, McNab, but you are just too closely involved for us to ignore you.'

153

They stood up. McNab remained sitting, his hand around the glass of beer.

'A long life,' said Parkington. 'And I don't mean the beer.'

They went out. McNab heard the Cord start. He stood up and looked through the window, watching them drive down the track. The moving dust cloud swirled and then settled. Heat beat down on the dry, parched ground. He opened another tin of beer and carried it out on to the patio and then went upstairs to the flat roof. The view was magnificent – the sea to the south and the mountains to the north – and he leaned on the wall, feeling its warmth through his thin shirt. There seemed no sign of life, but a donkey was braying somewhere out of sight, so some locals must be about. He guessed they had brought a donkey and cart to collect almonds and then released the donkey and hobbled it while they flayed the trees with sticks to bring down the almonds.

He went down the stairs, and stood irresolute, still holding the beer, looking at the dappled blue water of the swimming pool. He still felt uneasy. The heat and silence and solitude all increased his fear.

Who had put up Hood to try and find the package? Could it be these two men – or was it someone else? He glanced at his watch. He had missed the morning train but he could easily catch the one that left Lagos at ten past five. Why not get out now – which he could? Why not walk – or run – down to Luz, catch a bus or a taxi to Lagos or hire a car and be away? He had seen an Avis sign in the village on the way here. He had received half the money promised, and even if he never got the other half, he would still be in profit. He could not believe that whoever had given him the package would kill him. After all, he was only the courier. And yet . . .

What if more than money was involved? He would have to risk that. He had been in tight corners before, and survived. He would leave now, while he had the time and the chance. These men might be who they said they were, or they might not. He could not be certain, and if he delayed until they returned, it would be too late. His mind made up, McNab

154

opened the front door again and then leaned against it, weak with surprise.

A girl was standing in the porch. He had not heard her arrive. Who could she be?'

'Is Dr Love in?' she asked him.

'No. He has just stepped out,' replied McNab. 'I am leaving, too.'

'Who are you?' asked the girl.

'A friend of his. And you?'

'A friend, too. Victoria Forbes.'

'My name's McNab. Jock McNab.'

They shook hands formally.

'When will Dr Love be back?' she asked him.

'Soon, so he said. But I wonder if you could give me a lift down in your car, if you are going to Luz?'

'I am actually going in the other direction. To Burgau. But I'll certainly give you a lift to the main road. Luz is only a short walk from there.'

They climbed into her car and bumped away down the track.

'I have a speedboat in Burgau,' Victoria explained, making conversation. 'Dr Love was going to hire it for the afternoon. He has probably gone ahead to meet me there?'

'Very likely,' said McNab. He looked at her, a thought forming in his mind.

'How big is your boat?'

'Eighteen footer. Volvo engine. I hire it out for fishing parties. There's a lot of tunny beyond Sagres.'

'So I've heard. What's its range?'

'Oh, a hundred miles or so on the main tank. And I carry a reserve of fuel, of course.'

'Listen,' said McNab urgently. 'Never mind Dr Love for the moment. I'll hire your boat. How much do you charge an hour?'

'That's negotiable.'

'Let us negotiate then.'

'What do you want it for? Fishing?'

155

'No, to catch up with a ship. How much would that cost?'

'Depends how long we take. Let's work out a figure,' said Victoria, and stopped the car.

*   *   *

Love pulled his Cord off the main Sagres road into a clump of trees and switched off the engine.

'How do you think the Scottish engineer reacted?' he asked.

Parkington shrugged.

'Hard to say. Think he's wary, though. I certainly would be, in his position. But whether we've frightened him enough, only time will tell.'

'Time tells everything,' retorted Love. 'But sometimes to the wrong people.'

He reached down behind the seat and handed a cellophane carrier bag to Parkington. Parkington ripped off his check shirt and pulled on another shirt, the same blue as McNab's. He pulled down a denim yachting cap over his head, put on an alpaca jacket. Love handed him a pair of dark glasses.

'From a distance,' he said, 'you could pass.'

'My Scottish accent isn't so good,' said Parkington.

'So be thankful this isn't a talking part.'

They drove on in silence to Sagres.

A handful of fishing boats rode at anchor in the harbour, and some tourists were taking photographs of each other posed against a mooring bollard. Love stopped his car in the shade of the cliffs. They both climbed out. He buttoned down the tonneau cover and followed Parkington along the stone finger of the jetty. A blue and white speedboat, with a cuddy and half decking, and a long chromium bow rail, was tied up against one side. Her engine was running; the exhaust blew bubbles into the oily sea.

Diaz saluted Parkington.

'Your vessel, senhor,' he announced.

'Thank you,' said Parkington. 'Will you join us?'

'If you will excuse me, I have other business,' said Diaz.

'Although I come, like you, from a seafaring nation, I do not like the sea. In fact, it makes me ill.'

Parkington climbed down the metal ladder into the boat. Love followed. He checked fuel levels in the tanks, glanced expertly at the oil pressure and temperature gauges.

'Cast off,' he called to Diaz.

The tourists waved as they moved out to sea. Love waved back. A few fishermen splicing nets also watched them go, and then went on with their patient work. Up on top of the cliff, at the side window of his parked Caravette, Heinz followed their progress through his binoculars.

Three hundred yards to the right, in an upper window of a rented house, another man also kept his glasses trained on the little boat. He made a note of the time and the direction of their course on a pad of paper and then reached for the telephone. In an hotel bedroom in Lagos, Jarrold lay on a rumpled bed waiting for the call. He had kicked off his shoes and was smoking a Cintra cigarette, looking up at the ceiling through the curling wraiths of smoke.

As the telephone rang, he scooped it up instantly.

'Two men have put out to sea by launch. One is the English doctor who owns that old car,' the watcher reported from the house overlooking Sagres Harbour.

'And the other?'

'I could not see his face clearly, because he is wearing a cap and sunglasses. But it looks like the engineer McNab.'

'How big is the launch?'

'It was hired by a local from Lagos. A Portuguese journalist, well thought of, apparently. Senhor Diaz. He told the owner a friend wanted to go tunny fishing. They're carrying enough fuel for 150 miles.'

'I want you to stay where you are until that boat returns. Then report to me who leaves it. And whether they are carrying anything.'

'What am I looking for? A big parcel? A box, or what?'

'I cannot be more specific. But I think one or other of them will bring some package back from wherever they are going.'

157

'What if they don't come back?'

'I will ring you at twenty hundred hours precisely,' Jarrold told him. 'If they have not returned by then, we can make other arrangements.'

He replaced the receiver and lit another cigarette and lay back, looking up at the ceiling. Things were going his way, no doubt of it. By this time on the following morning, he should hold all the cards in the pack. It was a pleasant feeling to imagine that literally within hours he would have the key to wealth and power.

He allowed himself a thin smile at the prospect.

*   *   *

The speedboat came out of the protected harbour water and hit the heavy Atlantic swell with the shock of a train ramming buffers at the end of the line. Her fibreglass hull trembled at the long, hard waves.

Parkington sat in the stern, feeling as ill as he looked.

'Diaz was right,' he admitted. 'The sea makes me sick, too. Don't you carry any pills?'

'Not for your trouble,' retorted Love, holding the wheel so that the speedboat hit the waves head on and did not turn or roll in the troughs between them.

'How far do you reckon *Princess Rosael* is from here?'

'We'll soon find out. But I don't want to go too far out to sea because it's so damned rough.'

'Now I know why the ancients called this the end of the world,' groaned Parkington.

Love kept in sight of the rocky cliffs, grey and high and forbidding. Here and there, white houses peered over the top. A forest of radio masts sprouted near Cape St Vincent. Farther out to sea they saw the distant shapes of cargo vessels and a tanker and then, far ahead, but closing slowly, the old blunt stern of *Princess Rosael* leaving a trail of orange peel and splintered box wood and bobbing beer cans.

Love slowed the engine and Parkington leaned over the side, picking up some of this debris. He shook the water out, and then crammed some tins and pieces of wood into the leather bag Diaz had provided. When the bag was full and zipped shut, and in the back of the boat, Love increased speed until he was alongside the cargo ship, on her port side, and shielded by her bulk from the shore.

On top of the cliffs, Heinz had parked his Caravette, bonnet towards the sea. Volkoff was with him and set up a tripod behind the driver's open door, which sheltered him from the wind. On the tripod he mounted a naval telescope, focused on the *Princess Rosael*. He saw the little boat come up behind the old cargo ship. Two men were clearly visible: one at the controls, and the other in the stern, but moving forward. Then Volkoff saw the speedboat disappear on the ship's far side. He checked with his watch. The *Princess Rosael* did not slacken speed. Seven minutes later, the speedboat dropped behind and then turned back in a white arc of foam. This time, only one man was visible aboard, at the wheel. Volkoff removed his telescope and folded up the tripod.

'He's going back to Sagres,' he told Heinz. 'Let us be there when he arrives.'

*　　*　　*

The telephone rang again in Jarrold's hotel bedroom. His bags were packed now, his bill paid and he was ready to move.

'The English doctor has just come ashore. Alone,' reported his caller. 'He talked to Senhor Diaz, who has gone off with the owner of the boat, out to sea again. I understand that someone wishes to hire it along the coast.'

'Never mind them,' said Jarrold impatiently. 'Was the doctor carrying anything?'

'Yes. A leather bag with two handles. Like an airline bag. It seemed to be fairly heavy. He put it in the boot of his car, which was parked on the quay. He has just driven off.'

'Do you know where?'

'No. But from my window I can see the crossroads outside Sagres. He has taken the Lagos road.'

'Right. You come into Luz with Mario and Renato. Cover

159

the doctor's house. But use discretion. We cannot afford anything to go wrong now, and we don't want to use violence unless we have to. We want that leather bag – intact.'

He replaced the receiver without waiting for the other man to reply. It was time to go.

He dialled Room Service and waited for the porter to carry down his pig-skin bags. The commissionaire had brought his hired car to the door. Folded notes changed hands discreetly, arms were raised in respectful salutation. Jarrold climbed in behind the wheel, then drove through the town along the coast. He took his time. There was no need now for needless rush and hurry. All he had to do was to collect what was being brought to him.

*   *   *

Love turned off the main road in the small coastal village of Burgau, three miles from home, and bumped along an unmade surface until the houses fell away and he was in the middle of rough country. A few small whitewashed houses crouched on the hills. An old man walked beside a donkey that had two earthenware pitchers of water across its saddle. There was something timeless about the scene; it could be set in almost any century. Love parked off the track, on the shady side of a fig tree, and waited.

After nearly half an hour, he saw a moving cloud of reddish dust far ahead of him along the track, quickly coming closer. The sun glinted on a windscreen under the dust, slowed and stopped. Senhor Diaz and Parkington climbed out of their car and came towards him.

'We landed on the beach a couple of miles up,' explained Parkington.

'Anyone see you?'

'Half a dozen nude campers playing volley-ball. Otherwise it was deserted.'

'Good.'

Love opened the door of his car; Parkington climbed inside.

'Anything more for me, senhor?' asked Diaz, hoping his

duties at last were ended. He had an article to write on the political affiliations of students at the University of Coimbra, that was already overdue.

Parkington looked enquiringly at Love.

'There is one thing you can do, Senhor Diaz,' he began. 'Something of the utmost importance, which can only add to your reputation here – as a citizen as much as a writer.'

'Yes, senhor? And what is that, please?'

Love handed him an envelope.

'Read this when you are back in your house. And please follow the instructions *exactly*.'

Diaz put the envelope in his pocket.

'That's all, then,' Parkington told him. 'Our editor, Mr MacGillivray, will be in touch about your contract with us. And my warm thanks again for all your help.'

Diaz stood waiting until they were out of sight, and then he climbed into his car to follow them back on to the main road. It was neither pleasant nor fitting for a man of distinction to drive in another man's dust.

Love drove back to Burgau, past the Casa Grande on the left, an elegant old house turned into an hotel and restaurant. The road dipped and turned; he picked up speed, enjoying the feel of the heavy car on the straight stretches. And then, parked on the right hand side, around one of the few corners, he saw a small grey car with boot and bonnet lids open, and the red protective triangle set up behind to show it had suffered a mechanical breakdown.

Someone waved from the shade of trees by the side of the road. Love slowed and stopped. A man whose face seemed vaguely familiar came towards him. Who was he? A patient, an old car buff? Love's mind tried to slot the face into his memory and failed.

The man said, 'Hullo, doctor. I thought it must be you in this car. We met briefly the other night at the Ross's party. I told you I could remember the days when vintage did not mean an old motor car but an old wine. Remember?'

'Ah, of course,' said Love. He remembered the man now.

161

Ross had said he thought he was a friend of a friend.

'I didn't catch your name,' said Love, climbing out of the car.

'Jarrold. Tom Jarrold. I wonder, have you by any chance any tools aboard your barouche? The hire people have only given me a jack and a wheel brace.'

'What's the problem?'

'I am not mechanically minded,' Jarrold explained. 'All I can say is, it's stopped.'

'Switch on.'

Jarrold turned the ignition key. Love checked the key was in neutral and pressed the solenoid button. The distributor vibrated slightly as the engine started.

'Switch off,' said Love. He gripped the distributor. It was loose.

'Any trouble with it before?' he asked.

'None,' said Jarrold.

Love glanced at the nut and bolt that should lock the distributor in position. The whole engine was covered with a thin film of oil on which the dust of a hot summer lay thick and sandy. This dust lay everywhere, in fact, except around the edge of this one nut. Someone must have loosened this nut deliberately, and probably in a hurry, otherwise he would have cleaned the dust from the rest of the engine.

Love went back to the Cord and opened the boot. Jarrold followed him around and stood smoothing his hand appreciatively over the white paintwork. Love took out the tool kit, selected a spanner, moved the distributor while Jarrold pressed the starter, and then tightened up the nut. When the engine was running satisfactorily, he wiped his hands on a square of cotton he carried for such emergencies.

'There you are,' he said. 'No charge. One vintage man to another.'

'I am going into Luz, and I'd be very pleased if you both would join me for a drink,' said Jarrold.

'Thank you,' said Love. 'But we have another engagement. Another time, perhaps?'

162

Senhor Diaz swept past in his car – slowed briefly at the sight of the two parked cars, saw Parkington's reassuring wave and went on thankfully. He hated to be late with literary work.

'Of course. I am here for several more days. I will be in touch.'

Love climbed into the Cord and accelerated away.

'What do you make of that?' he asked Parkington.

'I haven't a mechanical mind.'

'That is what the man said. But he knew how to undo a nut to stop an engine. So why stop us?'

'To find out where we are going – or what we were carrying.'

'Exactly. Which is why he wanted to look inside the boot. And why I made sure he had a good *dekho* at the bag. I think we had better put the next stage of my plan into gear.'

He swung the heavy car off the main road, up between the white houses in Luz Park. Sprinklers sprayed lawns and holidaymakers sat on white fibreglass chairs, as advertised in the Sunday newspaper colour magazines. Except for the heat, they could have been sitting in the neat back gardens of Pinner or Bromley.

Beyond these houses the road petered out and became a dusty track, leading by twists and turns to his rented house. He stopped the car and climbed out. Parkington slid across the seat, behind the wheel, and drove on alone. Love found a gap in the cactus, planted as a hedge along the track, and started to walk over the rough stubbly earth towards Luz. Here he went into a bar, ordered a Sumol, and then dialled a number on the telephone.

The Portuguese telephone system possesses a peculiarity in that the engaged tone sometimes sounds as one lifts the receiver to make a call. And so on this occasion Love stood, lips pursed with annoyance, as the busy signal sounded in his right ear. A second and a third attempt produced the same result.

Love finished his drink, left the bar and tried a public telephone in a glass booth on the road outside. A different electronic malady affected this instrument; it stayed silent as a tongue-less woman. There was only one thing to do – try his own telephone back in the house. Maybe he should have done so in the beginning?

He started to climb up the long hill out of Luz. The sun was still hot, and tourists were walking down towards the beach, carrying beach bags. On the right beyond the houses lay the cemetery ringed in by a high white wall with a carved cross over the entrance gate. Above gravestones, the eyes of the dead stared from glazed photographs. The ground around the cemetery was dry and hard, ridged by last year's ploughing, but it was quicker to cross it than to follow the roundabout road to his house. Prickly thistles stung Love's ankles; burrs stuck to his trousers. Half a mile from the cemetery, he paused to wipe sweat from his forehead. In that second, he heard the faint sound of a dry twig snapping.

There were no birds in the bright still air and no rabbits in the dry undergrowth; and in any case surely no wild creature would break a twig? Sometimes, however, locals hobbled their donkeys while they collected edible snails, or knocked down almonds. He looked around him but could see no-one. The fields were dotted with almond and fig trees, but seemed deserted. He walked on for a few paces and then turned suddenly.

Two men stood watching him on either side of a dead juniper tree. They might have been models for a Van Gogh landscape, with the sun behind them, their faces brown under raffia hats. But these were not peasants; they wore expensive short-sleeved shirts and well-cut lightweight trousers. They watched him without speaking, legs slightly apart, hands easily by their sides, as though equally ready to attack or defend. Love felt the small hairs prickle on the back of his head.

'I thought I heard a movement,' he said casually. 'Wondered if it was a donkey that had got loose.'

Neither of the men spoke. They just stood in silence, watching him. He turned and walked up the hill, but now he walked with the uneasy feeling that two potential enemies were behind him.

164

The hill seemed steeper now, and the thistles thicker; sharp thorns he would previously have ignored, slashed his shins through the thin stuff of his trousers. He knew that the threat of danger had sharpened his senses: adrenalin pounded through his body.

The hill had a false crest, and when he reached this he could see the white mosque-like chimney of his house. More important, Parkington would be within shouting distance. A hundred and fifty yards more and he would be safe. The two men probably also knew this, so now the risk of attack – if they planned to attack him – would be at its height. He must meet it head-on. He paused and turned. The two men were still behind him, keeping their distance. They also stopped and looked at him.

'Is there something you want?' he asked them.

They did not reply.

'You speak English? Portuguese? Parlez vous français? Habla espagnol?'

This exhausted Love's gift of tongues. Perhaps they were harmless and simply using him as a guide to reach the top of the hill? The thought was infinitely reassuring, but instantly dispelled by the realization that nothing lay at the top of this particular hill apart from his house. And what if others had been waiting there for Parkington?

Love started off again, but now he glanced about for something he could use as a weapon. A stone would be better than nothing, and a stick better still. Against an almond tree he saw a long forked stick that locals used to shake upper branches and bring down the nuts. As Love gripped it, the man on the left jumped him from behind.

Although Love was half expecting the attack, its ferocity surprised him. He staggered and almost fell under the weight of the man's body. The attacker held both his arms around Love, hands locked in front, pinning him by his wrists. The stick hung at a useless angle, one end scratching the dust. Love kicked back and up with the heel of his right foot against the man's shins. His attacker screamed at the unexpected agony and, for an instant, relaxed his hold. In that instant Love swung around and gave him a sharp atemi blow across his neck with the edge of his hand. He had seen other Black Belts split planks of wood with such a move, for the whole force of a man's body is concentrated on the edge of a hand less than half an inch across. Love's attacker dropped, sobbing for breath. His companion leaped at Love with a flick-knife in his hand. Love gripped his stick with both hands, holding it across his body, parallel with the ground.

The man came close in, knife blade at an upward angle, ready to slice open Love's body from navel to neck.

Love took a step back and dropped the stick quickly to ward off the blow. The man cursed as his wrist hit hard wood. Love brought up the stick sharply, and rammed it hard under the man's chin. He staggered back, and fell, still holding the knife. Love jumped on his wrist. The hand opened and the knife dropped. His companion began to crawl like a beetle in the dust, coughing and choking. His right hand went towards his back trouser pocket, but Love struck his elbow with the stick. The man collapsed.

'Now,' he said. 'Who the hell are you, and what do you want?'

'I think the reply is academic,' said a voice behind him. 'For if we don't both get into the house in short order, we'll not live to hear it.'

Love turned. Parkington stood twenty feet away, a cigar in mouth, surveying the scene quizzically, arms folded.

'Others are coming up through the paddy on the far side as fast as they can run,' he explained.

'Who do you think they are?'

'Ours not to reason why. Ours but to run – or die,' replied Parkington. 'Now, *move*!'

Love bent down, picked up the knife, removed a pearl-handled automatic from his attacker's back trouser pocket, and then followed Parkington up the hill. The wall that ringed the garden and the house stood twelve feet high, pierced by a small green-painted wooden door, now open. They went

166

through this door, locked it, and shot the two bolts behind them.

To their left was a red-tiled building containing the pumping machinery for the pool, and a changing room. Across the pool, on the far side, stood another corresponding building of the same height, with a built-in barbecue. The level of the garden was about six feet higher than the land outside the wall, because when the swimming pool had been dug, the earth excavated had been levelled off around it.

'Follow me,' said Parkington, leading the way up the stairway to the top of the house.

'Where are these other men?' Love asked him.

'Here are three for starters.'

Parkington pointed to the brow of the hill. About 500 yards away, three men were walking slowly through the dry grass towards them.

'They are probably only tourists,' said Love hopefully. 'They look harmless enough.'

'Like the fellows who followed you? I think we are in for a siege.'

'Is the 'phone working?' asked Love.

'No, it's dead.'

'I thought it might be. That's why I went to Luz, but I couldn't get through from there, either.'

'So we're set for a rough night. And a dark one, for the current's off as well. Someone has cut the wires.'

'That means no ice for our drinks.'

'It also means that if these fellows – whoever they are – get in,' said Parkington grimly, 'we'll be lucky if we have throats left to put the drinks down.'

'Look on the bright side,' said Love.

'Can't see it from where I'm standing,' retorted Parkington.

They went down the stairs. Love checked that the front gates in the wall in front of the garage were locked and bolted.

'How can we stop them getting over the wall?' Parkington asked.

'Stay up on the roof with what weapons we have.'

167

'Which are?'

'The ones God gave us,' Love replied. 'Plus the automatic I have taken from one of those fellows down the hill. A knife. A boy's sling and a couple of dozen fire rockets left over from someone else's birthday party which are in a box of toys at the back of the garage.'

'I have a ·38,' said Parkington. 'And fifty rounds. But this still looks to me like Custer's last stand. Seven inches, and all stuck with arrows.'

'You seem to have forgotten my plan,' said Love chidingly.

'I'd forget it, too, if you can't even get through on the telephone.'

They carried the packet of rockets up on to the roof. In the hall, Love picked up a thin First World War brass shell case which had contained a decorative bunch of dry pampas grass fronds. They laid the rockets on the floor, six on each side of the shell case. Then they stood up, for the three walkers were now within twenty yards of the wall.

'I wonder if you could help me?' one of them asked. He was tall, wearing rope-soled beach shoes, a canvas shirt and jeans. Large sunglasses and a golfer's cap with a long peak shielded his face.

'How?' asked Love.

'I understand a doctor lives here?'

'That is true,' said Love, thinking: And he is going to keep on living here, too, come what may.

'You are the doctor?'

'Yes.'

'I would be grateful if you could come and treat one of my friends. He has twisted his ankle badly and we can't move him.'

Now Parkington stuck his head over the wall.

'Watch out!' he called urgently to the tall man. 'You've got one of these deadly bees on your glasses! *Quick!* Take 'em off! If it stings, you'll be blinded!'

The man tore off his glasses in a panic of surprise.

They were looking at one of the three men who had attacked Forbes in his house.

'Sorry about your friend,' said Love, 'but maybe I might do him more harm than good. Last time I was involved, I broke someone's arm.'

The man shrugged his shoulders, paused for a moment and then spat on the ground. He looked as though he was going to say something, and then he replaced his glasses and slowly walked away.

'Tourists?' Parkington asked Love sarcastically.

* * *

Jarrold turned his car off the main Luz to Burgau road, and drove up through Luz Park, along the track towards Love's house. When he was out of sight from the road and the houses, he parked in the shade of a fig tree, and started to walk across the rough ground towards the cemetery. The two men who had attacked Love were sitting with their backs against the white-washed wall. Jarrold looked from one to the other, noting their puffy, bruised faces.

'What happened?' he asked.

'We jumped him. But he was a lot tougher than we'd imagined. He had a stick, and got away.'

'Was he alone?'

'Another man came down from the house. They both ran back to it. This other person said more men were approaching from the far side.'

'More men?' repeated Jarrold in a puzzled voice. 'Who are they?'

'No idea. I caught a glimpse of some people in a grey Caravette going up the track. It didn't come to the house, so it must have stopped somewhere on the way.'

Jarrold turned and looked up the hill, shading his eyes against the sun. Somewhere out of sight, on the dead side of the hill, Volkoff would be putting his men in position. He must also have seen this English doctor come back from the ship with his bag, and knew or guessed what that contained. Volkoff must be deliberately breaking his agreement – as Jarrold was

169

convinced Marshall had done – and the presence of other men with him meant he was ready to use force to seize the bag and its contents. This was war, the break-up of an alliance; Jarrold's former ally had by his actions declared himself his enemy.

Jarrold considered the possibilities open to him. He could approach the doctor's house openly, overpower the doctor and his friend and make off with the bag now, and hope to deal with Volkoff and his men on the way down. Alternatively, he could wait for Volkoff to take the initiative and seize the bag, and then, with surprise on his side, ambush him and his helpers as they came down the hill.

There was much in favour of both approaches, but on balance Jarrold thought even more could be said for a third.

He would take his men up the road and meet Volkoff as a friend, showing surprise, even pleasure that Volkoff should be there. They would join forces and so more quickly overpower the two in the house. Afterwards, he would deal with Volkoff and escape with the bag.

'On your feet,' Jarrold told the two men sharply. They stood up and walked with him to his car. He unlocked the boot. Beneath a sack lay two shotguns with shortened barrels.

'You don't need a licence for these here,' he told them. 'If anyone stops you – but they won't – you are out shooting rats. Now, get in the back.'

'What's the plan?'

'I'll tell you on the way up,' Jarrold replied as he reversed the car into the road.

*   *   *

Six hundred yards away on the other side of Love's house, down a long, sloping hillside and out of sight even from the top of the roof, stood a deserted farmhouse.

Its threshing floor was overgrown with weeds, the well was long since blocked, and winter storms had blown out all the glass panes from the windows. Behind this building Volkoff had parked the Caravette. He stood outside it now, waiting impatiently for Heinz to return from his attempt to persuade the English doctor to leave the safety of his house. He did not think he would be successful but the attempt was worth making. The farmhouse was surrounded by a crude hedge of cactus plants. White-shelled snails dotted the leathery, spike-edged leaves. Volkoff plucked a ripe fig from a tree, peeled it and ate the soft inside as he waited.

From far down the track he caught a glint of sunshine on a windscreen. He put his hand in his pocket, moved the safety catch on his automatic to 'off'. The car was going very slowly. Three men inside it kept looking to left and right as though they were not sure of the way. He did not want anyone to go up to the house if he could help it; the fewer he had to deal with there the better. He came out from behind the Caravette and stood in the middle of the track. The driver stopped.

'Are you lost?' Volkoff asked him, the sun in his eyes.

'Not since I have seen you,' replied Jarrold.

'What brings you here?' asked Volkoff in surprise.

'I was about to ask you the same question.'

'It is quite simple,' replied Volkoff at once. 'The material that should be on the ship has been taken off – by someone not a hundred miles from here.'

'That is what I also heard,' said Jarrold.

'How?'

'Too complicated to explain now, my friend. The real question is, how are we going to collect it?'

'Who are these men?' Volkoff asked him, answering one question with another, indicating the two Italians who were climbing out of the car.

'Friends,' said Jarrold simply.

'What happened to that fellow's face?'

'He had a fight with an English doctor who lives up here. A man whose name, curiously enough, is Love.'

'Do they speak English?'

'Of course.'

'And they are involved?'

'Cartwright tried to doublecross us. I couldn't contact you,

171

because I didn't know where you were. But I had him taken out.'

Volkoff struggled to keep his feelings from his face.

'How do you mean, taken out?' he asked, as though genuinely puzzled. 'I thought he was back in the States?'

'He was. These Italians belong to the Family.'

'You mean, the Mafia?'

'Associated, shall we say? I had to act quickly. Had there been more time, things might have been different. But, as it was . . .'

He shrugged, one busy man to another.

'Then they came over to see if they could help me further.'

Volkoff pulled Jarrold out of earshot.

'Do they know what is at stake?'

'They know we have found something which could be of value to them. But not just how valuable – yet.'

'How many others know? I have got three fellows here from the Eastern bloc. Their principals are also interested.'

'I think we can come to some arrangement satisfactory to everyone concerned – once we have the papers,' Jarrold assured him.

'I hope you are right,' said Volkoff, doubt gripping his guts like a serpent's teeth. He leaned against the farmhouse wall for a moment, glad of its support. He had believed he had only Love and his companion to deal with, and in his own time. Now he had Jarrold and these Italians. And behind them would be others he did not know, who would not easily give up the search if he outwitted them. However, he had survived complex situations before; he could survive again. The essential thing was to get his hands on the professor's papers – first.

'What's your plan?' Jarrold asked him

'This man can tell us,' said Volkoff; he saw Heinz approaching.

'What did the doctor say?'

'He wouldn't come out.'

'Nor would I if I was in his situation,' said Volkoff. 'But it was worth a try. Some medical men are quixotic.'

172

'Who's this?' asked Heinz, indicating Jarrold.

'A friend of mine who is involved in this deal. He has two Italians with him. That makes six of us, not counting Kurt. He's a broken arm but he can still carry a pistol. And only two of them.'

'If we lose with odds like this, we deserve to,' said Jarrold.

'We'll not lose,' replied Volkoff confidently. 'Heinz cut the telephone wires and the electricity lines. They can't get a call out or in. And they'll have no lights tonight except candles or a hurricane lamp. I suggest we wait until dark and then approach from two directions. I'll go in from the front, and you take your men from the side.'

'What's the house like?' Jarrold asked him.

'Single storey. Steps lead up to the flat roof from outside. A high wall all around the garden, but that's no problem. There's even a ladder used for whitewashing hidden under a fig tree on the far side.'

'Are they armed inside?'

Volkoff shrugged.

'If they are, it can only be with pistols or pea-shooters. Anyhow, they can't cover the whole wall in the dark. Moon won't be up until after midnight, so visibility will be nil. It'll be all over in minutes.'

'I hope so,' said Jarrold. 'It certainly doesn't sound impregnable, from what you say.'

He started to walk to his car.

'Where are you off to?'

'Back to Luz. No point in all of us hanging around.'

'I propose we go in soon after dark,' said Volkoff.

'No,' replied Jarrold. 'Let them wait for several hours. Tire 'em out. They'll start to get jumpy. And *then* we'll go in.'

*   *   *

Victoria drove up the road from Burgau and turned off the track towards Love's house. She hoped that he and Parkington would be at home, for she had something of interest to tell them about McNab's return to the sea.

173

A local stood in the track, shaking the branches of an almond tree with a stick. He moved to one side, and courteously acknowledged her thanks by raising his black felt hat. She drove on around the first bend, and then the second.

A man stood in the middle of the track peering towards her, a puzzled expression on his face. He held up one hand for her to stop. She wound down the window she had closed to keep out the dust.

'Something wrong?' she asked him. 'Can I help you?'

He was dressed in short-sleeved shirt and lightweight trousers. His shoes, under their film of dust, looked expensive and well cared for.

'I hope you can. I am a bit lost up here. I am looking for Dr Love's house.'

'I am going there,' she said. 'I can give you a lift.'

'Then please wait for a moment, and give a lift to my friend as well. He is resting out of the heat of the sun. He has not been very well.'

'I don't know that the doctor is treating patients,' began Victoria doubtfully.

'We will have to chance that.'

Volkoff moved to the rear of the car. As he did so, another man put his face through the driver's window. In his hand he held an automatic.

'Get out,' Heinz told her. Victoria froze with horror; he was the man she had recognized on the beach, one of the three who had beaten up her father. She jammed the gear into first and accelerated wildly. The car leaped forward. Heinz's automatic cracked twice like a rodeo rider's whip. The car trembled and bumped as both back tyres flattened. Victoria changed up to second gear and stamped her foot flat on the floor, ignoring the hammering of the wheel rims on the ground. She did not hear the third shot against this noise, but suddenly a fierce yellow flame erupted from the rear of the car with a roar as the third bullet punctured the petrol tank. Heat burned her back and singed her hair. The engine stalled, and the car stopped abruptly.

174

Victoria opened her door and tried to run, but Heinz was ready, and tripped her. The car was crackling like a blazing haystack. Heinz pulled her to her feet and dragged her behind the farmhouse.

'You should have waited,' Volkoff told her sadly, as though he regarded her attempt to escape as a grievous breach of social etiquette.

'Who are you?' Victoria asked him. 'What do you mean, shooting at my car?'

'I am Eugene Volkoff, and I did not shoot. I regret that deeply.'

'Volkoff,' Victoria repeated. 'I know that name. You were in Calcutta. Eric Cartwright came to see you. I worked for him. And now . . .'

'Now he is dead.'

'*Dead?* Eric?'

Her voice was a shrill scream of disbelief.

'Where? How?'

'At his home in the United States.'

'But *how*? Was it illness, an accident?'

'I have no details, only the sad fact.'

*   *   *

Parkington stood on the flat roof of Love's house, elbows on the parapet to steady his binoculars. He was watching a pillar of black smoke rise into the sky.

He heard the crisp crackle of flames and the dull boom of sheet metal expanding in the heat. From the smell of burned oil and paint and plastic a car must be alight and, from the direction, he guessed where it was. In other circumstances, he would have investigated, but now he hesitated. The fire had all the signs of a hoax, bait to lure him out of cover.

'Come down and see what I've fixed,' Love called. Parkington went down to the main room. A wire from inside the garage door stretched across the patio into the garden. It was bright and uncovered, insulated from the floor by resting on

175

books Love had placed several feet apart. From the patio this wire went up to a point beneath a row of tiles that capped the garden wall. Inside this wall, and about three inches from the top protruded a row of wooden stakes. The owner of the house had tied strings to these along which morning glory was being trained to climb. Love had wound the bare wire to these stakes so that it hung close to the top of the wall.

In the garage, the Cord's alligator mouth bonnet was open. Love had removed the high tension leads from the first cylinder of each bank of the V-8 engine, and connected them to the end of the wire.

'I found a huge roll of wire hanging on a nail,' he explained. 'It's meant for training creepers to climb along. It should train our climbers to keep away.'

Love fired up the engine. It ran lumpily on six instead of its usual eight cylinders. Parkington wrapped a handkerchief around his right hand and gingerly tapped the wire. He nodded and gave the thumbs-up sign to Love.

'A good charge going through,' he said approvingly. 'Anyone who climbs over that wall will get a healthy shock.'

'They'd have to pay dearly for that treatment in the West End,' replied Love. 'Here, they'll have it free. It won't kill them, but it should surprise them, make them give away their position. Then it's up to us.'

Love switched off the engine; there could be a long wait ahead and, even ticking over, the Lycoming had a deep thirst. He glanced at the dashboard clock. Seven-thirty in the evening. All over the Algarve now, visitors would be changing out of beach clothes and bikinis into smarter clothes for the evening. There would be parties on a thousand patios; within an hour, every restaurant would be packed. Later, as they emptied, the discos would fill up, and the beat of music would echo from the hills out to sea.

Yet here, ironically, on the edge of such pleasurable activities, an unknown number of strangers were calmly planning the siege of a private house, an undertaking that quite easily could end in death. Love, analysing his feelings, felt no dismay,

176

but instead a certain exhilaration. He relished the animal prospect of two brains pitted against the combined guile and ingenuity and violence of unknown and unnumbered adversaries. That the odds seemed heavily against them paradoxically increased this feeling.

'Let's have a drink before the sun goes down,' suggested Parkington. 'Then, to our posts.'

The day was still bright, but heat had left the sun, and already the wind of evening was ruffling the trees. Love mixed rum and lime juice with crushed ice and filled two glasses. Solemnly, they toasted each other. They had agreed that Love would start the vigil on the roof. He had a canvas chair raised on wooden blocks so that he could see over the top of the wall in comfort.

Parkington, with his automatic, and his pockets full of spare rounds, would wait in one of the cane chairs on the patio. From here, he could command a view of three-quarters of the garden wall, at least until dark. Love could cover from the roof the section of the wall that Parkington could not see. After dark, they would have to rely on the electric wire forcing intruders to give away their position.

Love finished his drink, went out into the garden and picked up a handful of pebbles. He put one of these in the sling and fired it at the far wall. After a few minutes of practise he learned how to make allowances for the weight and shape of different-sized pebbles, and felt confident he should be able to hit, if not hurt, a human target at ten to fifteen yards. He filled a cigar box with the small stones from the flower beds, washed them under the garden tap and went up on the roof with a hurricane lamp.

The sun was dropping now into the Atlantic. Silhouetted against the sea lay the long dark line of cliffs. Houses, with minaret-like chimneys and Moorish domes, stood stiff as cardboard cut-outs as the sun went down. Light faded and distance merged with darkness over the sea.

Love arranged his chair facing one wall, with the rockets and shell case near his feet. He removed the globe from the lamp,

177

and lit the flame. Sheltered by the wall from the wind, it burned steadily. He shook out his stones on the floor alongside it with the sling. All his armaments were ready, and so was he. Now, it was just a matter of waiting.

*   *   *

Darkness dropped more deeply over the trees and bushes. Their shapes dwindled and disappeared. Hours passed. It grew colder. The wind's long fingers searched out empty window frames in the walls of the deserted farmhouse. The chirp and rattle of crickets were almost the only sounds.

Heinz and Jan had pulled Victoria's burned-out car off the road. Parts of the metal were still warm. A strong acrid smell of burnt paint and plastic hung over the charred vehicle. The men had put on dark sweaters, and black leather driving gloves. Several wore peaked yachting caps under which they had packed loose socks or folded handkerchiefs to provide some protection against a blow on the head. They had torn branches from trees, or searched for pieces of wood to use as clubs in addition to their shot-guns and pistols. Now they formed a ring around Jarrold and Volkoff.

'I'll take my people over the field to the far side of the house, where I have already reconnoitred the area,' said Jarrold. We'll pick up the ladder from under the fig tree and see what's happening on the other side of the wall. If the moment is right, we will go over. If it isn't, Volkoff, you will take one man and go down in front of the house. A number of branches have been piled up for winter firewood, but not taken in. You can easily put these against the wall, climb up and be over. Someone else can wait this side of the house and come over the wall if you lose surprise.'

'How do we keep in contact in the dark?'

'Radio. I have three walkie-talkies. We will each take one and you, Kurt, stay here and listen-in on the third. You will also guard the girl, and if there is any trouble or if anyone comes prying about, you can warn us on the radio.'

'One question,' said Volkoff. 'What do we do when we have the bag?

'Report back here. Anything else?'

'No.'

'Then synchronize watches.'

They checked the time.

'We will move at twenty-three hundred hours. Allow one hour to get in position before the moon rises. Everyone clear on every point?'

The others nodded, and then, one by one, they melted away like shadows into the darkness. Their rubber-soled shoes made no sound as they moved across the dry scrubby thistles and grass.

Kurt switched on his radio and placed it against a tree, aerial fully extended. The speaker hissed and crackled asthmatically with static. He felt lonely left behind and leaned against the door of the Caravette, a cigarette cupped in his hand. Far away, over the hill, he heard a car engine start and then go on running, not cleanly, but labouring as though its plugs were dirty. The noise was not dangerous, but it was unusual. As such, it disturbed him. He took a long drag on his cigarette and wished he were elsewhere.

* * *

Love turned to Parkington.

'A quarter to midnight,' he said. 'And our guests still haven't arrived. We've another four hours before it's light.'

'Ours is an open invitation,' replied Parkington. 'An invitation they can't refuse.'

'I suggest I make a quick recce around the whole perimeter.'

'Keep away from the track,' warned Parkington.

'Of course. My intention is to go two or three hundred yards from the front of the house, and then beat round in a circle.'

'You won't see much in the dark. I have never believed that the night has a thousand eyes.'

'Maybe I can hear, then. Anything's better than just waiting here.'

179

'All right,' agreed Parkington. 'But it is lonely back here on the ranch on my tod, so don't hang about.'

'They won't arrest me for loitering, that's for sure. I'll give you a whistle when I'm coming back over the wall – just here – so you don't start shooting at me.'

Parkington watched Love go, carrying a steel crowbar from the Cord jack in his hand. Then he went into the garage. Running the big engine in such a confined space gave out a surprising amount of heat. The heavy boom of the dual exhausts echoed from the whitewashed walls. He glanced at the petrol gauge; the red needle hovered depressingly near the 'empty' mark.

Keeping away from the bare wires, Parkington came back through the living room, and stood for a moment on the patio, looking out towards the sea. The whole world was dark now; dark and quiet. The parties were over and the revellers in bed – their own or someone else's. Parkington envied them.

To the left, a faint amber glow lit the sky from the lights of Lagos, and far to the right an even fainter glow hung like a halo over Sagres. The lighthouse at Cape St Vincent swung its beam out to sea and back again with a steady, monotonous regularity.

He climbed the stairs to the roof. He could see nothing, hear nothing but the wind in the trees and faint brassy music of a distant fair or fiesta. He went down again to the patio, and sat, pistol in his lap, waiting uneasily for the attack which every moment, every beat of his heart, brought closer.

*   *   *

Love counted his paces and when he reached 300, paused, listening. There was no sound except for the distant beat of music, and the rumble of the Cord engine. The wind was blowing out towards the sea, so he turned, keeping this on the left of his face as a means of knowing his direction. He began to walk slowly over the fields, picking his way carefully to avoid dry twigs and ridges left by that season's ploughing.

180

Once he thought he heard a movement and he paused, crowbar poised to strike, but the noise was not repeated. Perhaps he had imagined it. He walked on more slowly, more carefully.

Soon he was as near the track as he dared to go. The ground had been recently tilled and fewer thistles and barbed bushes tore at his trouser legs. He was now half-way round the perimeter, and still he had seen no-one and heard no-one. Yet surely they must be out here in the darkness, waiting and watching? Perhaps even now they had gathered outside the wall?

A tiny noise made him stop and hold his breath. This time it was not imagination, for the noise was repeated: a metal door was being opened. It did not sound like a car door, for it slid on rollers and did not turn on hinges. What car had a sliding door? A Bentley had been exhibited at a pre-war Motor Show with such a conceit, and before that Voisin, the individualistic French manufacturer, had offered these doors on some of his cars. The idea had then been taken up by the makers of motorized caravans. Love remembered the Caravettes at Carrapateira, and went forward carefully towards the noise.

Twenty feet ahead of him a tiny flame flared and died. He was now so used to the darkness that this momentarily dazzled him, although it was only a match. A man was lighting a cigarette. Love saw a brief flash of a grey Caravette behind him, and also the man's face. He was one of the men he and Parkington had found in Forbes' house. Love put his right hand in his pocket, took out one of the round pebbles and his sling. He closed his eyes tightly for a moment to accustom them again to darkness, and although it was now impossible to see the man, he aimed slightly to the left of where he had last seen him. The stone boomed like a gong against the metal side of the van. Love quickly fired a second pebble, and then a third. A muttered curse of surprise and a threshing of feet in the undergrowth, then both men held their breath, listening for some movement that would give away the other's position.

Love half turned and fired two more stones away into the darkness. They landed on the ground. He heard a crash of twigs as the man moved in their direction. Love tiptoed as quietly as he could towards the vehicle, hands outstretched like a blind man until he touched the smooth, dusty metal. He tapped lightly on one of the windows. To his surprise, he heard a faint moaning from inside. Someone was being held prisoner in the van.

The tapping alerted Kurt; he knew now that this stranger was standing alongside the Caravette. He cocked his automatic. Love heard the oiled metallic click and recognized that the other man carried a gun. But would he dare to fire it, for the sound would carry far in the still night? This was a risk Love had to take. He put away his sling and turned to face the direction from which this new noise had come. Now he heard breathing, controlled, but swift. To his medical mind this indicated that the breather was nervous, and trying hard to conceal his fear.

He raised his crowbar two feet in the air, and holding it by one end at arm's length, peered into the darkness, trying to force his eyes to decipher the first faint movement of his adversary; but there was nothing. Then he heard a sharp intake of breath closer than he had expected, and smelled the sharp animal scent of fear. Love brought the bar down sharply at a level with his shoulder. He heard the crack of a collar bone breaking, then a scream, the clatter of a metallic object falling, and the scrabble of someone on the ground gasping in agony and yet desperate to keep silent.

Love shone his pocket torch towards the noise. Kurt was crouching, one arm in a sling and the other loosely by his side. He was armless and so harmless.

'Get up,' Love ordered him. The man shambled to his feet. 'Who are you?'

Kurt did not reply. Love had no time to waste. If he wouldn't talk, then he would keep him silent. Love brought the crowbar across the side of his neck with a light, firm tap. He dropped unconscious. Love picked up his automatic, searched through pockets for extra rounds, and found the Caravette's ignition key. He removed Kurt's belt and tied this around his ankles, and wrapped his handkerchief around his mouth. With a broken arm and a broken collar bone he would not be able to undo either.

Love now slid open the door of the Caravette and shone his torch around the interior. Victoria was sitting in one of the rear seats, her hands bound behind her back, ankles tied with a nylon towrope. Love undid the knots and massaged her wrists and ankles.

'What happened?' he asked.

'I was driving to see you. Someone stopped me and asked where you lived. He told me his name. It was Volkoff – from Calcutta.'

'And then?'

'One of the men who beat up my father pointed a gun at me. When I tried to drive away, he shot my tyres and then hit my tank. The whole car caught fire. It's a total loss.'

'Don't worry. If it's not fully insured, it soon will be. After I've had a word with Dick Parkington.'

'Then they tied me up in here with that man outside to guard me. He's got a walkie-talkie, by the way.'

'Well, he won't be walking or talking for a while yet. What happened before all this?'

'Senhor Diaz fixed me up with a speedboat at Burgau, as you told me you'd arranged. Then I called at your house, as we agreed. There *was* a Scotsman there, and he begged a lift – just as you thought he would.'

'And then?'

'I told him I'd got a speedboat, and he hired me to take him out to join his ship.'

'The *Princess Rosael*?'

'No,' she said. 'The one behind. There are two old ships going back to be broken up.'

'Now that *is* good,' said Love approvingly. Items were falling into place like flakes in a child's kaleidoscope. Soon what had been obscure would be a clear picture; or, at least, significantly less misty.

'How many men are here altogether?' asked Love.

'Six, not including the guard you've dealt with. Some of the others appear to be Italian.'

'Now listen carefully, Victoria. Take this Caravette – here's the key – but don't put on any lights until you reach the main road.'

'And then?'

'Then I want you to do certain things. I tried to reach you on the 'phone this afternoon, but I couldn't get through. Follow the sequence exactly, as you did with McNab. There is no room – or time – at all for error. It's a split-second affair.'

'Better than no affair,' she said. 'Start talking.'

*   *   *

Volkoff paused. He and his companions were within fifty yards of the garden wall around Love's house, but his ears were sharp for distant sounds of possible danger.

'I heard a noise,' he whispered. 'A door opening or shutting.'

'A courting couple?' suggested Heinz.

'No. Too far for them to come up here. They'd go on the beach. It was from the direction of the van.'

'Maybe Kurt's gone for a pee. Come on. It can't be anything to worry about.'

They moved forward again. Dust swirled around their feet like sifted flour. Although the wind was cool, the effort of climbing the hill as silently as possible, strung out in a line and not able to see plough furrows, big stones or even trees clearly, was hot and tiring. Finally, they reached the crest of the hill, and, against a faint luminosity from the sea, could see the dark outline of the house. A car engine was running unevenly in the garage, as it had been for some time now. Again, the incongruity of this disturbed Volkoff.

'Think they're going to try a getaway?' he asked.

'No,' Jan replied. 'If they didn't risk it in daylight, they won't chance it now.'

Volkoff turned to his companions.

184

'On your way,' he told them. 'You have twelve minutes to get in position.'

*   *   *

Three hundred yards away to the left, Jarrold was creeping towards a huge fig tree that grew near the wall. He crouched under its branches and felt around with his fingers for the ladder. He touched a rung and gripped it, and then pulled the ladder towards him.

Renato took the other end, and together they placed the ladder against the wall, taking care not to touch the tiles on top in case they were brittle and broke beneath the weight. Then they waited, listening for the sound of any movement inside the wall. Jarrold checked the time; three minutes to go.

The sound of the Cord's engine came up louder as the wind changed. Leaves about their heads rustled metallically in the breeze. Jarrold was also puzzled by the fact that the engine was running, and running so badly. As he passed the double green gates let into the wall in front of the garage he had checked that they were bolted. They were, and so would take a few moments to open. The two men inside the house could not make a surprise run for freedom. But just to put his mind at ease, he ordered his men to place two large stones the size of pumpkins up against the gates, to prevent them being opened from the inside. Perhaps the doctor and his friend were hoping to smash through the gates without troubling to open them? If so, why give a hint of their intentions by starting the engine? If not, why run it at all?

Love stood 100 yards behind them and slightly to their right. It was impossible for him to see how many men were near the fig tree, for the wind stirred its branches and shadows became confused, but he could hear them. He moved towards the garage gates, noted the position of the stones, and followed the wall until he reached the place where he had told Parkington he would climb it. He whistled through his teeth and then hauled himself up and over. Parkington was waiting for him on the patio, glass in one hand, gun in the other.

185

'What kept you?' he asked ironically. Love began to explain and then stopped in mid-sentence. They both heard a faint movement by the fig tree. Parkington put down his glass, raised his automatic, gripping it with both hands, feet spread out to steady himself for a long shot. Under the rising moon, Love saw knuckles appear on the tiles, then a head and shoulders. A man lay along the tiles for a moment, left hand down to steady himself. Then his fingers touched the live wire.

He gave a shriek of surprise rather than pain, and rocked on the wall for a moment, trying to keep his balance. Parkington fired twice. One shot went low and blew a puff of whitewashed cement from the wall. The second hit the man in the shoulder. He rolled back over the wall, and hit the ground with a crash of branches. The ladder fell on top of him. Love and Parkington looked at each other. Parkington raised his glass.

'First come, first served,' he said.

Chapter Ten

There was no need now for concealment; they had announced their presence. Jarrold shone a torch on the wounded man. His shirt was stained with blood. Jarrold ripped it open and examined the wound as best he could. The bullet had penetrated the chest under the left arm. It was only a flesh wound; painful, but not serious.

'We'll strap you up,' Jarrold promised. 'You'll be all right.'

'The pain!' the man moaned.

'No worse than a wasp sting,' Jarrold told him sharply. 'Here.'

He opened a thin medical pack, took out a plastic hypodermic, pressed the plunger to exclude air, and then dug the needle into the man's chest.

'That's better, isn't it?'

'A bit,' the man admitted. He stood up. Jarrold began to bandage him.

'Doesn't affect your firing hand,' he told him. 'We'll keep our heads down now until the others start something. Then it's up and over the wall.'

*　　*　　*

Love bounded up the stairs to the roof, two at a time. All around the house the half moon had painted the dry grass silver. Nothing moved except the branches of the junipers. The scene was of peace and stillness. He was about to go down and rejoin Parkington, when he sensed rather than saw a faint movement about fifty yards to the left. He was shielded from view because his back was against one of the two chimneys on the roof, so he waited.

A man was moving slowly between the trees, carefully picking his way towards the house, pausing behind each trunk for cover, then coming on stealthily, leaning slightly forward as men advance under threat of attack. He was carrying what seemed like a stick or club in one hand. Then the moonlight glinted on metal; Love instantly recognized a sawn-off shotgun. This could be dangerous. He bent down and picked up a rocket, fed its thin wooden stick into the brass shell case and lit the touch paper from the hurricane lamp flame. Then Love carefully raised the brass case, aiming it like a gun barrel, slightly ahead of the moving man.

The blue paper fuse fizzed and spluttered. Love closed his eyes and bent down his head, and waited. A blood-red blaze against his eye-lids, a hot blast of air, and a strong, not unpleasant smell of gunpowder that reminded him of Bonfire Nights of his boyhood. He opened his eyes in time to see the rocket explode just ahead of the man in a shower of green and golden stars. The man screamed and dropped his gun and started to run, half blinded, hands clawing at his eyes, sparks cascading around his burning face. Then the rocket died.

'Two down,' Love called to Parkington.

'Get down yourself!' Parkington yelled back. 'They're coming over the wall in numbers!'

Love turned and saw the head and shoulders of one man above the wall. Parkington fired and missed. Then he fired again – and nothing happened. His automatic had jammed.

Love picked up a second rocket, lit it and rammed the stick into the shell case. He had not time to take accurate aim, and the rocket soared away harmlessly above the intruder. The man leaned over to steady himself. One of his hands touched the wire. He shouted at the shock and fell forward into a flower bed.

Love leapt down the stairs and raced around the pool. The man was up now, and ran at him, a pistol in his hand. Love gave him two quick blows about his shoulders with his crowbar to paralyse his arms, then stunned him with a thump on his head. The man rolled forward, face down, and his pistol slithered across the calcada, into the pool.

Three gone, but how many more to come?

*   *   *

Volkoff waited in the shadow of a giant fig tree. Pistol shots cracked like breaking bones, and he heard a cry of pain and a great splash. Someone had fallen into the pool. Then, in the background, he heard a deeper spluttering boom like the firing of a distant gun. It took him a second to realize this was not a gun, but a car backfiring. The Cord engine banged again and stopped. It was out of petrol. Volkoff began to run towards the wall. This must be the moment to attack.

*   *   *

Parkington surfaced in the pool, gasping for breath.

He had been running around the edge to head off another man who had just come over the wall, when a shot from the far side hit him. He reeled, staggered on the smooth calcada, and fell headlong into the water.

Love bent down and dragged him out. He could not see where Parkington had been hit, and there was no time to examine the extent of his injuries, for other men were already in the garden. Still kneeling by Parkington's side, Love fired at the nearest – and missed. The man raced towards him, firing from the hip. Love dodged to one side behind the barbecue building. The man fired again, missed, and then the hammer in his revolver rose and fell, clicking like a metronome. He had exhausted his six shots. Love fired, but his magazine was also empty and he had no more ammunition. He pushed his pistol into a pocket and raised the crowbar.

The intruder drew a knife and circled Love warily, waiting his moment to strike. Love gripped the bar with both hands and took a step back to gain better purchase. His heel left the hard calcada, sank into the soft earth of a flower bed, and threw

189

him off balance. He put out one hand to steady himself, and in that second the man leaped, knife at Love's throat. Love brought down the edge of his left hand against the man's wrist, but could not dislodge the weapon. It was all he could do to keep the blade from his windpipe.

Now the man had his other hand at Love's throat; his fingers gripped as tightly as a mole-wrench. As they struggled desperately, Love saw the sky deepen from blue to violet. A red mist spread before his eyes. Blood roared in his ears. And then the man suddenly collapsed and released his grip. His knife clattered on the calcada. Love stood up thankfully, sucking great gouts of fresh air into his lungs. Parkington, like some creature from the sea, knelt at the edge of the pool, steadying his pistol with both hands.

'Got him,' he gasped triumphantly, and collapsed.

But now the battle seemed all but over. Jarrold and Volkoff were in the garden, shining torches at both of them. Other figures moved in the moonlight.

'Put your hands on your head,' shouted Jarrold to Love. He ran round the edge of the pool, past the unconscious Parkington, to where Love was standing.

'Any others in the house?' he asked.

Love shook his head.

'No,' he said.

Jarrold smashed the handle of his revolver against Love's cheek.

'Up on your head, I told you,' he said angrily.

Love reeled from the blow and almost fell. He raised his hands and clasped them on the back of his head.

'You are damned lucky we don't kill you outright,' said Volkoff.

'You made a good attempt,' retorted Love.

'Where is the case?' asked Volkoff.

'What case?'

'The one you brought back from the ship.'

'The ship?' Love repeated, as though he did not understand the question. He was playing for time. There was nothing else

190

to play for now; no allies, no lucky breaks. The moon was dipping, the wind had dropped. In half an hour night would be in retreat and the sun burning up the sky to begin a new day.

Jarrold hit him again, this time on the other side of his jaw. Love tasted blood in his mouth, and spat out a broken tooth.

'When you took McNab back to the ship,' said Volkoff, 'you brought back a bag or a case. I saw you. We want it.'

'It contains private papers,' Love told him. 'Nothing to do with you.'

'Search the house,' ordered Jarrold. 'We can't waste any time with him. And it will be light in an hour.'

He kept Love covered with his revolver, while the others went from room to room, shining torches, pulling back curtains to get the benefit of growing daylight. They tossed cushions on the floor, tipped up chairs, ripped open cupboards, pulled books from shelves. Jarrold heard them go through the bedrooms, one after the other, opening drawers, tearing off sheets and mattresses. Volkoff came back to the patio.

'We can't find it,' he said.

'It must be in the house somewhere,' said Jarrold. 'We both know it must be here. I saw it myself in the back of the car.'

He paused, smiling.

'The car,' he repeated. 'Of course. Have a look there.'

Volkoff ran to the garage, lifted the heavy lid of the Cord's boot, and shone the torch inside. The leather travelling bag with the zip padlocked stood in the centre of the carpet. He pulled it out and brought it back triumphantly into the room. Jarrold felt the bag, his fingers searching for the outline of a metal box.

'Bring me a screwdriver or a spanner from the car,' he said. 'I'll break this padlock.'

Jarrold shook his head.

'The box is soldered,' he pointed out. 'We can't open it here even if we open the bag, without damaging the papers. We know it's there. That's all that matters. Let's get out now, before too many people are moving about.'

He turned to Love.

191

'Tie him up,' he ordered two of the men. One went into Love's bedroom and brought back several of his favourite New & Lingwood neckties. They bound his wrists with his hands behind his back, and tied his ankles together. Then they used a third tie to link the other two. He lay on his side on the floor, trussed like a broiler.

'Someone will find you,' Jarrold assured him, as he tore a bath towel into strips and gagged him. 'But not immediately. The maid will not be here at nine, as usual, by the way. I sent her a message on your behalf to say she could have the day off. But tomorrow, no doubt, she will arrive.'

It was much lighter now, and the sun was coming out of the sea, drying dew on window panes. Within half an hour, it would be hot.

Jan locked the kitchen and garage, then the bedroom and bathroom doors.

'Just in case you started to crawl around, looking for a knife or a pair of scissors,' explained Jarrold. He put the keys in his pocket, picked up the leather bag and turned to the others.

'Let's go,' he said.

He led the way out of the front door, pushed open the gates against the stones. In single file they started to cross the rough ground towards the ruined farmhouse.

Love watched them leave. Then he began to crawl, slowly and painfully, at first on his side, and then on his shoulders and knees, towards the patio. Parkington still lay unconscious where he had fallen. Someone had kicked his gun into the swimming pool. Love paused for breath, and then moved slowly and laboriously across the rough tiles until he reached the staircase For a few moments he crouched on the bottom step to regain his strength and then he swung his body around and raised his feet on to this step. Then, with his back braced against one side and his feet against the other, he moved himself up to the next step and so, carefully and steadily, he began to climb.

He reached the top and crawled across the floor, now growing warm under the sun, towards the flame of the hurricane lamp. He sat down on the tiles with his back to it, holding up his arms as best he could, until the ties were burned through. As he crouched in this ungainly position, he heard the noise for which he had waited since the first signs of dawn: the faint deepening rumble of an aircraft engine.

The flame singed his wrists, but no matter, his hands were free. He undid the gag around his mouth, bent down, untied the knot around his ankles, and then massaged blood back into his limbs. And all the while, the noise steadily increased, like the hum of a swarm of angry bees returning to their hive. He stood up, looking towards the sun, shielding his eyes against its shimmering brightness. Soon he could make out the wings of the Moth. Then the plane was down out of the sun, barely a hundred feet above the ground, a quarter of a mile from him.

Behind the house, heading back towards the deserted farm-house, he could see the men walking. They moved in the formation of an arrowhead, taking their time, picking a way through the sharp prickles of dried thorn bushes and thistles. They looked up towards the Moth, and then they went on. The little aircraft presented no threat to them; they had all seen it before.

The plane banked and turned, and came in ahead of them, in a wide circle. Love saw puffs of white mist blow from the rear edges of its lower wings, like giant fly-sprays in the sky.

The plane circled them again, and now the men increased their pace. Then they broke into a shambling run across the rough ground. He calculated they were probably three hundred yards away, with half as much again to go before the ground would begin to shield them from his view. He picked up the brass shell-case, rammed two rockets down its throat, lit the fuses and held the tube, eyes closed, pointing it up and beyond the running men.

The rockets erupted with a shriek and were gone, trailing spangled stars through the bright morning sky. They burst into a mass of green and orange flares that slowly sank to earth like balls of fire. They landed about twenty yards ahead of the

193

running men, behind the high dome of a fig tree. For a second, nothing happened. And then the whole area exploded in a sheet of flame fifty yards square.

The hot dry wind blew like a blast from a suddenly opened oven door. The Moth circled them once more, then flew back over the house. As it crossed the flat roof, Love waved both his hands at it in delight and triumph. The pilot raised a right hand in answer, waggled the plane's wings and then was gone, out over the sea before turning back to Lagos to land.

The dry undergrowth crackled like a machine gun battery. Shouts and screams of the men trapped in a ring of flame sounded thin and far away.

Now Love saw other figures wearing the familiar grey uniforms of the Portuguese police begin to appear. They came from the track, some with truncheons, others carrying rifles, all running in an extended line towards the flames. Someone blew a whistle. The game's over, thought Love, or should it be the game's up? He walked down the stairs. Parkington had got to his feet and was coming towards him, a dark stain of dried blood on his right cheek.

'We survived,' Love told him.

'Only just,' retorted Parkington shakily. 'Now, if you really are a doctor, prove it.'

He sat down in a cane chair at the edge of the pool. Love went into the house to find his first-aid kit – and a new bottle of rum.

*   *   *

Senhor Diaz had never entertained so many foreigners at one time in his small office. *Entertained* was probably not the right word, the *mot juste,* to describe his activity now, and he groped in his mind for one more suitable. Perhaps he should say he was receiving friends, or being host to them, or even, as Americans might say, hosting them? The English language was difficult when he did not speak it regularly, but now he was certainly having a lot more practice. Although he had no

194

alcohol to offer his visitors, there was an air of cheerfulness, almost euphoria, in the little room. It was as though they had all been drinking champagne.

Parkington, a large sticking plaster on his face, and still pale beneath his sunburn, sat with legs stretched out, on the only spare chair. Love stood, arms folded, his back against the one wall not covered by metal filing cabinets or book shelves.

A small man, with thinning hair and a saturnine expression, perched on the edge of Senhor Diaz's desk, drumming ringed fingers on its imitation leather top. According to Parkington, this gentleman, whose name Diaz had not caught, was a distinguished professor of Serbo-Croat from a British university. He had arrived late the previous evening.

Standing in the far corner, looking rather sullen, but with a stoicism which Diaz, who had known hard times himself, could not help but admire, stood the Scottish engineer, McNab. In the centre of the desk was a tin-plate box which a local silversmith had been instructed to open carefully with a delicate trepanning saw he used for his craft. By its side were four small piles of yellowing documents tied with faded pink ribbon. A fifth set of papers was untied. The writing was in a language that the professor could understand, and the pages were covered with neatly written notes and scientific equations. The professor tapped them as he spoke in his thickly accented English.

'The key, gentlemen,' he said, as though addressing a class of students, 'lies in the work of Nikola Tesla, one of the most remarkable scientists of this century.

'You may never have heard of him, so you must bear with me while I give you a few facts on his career. He was a Serb, born in 1857, in the village of Smiltan, in Lika province, in what was then a part of Austria and is now Jugoslavia. As a boy, Tesla had poor health. He suffered from epileptic fits. One severe attack seems to have damaged – or should I say, totally *changed* – his brain. For after it, he discovered he possessed an extraordinary mental ability. When faced with a complex scientific problem, Tesla could visualize the answer almost at once, and then he would work back methodically, stage by stage, to the basic query.

'He was educated in Prague and Paris, and specialized in electricity. As a young man, in Budapest, he invented a telephone repeater, but opportunities for advancement as an inventor seemed limited and when he was twenty-seven he emigrated to the United States and became an American citizen.

'Here he championed alternating electric current against the great Edison's faith in direct current. And Tesla saw his principles put into practice with the huge power plants at Niagara Falls.

'Tesla also developed a sophisticated arc-lighting system and a revolutionary type of transformer, known as the Tesla coil. But some of his greatest feats still seem inexplicable. He could transmit electrical power without any intervening connections or wires.

'He conceived a way of illuminating the depths of the sea as clearly as we can light up a tropical fish tank.

'He had a means of dispersing fog, and, above all, he devised a system of total weather control. But he did not make public the calculations behind these astonishing capabilities. He produced results, but carefully kept to himself the steps that led to these conclusions.

'Tesla's detractors therefore declared he was a quack, a faker. And certainly there was an air of showmanship about some of his experiments. For example, when he declared that by using what he called TMT – the Tesla Magnetic Transmitter – he could literally harness electricity from the air, his critics challenged him to do so. He accepted their challenge and in the foothills of the Rocky Mountains, he placed 200 carbon filament lamps, needing 10 kilowatts to light them, on a huge wooden stand. Tesla then lit them all from a dynamo 25 miles away, *without any wires*.

'As an encore, Tesla produced flashes of lightning, which observers noted were 135 feet long. He then held an electric lamp between his fingers and thumb – and the bulb lit up.'

196

'But how could he possibly do these things?' asked Love. 'Was his audience hypnotized into believing they actually saw them, when, in fact, they didn't?'

'Not so, doctor. I fully understand the scepticism of your calling, but the fact remains, this man conducted these experiments before hundreds of people. There is *a* scientific explanation, which is that Tesla had somehow discovered how to utilise the electric potential of possibly two billion volts that exists between the earth and the outer atmosphere. Tesla's belief was that once one could discover the right frequency, this electricity could be made to oscillate – and would then provide literally unlimited energy.

'He committed all his notes and results to paper and, when he died in 1943, in New York, he left these papers to a museum in Belgrade. But it was feared that not all reached that destination. Some are thought to be in Russian hands, because of certain incidents I will come to in a moment. Others, it seems – and from my brief reading of them, the most important ones – are here on this desk.

'These papers in this box, gentlemen, are the quintessence of Tesla's work. Whoever owns these papers could arguably control the world *without using any overt force.*'

'What proof have you for such a statement?' asked Love. 'I agree Tesla seems to have been a remarkable man – but that is a long way from being able to dominate the world.'

'I will give you two instances, gentlemen, out of the many to back up what I say, far-fetched as it may seem. In October, 1976, you may recall that a sudden and inexplicable blackout affected radio and radar systems all round the world? Interference and jamming occurred on an unprecedented scale. Nothing was working properly – and no anti-jamming equipment the West possessed could remedy the situation.

'The interference was traced to a source in Riga. Immediate enquiries and protests were made to Russia, and their reassuring explanation was that Soviet scientists had been conducting experiments on different frequencies in that area, but these were now concluded.

197

'The interference disappeared, but by the end of the year, it was again reported, this time from what we call "standing waves" – 1,000 miles long, pulsating irregularly several times a second – from places as far apart as Honolulu, Toronto and New Delhi. Again, more protests and more reassurances and then once more everything appeared normal.

'A few months after this, meteorologists on both sides of the Iron Curtain reported extraordinary changes in weather conditions. These extended from the Californian coast to Finland. Parts of Europe suffered unprecedented floods from rain as heavy as the Indian monsoon. Snow fell in Florida. There was such a severe drought in Britain that, as you will remember, restrictions were placed on the use of water. The usual seasonal changes in the weather were being blocked – that is the only word I can use. And these blockages appeared to be due to these "standing waves".

'Now I am sure you will agree that if any person or group of people could control the world's weather, and radio and radar, then they would already be a very long way on the road to controlling the world. This the Russians may be trying to do – and these papers contain details. And when I tell you of Tesla's equally successful experiments in other fields – you will even more readily appreciate the value of his notes. He was concentrating on a way to transmit sound from a great distance, direct to the human ear.

'Russia and the United States are both working on this problem, but so far have only succeeded over short distances, because of the immense cost and complications. The end result would be that the people to whom the sound is directed imagine it is actually originating inside their own head! The result can be a mental breakdown – madness. And Tesla had a scheme to transmit sound, without wires or receivers, on a world-wide scale, again by tapping the vast electrical potential of the atmosphere. Remember, gentlemen, these experiments were first conducted sixty or more years ago. Just think how modern science could improve on his basic equations. And with what cataclysmic results.'

198

No-one spoke for a moment; each was busy with their own thoughts about the man who had achieved so much so long ago. Then Parkington broke the silence.

'Volkoff and Jarrold both admit they showed some of the items here to potential buyers,' he said. 'Volkoff approached contacts in the Eastern bloc, and Jarrold tried to interest possible Italian-American buyers. Both parties instantly realized the value of the papers – and sent over their own representatives to keep an eye on things.'

'Which is why we were attacked by East Germans *and* Italians?' asked Love.

'Exactly.'

'So these papers really *are* worth a fortune?'

'They are worth life itself,' replied the professor quietly.

'And they only gave me 8,000 dollars for carrying them,' said McNab.

'You should accept that money in a kneeling position,' said Parkington. 'As I have already told you, it was extremely fortunate for you that you did not deliver them and claim the rest of your fee. You'd have no doubt been found dead in the harbour next day. You knew too much to be left alive.'

'Where exactly were you carrying them?' Love asked him.

McNab smiled wanly.

'I didn't like to risk hiding them aboard my own ship *Princess Rosael*, so I hid them, without anyone knowing, aboard another old tub that was just behind us, also bound for the breaker's yard.'

'Where are the principals and the others now?' asked Senhor Diaz, who felt he was being left out of things.

'Under guard in a military hospital,' replied Parkington. 'They were burned, not severely, but enough to incapacitate them a bit when Victoria flew over and sprayed them with paraffin. The police, who you so wisely alerted, senhor, were able to arrest them all without much trouble.'

'I don't doubt there'll be some diplomatic comings and goings,' said Love. 'But not of a very convincing nature. Anyway, Jarrold will face a murder charge over the deaths of

199

Marshall and Cartwright. And Volkoff has a number of questions to answer. Doubtless, the Midland Widows and the Western Mutual Nominees will be assiduous in asking them.'

'One thing still puzzles me,' said the professor. 'The explosion at Forbes' house. Who did that – and why?'

'Jarrold. He wanted to silence Victoria. He was afraid she might start talking, if she learned of Cartwright's death. He calculated she would be at home during the early evening, so he put some explosive with a timing device outside her bedroom. She missed it by minutes.'

'And that was when things started going wrong for Jarrold and Volkoff?'

'No. Much earlier, in fact. They realized in India that some very hard men were after them to acquire Tesla's papers without buying them, but they weren't sure of their identity. They could be Eastern bloc agents, or terrorists or even the Family. And they reckoned – rightly, I should think – that if they escaped from India, a reception committee would almost certainly be waiting for them in England.

'So they didn't go to England. They flew to Egypt from Delhi. Volkoff had bought some old ships in the Canal which he intended to insure and scuttle. He changed this plan and gave Tesla's papers to Mr McNab here. Jarrold knew of this, and couldn't resist doing down his partner. After all, it was for a matter of millions. When money's in, moralities are out.'

'His orders to me were to dump the box over the side beyond Sagres,' McNab interrupted dourly.

'You see?' said Parkington triumphantly. 'But then he saw Marshall quite unexpectedly in Portugal and instantly thought that Marshall must be trying something on his own. It takes one crook to distrust another. So he got rid of him – as he got rid of Cartwright. As no doubt, he would also have killed Volkoff, if he'd had the chance. That's why he came into his hotel bedroom in Sagres when you were there, doctor. So it would go on. Until, perhaps, in the end the buyers would kill him.'

'Instead of which, he and Volkoff have survived,' said Love. 'They have each other.'

'You make it sound like a husband and wife coming up for their 50th wedding anniversary. The police tell me the difficulty now is not to make them talk, but to stop them talking.'

'So much killing,' mused Love. 'It reminds me of the Scots proverb, "Hang a thief when he's young, and he'll no steal when he's old".'

'I feel I only played a very small part in all this,' declared Diaz modestly, hoping to be contradicted.

'Not so,' Parkington contradicted him warmly. 'I shall personally see that Douglas MacGillivray, the editor of the West European Press Alliance, is made fully aware of all the work you did. And, of course, in due course you will have a valuable world scoop on this whole story. When I clear it with the proper authorities, of course.'

'Of course, senhor,' Diaz agreed. So it had been a writing assignment after all. And to think that he had ever doubted Parkington's word!

Now Parkington turned to Love.

'As for you, my good doctor, if you hadn't been able to contact Victoria – and you damn nearly didn't, because the 'phones were out of order – things might all have ended differently.'

'Not in a different way,' Love contradicted him. 'Only in a different place. After all, the papers would still have been safely aboard the ship – instead of being right here on Senhor Diaz's desk.'

Love moved towards the door. The professor replaced the papers in the box. Parkington put this in a brief-case and padlocked it. A military aircraft had made an unscheduled landing at Lagos and was waiting for both of them. Within an hour they would be away. Within two, they should be back in London.

'Things will be quiet for you here when I've gone,' Parkington told Love.

201

'I'll find ways of enlivening them. Victoria is teaching me to fly.'

'Love in the air, eh?' asked Parkington – and just dodged Jason's judo blow.

*   *   *

Swallowcliffe, Wiltshire, England;
Waldport, Oregon, USA;
Praia da Luz, Lagos, and Sagres, Portugal.